*Also by Laurien Berenson
in Large Print:*

A Pedigree to Die For

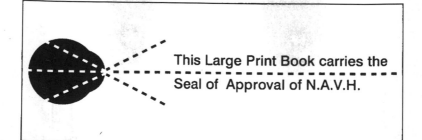

Hot Dog

A Melanie Travis Mystery

Laurien Berenson

Thorndike Press • Waterville, Maine

Published in 2003 by arrangement with Kensington Books, an imprint of Kensington Publishing Corp.

Thorndike Press® Large Print Paperback Series.

The tree indicium is a trademark of Thorndike Press.

The text of this Large Print edition is unabridged.
Other aspects of the book may vary from the original edition.

Set in 16 pt. Plantin by Christina S. Huff.

Printed in the United States on permanent paper.

Library of Congress Cataloging-in-Publication Data

Berenson, Laurien.
    Hot dog : a Melanie Travis mystery / Laurien Berenson.
      p. cm.
    ISBN 0-7862-5224-3 (lg. print : sc : alk. paper)
    1. Travis, Melanie (Fictitious character) — Fiction.
    2. Women private investigators — Fiction.   3. Women
    dog owners — Fiction.   4. Divorce — Fiction.   5. Dogs
    — Fiction.   I. Title.
    PS3552.E6963H68 2003
                                         2003040734

LT-M

Recently I was asked what I thought was the best thing about being a writer. The answer came easily. The best thing is knowing that there are people who read and enjoy my books. I've been fortunate to hear from many of my readers and one, Betty King, suggested the title for HOT DOG. I loved her idea and I hope you do, too.

Thank you Betty! And to all the readers out there — I'm enormously grateful for the response you've given my series. I couldn't do it without you.

Prologue

Show me a man who proposes on bended knee and I'll show you a man who's overcompensating.

As it happens the man in question, Sam Driver, had a lot to compensate for. Too much to be solved by a mere proposal, no matter how romantically couched. One look at the two-carat, emerald-cut diamond ring Sam thought he'd be slipping on my finger and any woman would have known that this was a guy with a guilty conscience.

Good, I thought. He deserved one.

Bear in mind that we were going through this proposal thing for the second time. The first, Sam had been on his feet, smiling that easy, knowing smile that always made my stomach plummet. He'd simply held out his arms and waited for me to walk into them, secure in the knowledge that there was nowhere else I'd rather be. There hadn't been any expensive ring; we hadn't felt the need.

This time around neither one of us was

feeling very secure. Six months earlier Sam had gone away unexpectedly — needing something, searching for something that he couldn't quite define. At the time, there had been some extraordinary events in his life; I knew there was much he needed to come to grips with. I'd even managed to tell myself that I understood.

And eventually I did. As the months passed I came to understand that the forces that kept him away were stronger than the ones that had bound him to me. Maybe that was all I needed to know.

So when Sam reappeared, I wasn't exactly ready to drop everything and take up where we'd left off. Not my son Davey. He welcomed Sam back with typical, unquestioning, seven-year-old exuberance.

In the interim, Davey's father, my ex-husband Bob, had come to Connecticut for a visit that had stretched into a two-month sojourn and ended with him buying a house only a couple of miles from our own. Summers were too hot in Texas, Bob had announced. He was ready to relocate to the northeast.

Now my son had two men vying for his attention and looking out for his welfare. Three, if you counted my recently married brother, Frank. I'd been a single parent for

8

so long, it was a little much to take in. Davey, of course, coped beautifully.

So when Sam proposed for the second time, I didn't have to worry about my son's feelings, just my own. For a brief, stirring moment, I held the ring in my hand. I felt the sharp, faceted edge of the diamond bite into my palm and thought about the commitments we honor and those we choose to walk away from.

Then I handed the ring back.

Sam was visibly shaken by my response. Evidently, he'd hoped that an expensive piece of jewelry and a proposal tendered with all sincerity would be enough to bridge the rift between us. For him, it seemed as though they were.

For me, it wasn't that simple.

The months we'd been separated had helped Sam heal. But while time had put him back together, it had torn me apart. Love endured, but faith eroded. I couldn't promise Sam my future when I didn't trust his past.

Maybe someday I'll change my mind and put his ring on my finger. Then again, maybe not.

We'll see.

1

Nothing sucks all the joy out of a glorious spring afternoon faster than the sight of a feisty, fifty-something ex-nun standing on the doorstep and glowering as though she has murder on her mind.

"Hi, Aunt Rose," I said. "Who do you want to kill?"

"Is it that obvious?"

She didn't sound distressed by this, my aunt who'd spent the better part of three decades known as Sister Anne Marie, wearing the solemn black habit of her order, turning to prayer in times of need, and taking her complaints directly to the Head Man upstairs. Actually she looked rather gratified by the effect her scowl had produced.

Stepping aside so I wouldn't get run over as she came marching in, I made a silent vow to tread carefully. With my relatives, that's always a good plan. As is keeping your back to the wall and your head down.

"Only to someone who knows you," I lied.

If she'd still been wearing the wimple and

veil, I wouldn't have been able to do that; habits ingrained in a Catholic childhood are hard to break. Instead Rose was casually dressed in khaki pants and a cotton sweater, with a silk scarf in a nautical print tied jauntily around her neck. She looked less like a Mother Superior than a busy Connecticut matron on her way to the supermarket.

Except for the frown, which had, if anything, intensified. It was now firmly aimed in my direction.

"You're a better liar than you used to be," Rose said. "I suppose Peg has been coaching you."

Peg was my other aunt. She'd been married to Max, Rose's and my father's brother, until his death three years earlier. The two women had been in-laws for decades, and animosity had sizzled between them for much of that time.

Any hope I might have had of spending a peaceful Saturday afternoon was rapidly fading. Aunt Rose was heading for the living room. I trudged along behind. Books and magazines littered the coffee table. A rawhide bone sat on the couch. Davey's wooden train set took up much of the floor.

"I should have known," I said. "What has Aunt Peg done now?"

"I'm sure I have no idea." Rose stepped

carefully over the wooden tracks, glanced at the chew toy, and wisely chose a chair. "Why? Is she in trouble?"

"I thought that's why you were here."

"Goodness, no. I haven't spoken to Peg in weeks. It's Peter who's giving me fits. I thought maybe you could help."

Other kind souls might have leapt in at that point to offer their services. I folded my hands in my lap and didn't say a thing. As it happens, I've been down this path of family obligations before. The scenery is often alarming, and there tend to be a surprising number of potholes along the way.

Peter was Rose's husband, an affable middle-aged man with an expanding paunch and a ready smile. He'd left the priesthood about the same time Rose had bid good-bye to the Sisters of Divine Mercy and they'd married shortly thereafter. Recently he'd taken a job running an Outreach program at a community center in downtown Stamford.

Peter loved his work, and I knew he was good at it. Whatever was bothering my aunt, surely it couldn't be too serious.

Before I could find out, however, I heard the back door slam. That noise was followed by the unmistakable sound of three youngsters — one human, two canine —

racing through the kitchen and down the hallway.

"Hey, Aunt Rose!" My son announced his presence with a delighted shriek. "When did you get here? Where's Uncle Peter? Want to go outside and play?"

Faith and Eve, our two Standard Poodles, greeted the guest with rather more dignity. The pair are mother and daughter, both black, and both bigger than many people imagine Poodles to be. Standards are the largest of the three varieties; and these two stood twenty-four inches at the shoulder. They also exhibited that wonderful Poodle temperament: lively, intelligent, mischievous, and highly empathetic.

Eve was an older puppy now at nine months of age. With her ear hair wrapped, her topknot done up in brightly colored rubber bands, and the profuse coat she was growing for the show ring making her appear bigger than she was, even I had to admit she was quite a sight. Aunt Rose didn't so much as blink. Instead she simply held out her hand, which Eve sniffed politely before spinning on her hind legs and bounding back to Davey's side. Faith, meanwhile, trotted around the coffee table and hopped up on the couch beside me, resting her head in my lap.

"Play what?" Rose asked, considering Davey's offer. "What sort of game did you have in mind?"

"Basketball," he suggested quickly. "Or maybe tag. Then Faith and Eve can play too."

"Your father should be here any minute," I pointed out. My ex-husband was picking Davey up and taking him out for the afternoon.

Davey made a production out of checking his watch, a recent addition to his left wrist. "He's late. He was supposed to be here already."

"How is Bob?" Aunt Rose's brow arched delicately. The small gesture was as close as she would come to expressing disapproval in front of Davey.

"He's fine. He's doing great. He's . . ." I stopped, shrugged. ". . . Bob. You know."

Rose nodded. She did indeed.

Davey headed for the front door. "I'll go out and check. Maybe I can see him coming."

"Good idea. Leave the dogs inside."

The backyard was fenced, the front wasn't. Davey knew the rules. So did the Poodles. Eve turned a small circle and lay down beside Rose's chair.

"Sorry about the interruption," I said.

"Bob was supposed to be here twenty minutes ago. He's usually pretty punctual."

"I'm glad he's late." Rose smiled. "I don't see nearly enough of my nephew. It always seems as though Davey has grown another three inches between visits."

That the rebuke was a gentle one didn't make it any less well deserved. Somehow my relatives and I have less in common with the Brady Bunch than we do with the tortured characters in *Hamlet*. Or *Monty Python*. Which never seems to stop us from beating our heads against that barred and shuttered door that somehow lies between us and familial bliss.

"I'm sure now that you and Peter are living in the area again, things will be different," I said hopefully.

Aunt Rose didn't look convinced. I imagine I didn't either.

"Let me tell you why I've come," she said. "I'm afraid I need some advice. Quite without warning, I seem to have become the caretaker for a rather young puppy —"

"You got a dog?" I must have sounded surprised. Faith lifted her head and gazed at me inquiringly. Having recently acquired her championship, she'd had her elaborate show coat replaced by an elegant pet trim. Now I could tangle my fingers in her topknot and ears to my heart's content. "That's great!"

"Yes and no. You see, this isn't our puppy. Peter and I are just taking care of it for a little while."

Oh. That didn't sound like nearly as much fun. Faith and Eve were members of Davey's and my family. We were great believers in the joys of dog ownership.

"What kind of dog is it?"

"A Dachshund. A smooth-coated red Standard." Rose paused, then added quite unnecessarily, "I bought a book."

"I can tell."

I didn't laugh. I didn't even smirk. Aunt Rose did not look amused.

"I read the book from cover to cover," she announced, "and I now know volumes about the history and function of the breed. However, I still know diddly about what puppies eat, why they feel the need to cry all night long, and how to stop them from doing their business in the house."

"Diddly?"

"Diddly," Aunt Rose confirmed. Her scowl was back. "Zip, zero, nada. My vocabulary is not what's at issue here, Melanie."

Of course not. "How old is the puppy?"

"Eight weeks, I think. Maybe ten. Or maybe three months, does that sound right?"

"They all sound possible." That was supposed to be an easy question. That Rose didn't have a ready answer wasn't a good sign. "Where did the puppy come from?"

"A man in Norwalk donated him to Peter's benefit auction." Rose plucked at a stray thread in her sweater. Her gaze, usually so confident and direct, didn't quite meet mine.

"Donated him . . . ?" Now I was the one who was frowning. "What auction?"

"It's a fund-raiser for the community center. Considering the amount of wealth that's concentrated in this area of Fairfield County, the resources available to Peter's Outreach program are a disgrace. And of course, you know Peter. He immediately set about to rectify the situation."

That sounded like Peter, all right. Though I still wasn't sure where a Dachshund puppy would have fit into his plans.

"Our first step was to drum up some support in the community and find sponsorship among the local corporations." Aunt Rose was a master at charity fund-raising. Now that she was back on familiar territory, her self-assurance was returning. "I have to say, both Peter and I are gratified by the response our efforts have received."

"When does the auction take place?"

"The second weekend in May. A hotel in Stamford has donated a ballroom and a number of area restaurants, and caterers have signed on to supply appetizers and finger food in exchange for prominent mention in the program. It looks like it's going to be quite an event."

"I can see why. It sounds like a great idea."

"Thank you." Rose was pleased. "Now back to the puppy —"

"Which is not a great idea," I said firmly.

My aunt's chin lifted. "Why not?"

"You can't simply hand a living, breathing animal over to the highest bidder. Puppies aren't an impulse purchase. They need to go to carefully selected homes where their new owners are prepared to devote the time and effort necessary to their upbringing. . . ."

Aunt Rose didn't seem surprised by what I was saying. Indeed, she looked rather resigned. My voice faded away as a suspicion slipped, unbidden, into the back of my mind.

"Aunt Peg already told you the same thing, didn't she?"

"Yes," Rose admitted. "And rather less politely."

She would have, I thought. Aunt Peg was Margaret Turnbull of Cedar Crest Kennels, prominent in dog show circles for many years as breeder of the East Coast's top Standard Poodles. Aunt Peg's dogs were justifiably praised for their beauty, their excellent health, and their stable, fun-loving temperaments.

Faith had come, of course, from Cedar Crest. And I had bred Eve with Aunt Peg's careful guidance. Though Peg had made her mark as a breeder and owner-handler, she had recently added another feather to her cap when she'd gotten her judge's license over the winter. She'd already performed her first few assignments and was fast gaining a reputation for being tough, knowledgeable, and fair.

Peg didn't suffer fools gladly. Not in the show ring and not in her own family. I couldn't imagine she'd have been pleased to hear Aunt Rose's tale of the giveaway puppy.

"To be perfectly honest," said Rose, "I suppose I hadn't thought things through. One would assume that the puppy's breeder knew what he was doing. According to Peter, this Dachshund is very well bred. He even has a pedigree."

"Aunt Rose," I said patiently, "most purebred dogs have pedigrees. All that really means is that someone has written the

19

names of their ancestors down on a piece of paper."

"Well this little dog has illustrious ancestors. Champions even."

I sighed. Unfortunately it wasn't unheard of for dogs even as little as one generation removed from reputable breeders to fall into the hands of the puppy mills that wholesaled puppies to pet stores. The American Kennel Club has created the option of limited registration to try to fix the problem, but it hasn't accomplished nearly enough.

"Not only that," Rose continued, "but a number of the donations that we've received for the benefit are rather grandiose. There's a very good chance that whoever takes this little fellow home will have paid quite a high price for the privilege. I saw Peter's notes about the puppy. I believe they said that his sire had won Best of Breed several months ago at that big dog show in New York."

"Best of Variety," I corrected automatically.

Dachshunds, like Poodles, come in varieties. In Poodles, the distinctions are made by size, Toys being the smallest at ten inches and under, Miniatures standing between ten and fifteen inches at the shoulder, and Standards being anything above that.

In the case of Dachshunds, things are

even more complicated. Their varieties are divided by coat: smooth, wirehaired, and longhaired; and they also show in two different weight classes, Standard and Miniature.

Abruptly, incredulously, I realized what she'd said. "You don't mean Westminster, do you?"

"That sounds right. I believe Peter and I watched the show on television. If you ask me, it seemed like rather a lot of hoopla over a bunch of dogs."

Yes, well, dog shows sometimes did seem like that to people who didn't understand their inner workings. But I was still back on my aunt's earlier point. How had she and Peter come into possession of a puppy whose sire had just been awarded Best of Variety at Westminster? What kind of breeder would have donated such a puppy to a charity auction?

"Mom, come quick!"

Before Davey had even finished yelling, I was already on my feet. There are certain things that make a mother's heart race and her hands grow cold. The sound of a child shrieking pretty much tops the list.

I scooped Faith up, thrust her aside, and wiggled out from between coffee table and couch. When I reached the hall, Aunt Rose and the Poodles were right behind me. Davey hadn't bothered to latch the front door. Yanking it open, I nearly knocked myself over.

Anxiously I scanned the yard. Blood I can deal with, even broken bones. It's the unknown that makes me quake.

I spotted Davey immediately. He was standing by the driveway. His body was angled toward the street, and he was gazing back over his shoulder at the house, waiting for me to appear.

Quickly I cataloged all visible body parts. Everything seemed to be intact. Indeed, my son was smiling.

Relief washed through me, followed improbably by irritation. While I was happy it was a false alarm, I'd have been happier still with no alarm at all. I pushed open the storm door, dropping a hand to catch Eve before she scooted out.

"What?" I demanded.

"Look!"

Davey waved grandly toward the street. For the first time I noticed that my ex-husband's cherry red Trans Am was parked along the curb. Pulling in behind it was another vehicle, a white dually pickup truck towing a horse trailer.

My first thought was that the driver must

be lost. Our neighborhood is more suburban than rural: small cozy houses tucked side by side on quarter-acre lots. We're fortunate to have wide sidewalks, plenty of trees, and not much traffic, but still, there's no place around here to keep a horse. Or even to ride one. Then I saw Bob walk around the side of the truck and confer with the driver as she parked.

For the second time in less than a minute, my stomach clenched.

"Isn't this the greatest?" Davey crowed. "Dad got me a pony!"

2

He had to be kidding.

A pony? No way.

Oh I understood the concept readily enough — small equine, shaped like a horse, useful for riding and eating grass. But what I couldn't seem to wrap my brain around was how that was supposed to apply to me and my family. What could Davey possibly want with a pony?

Like every child he'd had the occasional photo-op pony ride. But he'd never demonstrated any desire for riding lessons. Until Faith had arrived, we'd never even had a pet. Some people — notably my Aunt Peg — might say that we were still learning how to be responsible dog owners. So what did that say for our ability to deal with a pony?

"No." Nobody seemed to be paying any attention to me, so I repeated the word for good measure. "No. This is *not* happening."

Aunt Rose gave me a pitying look. Outside, Davey was already running toward the trailer. Not only that, but the news seemed to have zapped like radar through the neighborhood. Other kids were beginning to appear.

"We can't take care of a pony," I said firmly. Like my opinion mattered. Like anyone was even listening to me. "We have no place to keep it. We have nothing to feed it." I spread my hands helplessly. "The whole idea is impossible."

This was *so* Bob. Leap first, and ask the practical questions later. Or never, if you could get away with it. His grand gesture would make him look like a hero, while I'd end up being the bad guy who had to send the pony back to wherever it had come from.

Leaving Faith and Eve locked in the house, I strode down the steps and across the yard. The woman who'd been driving the truck had gotten out and disappeared around the back of the trailer. Judging by the clanking noises I heard, she was unhooking the ramp. Several kids, Davey among them, were clustered in an excited knot by the sidewalk. Bob came across the lawn to meet me.

"Hey, sorry I'm late, but this is pretty cool, huh?"

"Cool?" My tone indicated pretty clearly what I thought of that description.

Bob slowed, then stopped. His grin faltered briefly, then returned full strength. My ex-husband had charm to spare. He not only knew it, he was an expert at using it to great effect.

What he often lacked, however, was the maturity to see both sides of an issue. Thick, sandy-colored hair, so like his son's, ruffled in the April breeze. His dark brown eyes found mine with a beguiling gaze. There'd been times in my life that I'd have given him anything when he looked at me like that. Fortunately, they were long past now.

I blinked and looked past him. "Bob, what's inside that trailer?"

"Wait until you see. I bought Davey a present. Every kid in the neighborhood is going to be jealous."

I tipped my head to one side, wondering why he seemed to think that was a good thing. "Bob —"

"Hang on a minute. Let me get Pam over here. She'll explain things."

Pam, presumably, was the woman who'd been driving the truck. Bob jogged back to the trailer, helped her finish lowering the ramp, then brought her over and introduced us. As if that was going to help.

"Nice to meet you," Pam Donnelly said. The pleasantry sounded perfunctory, but then I'm sure I didn't look very pleased to see her either.

She was an athletic-looking woman in her mid-twenties with a purposeful stride and a long braid of thick, dark hair that hung down the middle of her back. Pam rubbed one hand down the side of her jeans before offering to shake. Her nails were cut short and her grip was firm.

"Bobby has excellent taste. He picked out a wonderful pony for your little girl."

Bobby? I leveled a glare at the man in question who was doing his best to look as though everything were going according to plan.

"Little boy," I corrected.

"Huh?"

"Davey is a little boy."

"Oh yeah, right." Pam glanced over at Bob and smiled. "He's going to love Willow. Let me just go and get her out of the truck."

"Wait!" I cried. "Bob said you were going to explain."

"Explain what?"

Good question. Did I dare answer *everything?* Probably not.

"Pam runs Long Ridge Pony Farm," Bob said. "Maybe you've seen it?"

I thought for a moment. The name sounded familiar.

"I'm about three miles north of here," Pam supplied. "We've got ten acres and a little barn with a bunch of ponies. I do some breeding, give riding lessons to local kids, and run a camp in the summer."

"That sounds like fun," I said, forgetting for a moment that I was talking to a woman who was about to unload a pony into my driveway.

"Yeah, it is." Pam grinned. "I met Bobby a couple of weeks ago at the Bean Counter."

The Bean Counter was my brother Frank's coffee bar, a project he'd been involved with from the initial construction phase to a successful opening eighteen months earlier. Since Frank wasn't known for his perseverance, or his work ethic, I was delighted that he'd finally found a career he wanted to devote his life to. Not only that, but the Bean Counter had utterly defied my expectations and become a popular hangout for area singles, a gathering place for teens, and *the* place for anyone in North Stamford to grab a gourmet snack on the go.

It sounded as though Pam's farm and the coffee bar were in the same neighborhood. Since Bob lived in the other direction, however, I wondered what had taken him all the way across town for a cup of coffee.

"That was a stroke of luck," I said.

Bob caught my ironic tone. "Actually, that's something else I need to talk to you about."

My gaze flickered toward the trailer, then back up to the steps of the house where Aunt Rose was watching the proceedings with amusement. Behind her, both of my Poodles had their wet black noses pressed hard against the front window. Their chagrin at being denied a place in the afternoon's festivities was obvious, yet another issue I'd have to deal with shortly.

That made three problems and counting. How could there possibly be something else?

"Excuse me," said Pam. "I'll just go and get Willow out of the trailer while you two talk."

"Great idea," said Bob. He turned and watched her walk all the way back to the curb. My ex, the king of the delaying tactics.

"Bob, what's going on?"

Slowly, he brought his attention back to me. "It happened pretty much the way Pam said. She and I met a couple of weeks ago. We got started talking and one thing led to another. She invited me out to her farm, and when I got there, all these kids were running around having a great time. It made me think about the things I missed out on in my own childhood. Growing up in the city —"

"I thought you liked the city."

"I do. But I used to watch Roy Rogers and the Lone Ranger on TV, and I really wanted to be a cowboy."

Yeah, right. I'd known Bob for years. This was the first I'd heard of any unrequited cowboy fantasies. The current bout of nostalgia notwithstanding, I'd be willing to bet he'd outgrown them by the time he was five.

"Anyway, you know how it is with kids these days. They're all growing up way too fast. There I was at Pam's place watching children who weren't in front of a TV, or playing video games, or hooked to a computer. They were laughing, and dirty, and outside in the fresh air just having good old-fashioned fun. So I put two and two together and came up with — "

"Four," I admitted. The picture he painted was pretty appealing.

"Not that Davey doesn't already have a lot of great stuff going on in his life," Bob said carefully.

As divorced parents who'd been living apart, with only minimal contact since our son was less than a year old, Bob and I were still learning how to do the parenting thing as a team. For Davey's sake, both of us were determined to make the new living arrangement work; and so far, we'd managed to keep things running fairly smoothly. Of course this was the first time — ever — that Bob had made a major decision about Davey's life without consulting me.

If I ranted and raved, I could probably make him back down. Or I could just hang loose for a little while and see how things were going to play out. Bottom line, was I mature enough to be ready to give up some control over my son's life?

Out on the street, Pam was backing Willow down the ramp. A bushy white tail appeared, followed a moment later by a golden palomino rump. The pony was of medium size, her back standing level with Pam's chest. Her white mane was just as thick as her tail, and a silvery forelock hung down over her dished face from between two tiny ears. Her eyes were big and brown, and she had a star on her forehead as well as high white stockings on both hind legs.

Calmly the pony continued her descent until all four hooves were on the road. Immediately she was surrounded by excited children. I held my breath, afraid she might spook, but Willow merely flicked her ears at the attentive horde and began nosing pockets for treats.

31

"Oh my," I breathed. "She's adorable."

"Isn't she? Davey's going to love her."

Yes, he would, I realized sadly. For a few minutes, I'd been so distracted by the utopian vision Bob had created, not to mention the pony herself, that I'd forgotten all about practical matters.

"Unfortunately that doesn't change the fact that we don't have any place to keep a pony. Nor do I have any idea how to take care of one."

"That's the great part," said Bob. "You don't have to do a thing. Pam just brought Willow over here today for fun. After Davey has a ride around the neighborhood, she'll load her back up and take her back to the farm. Willow will stay there and Pam will take care of everything. A couple times a week, I'll take Davey over for riding lessons."

"It sounds as though you have this all worked out."

"I do," Bob said earnestly. "Trust me."

Trust him? Now there was the rub. Trust wasn't something I came by easily. A defense mechanism to be sure, but one that had served me well when I remembered to use it. Unfortunately, where men were concerned I hadn't remembered nearly often enough.

Ah well, I thought. Once more into the fray.

"All right —"

"Excellent!"

"Just one thing."

Bob's celebration stopped mid-stride.

"What was the something else you were going to tell me a minute ago?"

"Oh, that. It's more good news, actually."

Pardon me for thinking I'd had about as much good news as I could stand for one day.

"Frank and I are going into business together."

"You . . . *what?*"

"I'm buying out his partner's share of the Bean Counter. Now that I'll be staying in Connecticut permanently, it seemed like a good idea to line up a job. With the coffee bar being such a success, Gloria had been talking to Frank about cashing in her share. She wants to retire to Florida and take her profits with her. Frank and I sat down last week and ran the numbers."

Of course he would do that, I thought. Bob was an accountant. Or at least he had been until he'd moved to Texas and taken a share in a wildcat drilling company in return for bookkeeping services. Who would ever have expected that his oil well would actually come in?

"It looks like a sound investment to me," Bob was saying. "And Frank likes the idea of keeping the business in the family. Who knows, another year like this last one and we might even start looking to expand."

"Expand?" I said weakly.

It was all a little much to take in. Not that long ago I'd despaired of my little brother ever finding a job he would stick with long enough for benefits to kick in, not to mention a woman he might see for more than two weeks in a row. Now suddenly Frank was not only married to a wonderful woman named Bertie, he was also, apparently, turning into something of an entrepreneur.

"Melanie." Rose tapped me on the shoulder. "Could you give me just a minute?"

"Sure, Aunt Rose," I said guiltily. The poor woman had been standing in front of the house waiting for me for the last fifteen minutes.

"About the Dachshund puppy . . ."

Of course, the puppy.

"I'll be right back," I told Bob. Rose and I went inside. "Let me get you a crate. I have a little one in the basement that I used for housebreaking Eve last fall. It should be just the right size."

On the way, I gave my aunt a crash course

in puppy management. We covered feeding, teething, crate training, and basic discipline, with Aunt Rose nodding thoughtfully as each new topic was outlined. I'd seen my aunt in action before. Now that she knew the fundamentals, I had no doubt that she'd turn the little Dachshund into an upstanding member of society in no time.

"Call me if you have any questions," I said as I walked Rose out to her car. Over by the curb, Pam was putting a saddle on Willow's back while Bob led the kids in a game to guess the pony's name. "I'm sure you'll do fine."

"Yes, we will," Rose said firmly. "You know, I've never had a dog before. I had no idea they could be so endearing."

I smiled, enjoying the notion of my very proper aunt being wrapped around the tiny paw of a Dachshund puppy. "Have you given him a name yet?"

"Not a real one. Because, of course, he isn't ours. Peter and I have just been calling him Dox for short."

I stowed the crate in the back of her car. "Good luck."

Aunt Rose cast a meaningful glance toward the melee at the curb. "You, too."

As she drove away, I lingered by the side of the yard. Pam had finished tacking up the pony. Davey, wearing a huge grin, was holding Willow's reins and waiting to see what would happen next. After rummaging in the back of her truck, Pam produced a white plastic safety helmet which she fitted to Davey's head. A strap fastened under his chin.

Bob walked over to join me. "He's just going to take a little ride around the block. Then we'll load Willow back up and take her back to the barn."

Pam looked over at Bob, waiting for permission. "Ready?"

"No!" I cried suddenly. "Wait!"

I ran back to the house and emerged a minute later with the camera, freshly loaded with film. "Okay, now."

Pam led Davey around the pony's left side and boosted him up into the saddle. He landed lightly and clutched almost immediately for Willow's bushy mane. Pam gave him a minute to get comfortable, then showed him how to fit his feet into the stirrups. Though she put the single rein in Davey's hand, a lead rope snapped to the side of the bit gave her control. I shooed Bob back over to stand beside them and lined up my shot.

"Smile!" I said.

The command was wholly unnecessary.

All three looked enormously pleased with themselves. The adults stood on either side of the pony, and when Bob reached a hand around his son's back, Pam did the same. They linked arms, cradling Davey between them. Willow lifted her head and pricked her ears, and I took the picture.

"Be back in a bit." Pam's braid swung between her shoulder blades as she turned the pony in a small circle away from the trailer.

Bob flashed me a "thumbs up," then steadied Davey as Willow began to walk. The other kids skipped alongside, forming a neighborhood parade. I thought about going with them, but Pam and Bob, who were now chatting across Willow's back, seemed to have the situation well in hand.

Besides, I could hear Eve barking in the house. The Poodles didn't take kindly to being locked away when there was something interesting going on. Exciting as the new pony was, I had other priorities.

"Davey, wave!" I called.

He did and I snapped another picture. Then I went in the house to see to my dogs.

3

According to American Kennel Club rules, Eve wasn't eligible to be shown until she reached six months of age. Since she was a Poodle, however, preparations for her career had begun much earlier than that. For starters, I had to register her with the AKC, which meant coming up with a show name. Because Faith's litter was the first I'd ever bred, it also meant that I needed to choose a kennel name for myself.

A kennel name is a very useful thing to have, even for someone like me who is in all likelihood never going to be more than a small, hobby breeder. For one thing, it makes for easy identification of a dog's origins. Any Standard Poodle owner looking back through his dog's pedigree and finding such kennel names as Rimskittle, Syrena, Alekai, or Graphic can rest assured that his Poodle descends from quality stock produced by breeders who placed a premium on doing right by the breed.

Secondly, affixing your own kennel name

to stock you've bred is a matter of personal satisfaction. It announces to the dog show world that these are animals you are justifiably proud to be associated with.

Many people chose prefixes that derive in some way from their own names, or those of their children or loved ones. This tendency accounts for the proliferation of monikers such as Car-bob, Suestan, ShirlRob, and Brendawyn. Having tried out a couple of possible combinations, notably Meldave (sounded like the name of a character on *Seinfeld*), Mel-tra (definitely an alien planet), and Samanie (not going there!), I quickly decided to follow Aunt Peg's example and simply opt for a name that sounded agreeable. With high hopes for the future of my small endeavor and a nod toward the joy my two Poodles had already brought me, I chose Elysian. Eve became, in the eyes of the American Kennel Club, Elysian Eve.

Like her dam, Eve was blessed with a profuse, fast growing coat, and when it comes to getting a Poodle ready for the show ring, hair is all important. Poodles are allowed to be shown in three different trims. The continental and the English saddle are the more ornate clips, worn by adult dogs, and familiar to anyone who has ever seen a Poodle being exhibited. At nine months of age, Eve was wearing the puppy trim which allowed for only her face, her feet, and the base of her tail to be clipped. A thick blanket of hair, shaped to follow her outline, covered the rest of her body.

So far we'd been to a handful of shows together. Young as she was, Eve was showing mostly for socialization. The point of the exercise was simply to go and have fun. Unfortunately, that didn't mean I could skimp on the preparation. Saturday night, I gave Eve a bath and blew her coat dry, an exacting process that takes every bit as long as it sounds like it would. I also fielded a quick call from Sam, home at his house in Redding doing the same to his Standard Poodle, Champion Cedar Crest Scimitar, more familiarly known as Tar.

Sam said he was just calling to check in. I thought — but didn't say — that I'd have appreciated the sentiment more if it had taken place during the time at the end of the previous year that he had been missing from my life. Then there hadn't been any phone calls at all.

Once he was back, Sam seemed to think that we should simply take up where we'd left off. Pardon me, but I'm not quite that easy.

I'd resisted; Sam had pursued. Eventually, that bit of yin-ing and yang-ing around had led to the unlikely arrangement we now found ourselves in. We were — once again — dating, and trying to redefine the state of our relationship one step at a time.

All I can say is that it's a sad commentary when your love life has been reduced to an agenda more befitting to recovery.

Sunday's dog show was being held in Rhode Island. Aside from Eve and Tar, Eve's littermate Zeke, now owned by Aunt Peg, was also entered. As a champion, Tar would be entered for Best of Variety; and since the classes were divided by sex, Eve and Zeke would not compete against each other except in the unlikely eventuality that each of them managed to beat the competition for Winners Dog and Winners Bitch. Optimally, we all had a shot at winning. Practically speaking, however, things never seem to work out that way.

With the excitement of Willow's arrival fresh in his mind and the promise of another ride on Sunday, Davey had opted not to come with me to the dog show. Instead, he'd spent Saturday night with Bob, another of our new arrangements that I'm trying — with varying degrees of success — to act like an adult about. Davey had taken Faith with him to his father's house. I was planning to meet up with the three of them there later that evening.

The car seemed curiously empty as Eve and I followed the thruway up the Connecticut coast. My son is one of those rare children who doesn't mind long car trips, perhaps because he was indoctrinated at an early age. He watches the scenery, plays automobile bingo, and almost always feels compelled to entertain us with warbled renditions of whatever song is his current favorite. He has even been known to induce Faith to howl along.

This car trip was quiet by comparison. I was actually able to hear the radio, and the only other sound was Eve's gentle snoring in the back seat. I'd thought I'd revel in the peace and quiet. Instead the damn trip seemed to take forever. Go figure.

I wasn't running late, but, true to form, Aunt Peg had gotten to the show site early. It was a good thing, too, because the facility was tiny and grooming space was at a premium. I found Aunt Peg and Sam set up together, tucked away in the dark corner of an interior hallway. They'd deliberately spread out their crates and grooming tables over a larger area than the two of them needed, thereby subjecting themselves to the scowls and disgruntled comments of latecomers who were having trouble finding room.

"It's about time," Aunt Peg said grumpily as I dragged my dolly over and began to unload. "I've turned away half a dozen people in the last fifteen minutes alone. I thought we were going to have a riot on our hands."

Trust me, there's nothing my Aunt Peg would have enjoyed more. She may be in her sixties, but Peg maintains a schedule and a social life that would run a twenty-year-old ragged. Very little escapes her steely gaze, and she's never been one to leave well enough alone.

All right, I'll be blunt. Aunt Peg is a trouble-maker. She's also one of the smartest, most determined women I've ever met. I'd never admit it to her, but I only hope I'm doing half so well when I reach her age.

"Don't tell me you've been stirring up the Bichon people again."

"Worse." Sam came around from behind his grooming table to lend a hand with the unloading. "This time it was a whole contingent of Dachshund exhibitors. They hadn't even asked if there was any room before she sent them packing."

"Who needed to hear the question? They

were eyeing our little corner like it was prime chicken liver. Wet washcloth dogs." Aunt Peg sniffed, obviously referring to the smooth-coated variety. "What do they have to groom anyway? They could blow on those dogs and walk them in the ring."

Well, not exactly, but I could see her point. Poodles have to be groomed right before they're shown. Many facets of preparation — brushing, putting in a topknot, scissoring, spraying — can't be done ahead; and indeed, the primping continues even while the dogs are in the ring. It can be frustrating to arrive at a show and find that all the available grooming space is taken up by exhibitors with short haired breeds who've put out a bunch of chairs and sat down to socialize.

"She's been on the warpath all morning," Sam confided in a loud whisper. He reached around me to set my tack box on top of a crate and managed to give my waist a squeeze in the process. "Now that you're here, maybe she'll settle down."

A year ago, we would have kissed hello. A year ago, a lot of things would have come more easily.

The one thing that hadn't changed was the frisson of awareness that hummed along my nerve endings whenever Sam was near.

During the time he'd been away, I'd almost managed to convince myself that I was over that. I'd hoped that when — if — Sam returned, I'd look at him dispassionately and wonder why I'd ever found his shaggy blond hair and rugged features attractive.

Unfortunately for the sake of my equilibrium, that hadn't happened. Instead, I'd taken one look and tumbled all over again. Mother Nature was enjoying the last laugh at my expense, no doubt.

"I heard that," Aunt Peg said. "And I am not on the warpath. I am merely annoyed." Her brow lowered into a frown. "Extremely annoyed."

"What happened?"

"Judge change," said Sam. "Mike Zinman didn't make it."

"Who did?"

"Rachel Lyons."

That wasn't good. The sole reason that the three of us had made the effort to drive several hours to this godforsaken little dog show was because Aunt Peg had approved of the judge. "Good hands on a puppy," she said. It was one of her highest accolades.

I knew there would be no such praise accorded Rachel Lyons. The woman was a Dalmatian breeder and a member of Aunt Peg's kennel club. The two had known each other for years, and when Rachel had decided to expand the number of breeds she was approved to judge by applying for the remainder of the Non-Sporting group, Peg had offered to share her vast knowledge of Poodles.

Not to worry, Rachel had replied blithely. She'd been watching poodles from outside the ring for years. Besides, the AKC had a video available. She was sure she already knew quite enough to pass judgment on Peg's chosen breed. My aunt had hidden her outrage well, but I doubted that the two women had spoken since.

"You could go to the superintendent and get your money back," I pointed out.

"I'm here now." Peg's tone was heavy with disgruntlement. "The entry fee is the least of my worries. Zeke is bathed and trimmed and I've driven all this way. There's nothing to do but chalk it up to experience."

All too often, that's showing dogs in a nutshell. Nine parts frustration for every one part elation.

"Is that all your stuff?" Aunt Peg asked. "Where's my nephew?" She peered around the setup as if she expected to find Davey hiding behind Eve or tucked inside a crate.

"Home with Bob. Much to my surprise, we have a new addition to the family."

"Oh?" Sam, who'd gone back to working on Tar, swiveled to face me, suddenly attentive. "Is Bob getting married again?"

And they say women are catty.

"Not quite." I smothered a grin.

Now that Bob is back in the neighborhood, there's a definite undercurrent of rivalry between the two men in my life. Sam feels it was underhanded of my ex-husband to put in an appearance soon after he left town. Bob believes that Sam was a cad for leaving Davey and me hanging.

So if my ex's name slips into the conversation a little more often than necessary when I'm talking to Sam, I'm not entirely sure I should be held accountable. Payback's a bitch, isn't it?

"Bob bought Davey a pony," I said.

"A pony?" Aunt Peg looked up from unwrapping Zeke's ears. "Isn't that lovely? I had a pony when I was a little girl."

"You did?"

"You shouldn't sound so surprised, Melanie. I'm sure there are scores of things you don't know about me."

I was certain there were. And equally certain that I was better off not knowing most of them.

Sam and Peg already had their two Poodles brushed out. I patted the top of my rubber-matted grooming table and hoisted Eve up into place, then opened my tack box, got out a bunch of supplies, and quickly went to work.

"Speaking of surprises," I said. "I had a visit from Aunt Rose yesterday, too."

"Don't tell me," said Peg. "She wanted you to take care of that puppy, didn't she?"

"What puppy?" asked Sam.

"A Dachshund. Just like the ones Aunt Peg shooed away so rudely earlier."

"Aha." Sam nodded knowingly.

"Now listen here, both of you." She shook a comb in our direction. "For once, you can't place the blame on me. This problem is all Rose's doing."

"With a little help from Peter and the puppy's breeder," I said.

Peg had finished unwrapping Zeke's head and ears. Now she picked up a knitting needle and deftly parted the hair, resectioning so that she could put in the tight topknot he would wear into the ring. "I can't imagine what they were thinking. Anyone with an ounce of sense would know that the very idea of offering a live puppy at a charity auction is perfectly abhorrent."

"I have to agree," said Sam. "Where did the puppy come from?"

"I didn't find out," I told him. "Though

Rose said that he was very well bred. Apparently his sire won the variety at Westminster a couple of months ago. I was still trying to get the rest of the facts when Bob pulled up outside with the pony."

"He brought a horse to your house?" Sam asked incredulously.

"I think that's sweet," said Peg. "Stupid, mind you, but sweet."

Eve was lying flat on the grooming table. I reached down and flipped her over so I could line-brush her other side. "Not a horse, a pony. They're the smaller version. Her name is Willow."

Sam shook his head. "Where are you going to keep this pony, in the garage? The backyard? Maybe you could tie her to Davey's basketball hoop."

"Actually, she already has a home. Willow's going to be staying at Long Ridge Pony Farm with a woman named Pam who teaches kids how to ride. They just stopped by for a visit."

"Much like Rose," Peg said disparagingly. "She had no idea who'd bred that puppy when we spoke, so I called Peter and asked him to check the name on the blue slip. It came from Marian Firth."

The name meant nothing to me, but Sam looked surprised. "I've seen her show in the

49

group," he said. "She has some very nice dogs."

"She does indeed," Aunt Peg agreed. "She's a second-generation breeder, and her Dachshunds are every bit as lovely as her mother's were. Marian certainly knows better than to let a puppy of hers be offered as a prize to the highest bidder. Whatever's going on with that puppy, I can't imagine she would have agreed to it."

"Excuse me! Coming through!"

There was a commotion at the end of the crowded hallway. A young woman holding a microphone, followed by an equally young man toting a video camera on his shoulder, elbowed their way toward us. Her gaze scanned the three of us briefly and came to rest on me.

"Are you Melanie Travis?"

So help me, I thought about denying it. If I'd had any inkling of what was to come, I'd certainly have done so.

Instead I nodded.

"Well, it's about time. Rich, get up here and get a shot of this. We've been all over this damn dog show looking for you."

4

Startled by the disturbance, Eve slipped out from beneath my hands and leapt to her feet. Faith was trained to overlook such things, but Eve was just a puppy. If someone was playing a game, she wanted to play too. I placed a restraining hand gently on her withers to calm her as she danced in place on the rubber-matted tabletop.

"You've been looking for me? Why?"

The woman thrust out a hand. "I'm Jill Prescott from KZBN Cable in Norwalk. I want to do a story on you."

"You're kidding."

"No, I'm not," Jill said earnestly. A tiny frown line furrowed her brow, but considering that she barely looked eighteen, it was going to be years before Jill Prescott had to worry about wrinkles.

Her ash blond hair was swept back off her face and held in place by a velvet headband. Her nails were manicured; her lipstick, perfect. Her smile was wide enough, and bright enough, to light our dark corner of the hallway.

"This is going to be so great," she enthused. "Meet Rich, my cameraman."

Rich had broad shoulders, spiked hair, and a pierced eyebrow. He held up a laconic hand in greeting. "Hey."

As his arm lowered, it reached toward Eve. It didn't take a genius to see that he was about to mess up the hair I'd just finished brushing. I caught his hand before he could touch her and moved it gently away. "Sorry, I'm getting her ready to go in the ring."

"Perfect!" cried Jill. "We'll get footage of that, too."

"Footage for what?"

"To go with the interview."

"What interview?" asked Peg. She glanced at her watch and then at me. "Time is passing, Melanie. Keep brushing." Her gaze swung back to Jill. "Did you say you're from Norwalk, as in Connecticut?"

"Yes, KZBN Cable —"

"What are you doing in Rhode Island?"

"I looked on the Internet," Jill said brightly. "And this dog show was the closest, so I figured you'd be here."

A somewhat cockeyed assumption, I thought. But then again everything about Jill Prescott from KZBN Cable seemed slightly cockeyed. I picked Eve up, laid her down on her side, and went back to work.

"You really came all this way hoping to find me?"

"Of course. And now everything's going to work out perfectly because we can get some shots of you with your dogs. That's what you do, right? You show Poodles at dog shows. And you're a special needs tutor at Howard Academy in Greenwich —"

"Wait a minute." My hand stilled. "How do you know that?"

Jill looked affronted. "It's not as if I don't have my sources." She glanced at Sam. "Is this your husband?"

"No," I snapped, then added belatedly, "and it's none of your business."

"Don't mind me. I'm just nosy about things like that. And I figured since you have a child —"

"Stop right there!"

"Yes?" Eve lifted an ear at my tone, but Jill's smile never even wavered.

"Who *are* you and what do you want?"

For just a moment, she finally looked unsure. Not of herself, I was betting. More likely, Jill was questioning my mental capabilities.

"I'm sorry," she said. "I thought I explained all that."

I crossed my arms over my chest. "Try explaining it again."

Tar was lounging on his table now, finished except for the final hair spray, which would be applied shortly before he went in the ring. Sam nudged me aside, picked up the brush I'd been using, and went to work on Eve. Thank goodness the puppy didn't have much hair yet. At the rate things were going, it would be a miracle if she was ready in time.

"I want to do a story about you for KZBN Cable television."

The announcement didn't make a whole lot more sense the second time she said it than it had the first.

"Why me?"

"Well, because you're a local celebrity."

I most definitely was *not*.

"You know," Jill said in a wheedling tone, "with your crime solving and all. You've been written up in the newspaper lots of times."

Once. My name had been mentioned once. Well, twice if you counted the time I'd gotten hurt in a fire at Howard Academy. But that wasn't crime solving, it was more a matter of being caught in the wrong place at the wrong time.

"I don't understand what's going on," I

said. "Where did you get my name? Why do you know all this stuff about me? I have no idea what producer gave you this assignment, but I can assure you he or she was mistaken. I'm not a celebrity and there's nothing noteworthy about my life."

"But there *is*," Jill persisted.

She turned around and handed her microphone to Rich. Like we were going to be talking woman to woman now. Like we were friends.

"Look, let me be honest with you."

"That would be nice."

Aunt Peg lifted a brow at my sarcastic tone. Sam merely grinned and kept brushing.

"Nobody assigned this story to me. I found it for myself."

A throat cleared loudly in the background.

"All right," Jill amended, "Rich and I found it together. Do you have any idea how hard it is to get started in the entertainment industry? I went to college and majored in broadcast communications. My credentials are as good as anybody's. But I can't even get my foot in the door at the major networks. So I decided to start a little smaller."

Presumably KZBN fit the bill. I lived two towns over from Norwalk and I'd never heard of the station.

Jill tossed her head. The artfully arranged blond hair fluffed and resettled. "So here I am, out in the boonies, working for a pittance, and I still can't get any on-air time. I want to be a reporter, but all the good assignments go to the people who have been there for years. Years! Let me tell you, I have no intention of devoting years of my life to moving up the ranks at some backwater cable station."

"So you decided to speed up the process."

"Exactly. That's where you come in. You're going to be the story that gets me noticed."

"There's only one small flaw in your plan."

Sam had his back to us, but it didn't matter. I could still see his shoulders shaking. He was laughing, damn him. Even Aunt Peg looked amused by this turn of events.

"I am *not* a story."

"Sure you are." Jill's sunny smile was back. "You're The School Teacher Mom Who Takes a Bite Out of Crime in Her Spare Time. Doesn't that sound great? I think that's going to be my lead."

Her perkiness was really beginning to get on my nerves.

"Listen," I said. "I understand your

problem. But what I still don't see is why you've come to me. There are plenty of celebrities living in Fairfield County. Real ones, like Diana Ross, Paul Newman, and David Letterman. Those are the people you should go after. Not me."

Jill hesitated briefly. Her cheeks grew pink. Obligingly, Rich leapt in to fill the silence.

"Those people also have managers, and publicists, and gated driveways," he said. "You don't."

Right. I should have known.

"I guess that means I wasn't your first choice."

"Hell, no," said Rich. That admission was followed by a yelp as Jill stuck a leg under the grooming table and kicked him in the shin. Maybe she was hoping I wouldn't notice.

"You were very near the top of the list," she said determinedly.

"Well, I'm sorry to disappoint you, but like the other candidates who turned you down, I'm afraid you're going to have to take me off your list. There's no story here."

"There is," Jill insisted. "There has to be."

Let me guess, I thought. This was what it felt like to be someone's last resort.

"Melanie?"

I looked over at Aunt Peg and saw that Eve had her topknot in and Sam was scissoring a finish on her trim. Considering her youth, there hadn't been that much preparation to do. Still it was nice of Sam to cover for me.

"I'm going up to the ring to get our numbers," said Peg. "Be ready to go when I get back." Figure this problem out, her tone implied. And make it go away.

I couldn't have agreed more.

As she left, I turned back to Jill and Rich. "Look, I don't have time to argue with you right now. My life is not the story you want, and I'm not going to do any interview."

"Fine," said Jill.

Her acquiescence came entirely too easily. A moment later, I realized why. Rich and Jill exchanged a look.

"Backup plan," said Rich.

Jill nodded.

That didn't sound good.

I knew I'd probably kick myself later, but I had to ask. "What's the backup plan?"

"You don't have to talk to me." Jill stepped away, and Rich followed. "In fact, feel free to ignore us completely. We'll just be over here, blending into the background."

"And doing what?"

"Observing," said Jill. "That's all. You're convinced there's no story. I think there is. Let's see who's right. According to my sources, you have a remarkable propensity for stumbling over dead bodies."

If I'd had the time, I might have taken exception to that characterization. Instead, I was busy stuffing my pockets with dried liver and squeaky toys that I would use to get and keep Eve's attention in the ring.

"One might even think that you attract trouble," Rich interjected from his new post on the other side of the hallway.

Like that might make me feel better.

"So we'll just follow along and keep tabs on how things are going," said Jill. "And the next time you find yourself in the middle of a mystery, I'll be the one who breaks the news. I'm not just doing this for myself, you know. My story will make both of us famous."

"I don't want to be famous —" I broke off abruptly as Aunt Peg reappeared waving our numbered armbands and bearing the news that the Poodle ring was running early. Fast judging was often sloppy judging; I could tell Aunt Peg wasn't pleased. "Then again, maybe you'll get lucky and my aunt will murder the Poodle judge."

"That's not funny," Peg snapped. She

hopped Zeke down off his table and let him shake out on the ground. Now that she was a judge herself, she felt obliged to conduct herself with the utmost decorum.

"Who's trying to be funny?" I asked.

I patted my pockets and unrolled Eve's leash. Sam grabbed Tar, and we were off.

We arrived at the ring in a rush and found our judge having her picture taken with the previous breed's winners. That gave us a minute to catch our breath and regroup.

I used my long comb to flip through the silky hair on Eve's ears. Sam pulled out his scissors and rounded the pompon on Tar's tail. Aunt Peg put some more spray in Zeke's topknot. Poodle exhibitors are like gypsies; everything we own follows us around.

Jill and Rich, I was pleased to see, had found themselves a spot all the way over the other side of the ring. Maybe they really would be content to remain in the background. After a couple hours of that, I'd think anyone would be willing to concede that my life was every bit as boring as I'd said it was.

For most show dogs, the long road that leads to a championship begins in the Puppy Class. In most breeds, puppies are shown for experience and admired by the judges, but not often considered for points. Not so Poodles. Being a flashy, fast-maturing breed judged on their temperament and animation as much as their physical structure, Poodles do a great deal of winning as puppies. The fact that many people — judges and exhibitors alike — prefer the look of the puppy trim to the two highly stylized adult clips doesn't hurt, either.

All of which didn't help Aunt Peg one bit under Rachel Lyons. The two women locked eyes briefly as Peg led Zeke into the lineup for the first class. Mrs. Lyons managed a tight smile. It's considered bad form to acknowledge friendships in the show ring. In theory, judging is supposed to be bias-free and totally objective. Nobody really believes that, but we all do a decent job of pretending.

I watched as Aunt Peg put Zeke through his paces. There were only two puppies in the class. The other was several months older than Zeke and a good deal hairier, but with a plainer face and feet that tended to go flat on the slippery floor. He moved with reach and drive, however, and did not, unlike Zeke, bounce straight up into the air every time his handler squeezed his squeaky toy. Aunt Peg didn't look entirely surprised to be placed second of two, and she accepted her red ribbon with good grace.

With no entries in the intervening classes, Open Dogs was next, followed by Winner's Dog, then Puppy Bitch. Unless the puppy won Winner's and Aunt Peg had to take Zeke back in the ring to contend for Reserve, he was done for the day. Five hours of driving, at least that much time spent grooming, and all she had to show for her efforts was a scrap of satin ribbon.

Aunt Peg, however, wasn't displeased. "For a baby, I thought he acquitted himself beautifully," she said, rewarding Zeke with a piece of liver from the pouch on her belt.

Eve caught the exchange and wagged her tail hopefully. Poodles don't miss much, and staying one step ahead of them requires constant vigilance. I was supposed to be saving her treats for the ring, but I slipped her a small piece anyway.

"Beautifully," Sam agreed. His hand lifted and fell, mimicking the puppy's exuberant leaps. "Especially if Mrs. Lyons wanted to examine him at eye level."

"His loss doesn't bode well for Eve and Tar," I mentioned. All three of the Poodles we'd brought to the show were quite closely related. "If she didn't like Zeke . . ."

"Oh, pish," Aunt Peg said under her

breath. "I doubt if Rachel even formed a coherent opinion of the dog. She barely touched either one of them, did you notice?"

Now that she mentioned it, I had.

"You can't judge Poodles properly if you're going to be intimidated by hair," Aunt Peg said firmly. "What's underneath is far more important than the artful presentation on top. If Rachel had come to me, it's the first thing I would have told her."

"Hear, hear!" Terry Denunzio slipped an arm around Aunt Peg's shoulder and insinuated himself into our small group.

Terry was assistant to Crawford Langley, one of the Northeast's busiest and most successful professional handlers. He was impossibly handsome and totally gay and he reveled in both attributes. He was also charming, funny, and a genius when it came to hair.

"You weren't supposed to be listening to that," Aunt Peg said disapprovingly.

"Why not? You were right."

"Of course I was right." Peg refused to be appeased. "I was also whispering. Didn't your mother teach you that it's not polite to eavesdrop?"

"Good heavens, no. My mother's a politician."

"She is?" That was news to me.

"Hey, everybody's got to do something." Terry leaned down and kissed Eve's nose, careful not to touch the lacquered hair around her face and neck. "How's my pretty girl?"

"Not above listening to flattery apparently." The puppy's tail was wagging up over her back. "Where's Crawford?" I asked. "How come he doesn't have any Standards today?"

"We just brought Minis and Toys. Crawford couldn't see the point of trying to show anything bigger in a ring the size of a hatbox."

The excuse made sense, but I wasn't buying it. Not entirely anyway. Professional handlers make their money showing dogs. Good venues, bad venues, they're paid to cope. It's amateurs like me who usually wimp out.

"Besides . . ." Terry cast a meaningful glance in Tar's direction.

Now we were getting to the heart of the matter. Sam's dog had recently returned to specials competition after a long layoff and he was ready to win. Fortunately, the judges had been agreeing. In the last month, he'd been Best of Variety every time he was shown and had placed in a number of groups.

"Don't tell me Crawford's running scared?" I teased.

A handler's specials dog is his showcase. If they think they're going to get beaten, they stay home. Of course the whole point was never to admit to such insecurities.

On the other hand, one of the things I liked best about Terry was his big mouth.

"Excuse me." Aunt Peg poked me in the shoulder. Hard. "Not that I don't find all this chatter entertaining, but are you even marginally aware that Reserve Winners just finished and your class is next?"

I spun around and had a look. Of course, Aunt Peg was right. Back when I was showing Faith in the Puppy Class, I used to stand at ringside and agonize over each passing minute as my nerves grew taut and butterflies danced in my stomach.

Aunt Peg's annoyance notwithstanding, I had to say this was a better system. I took a few seconds to flip my comb through Eve's neck hair, smooth her ears, and ball my skinny little show lead up in my fist. Then I chucked her under the chin and we went sailing into the ring.

Time to have some fun.

5

It would be nice to think that I accomplished a great feat in winning my Puppy Class after Aunt Peg hadn't managed to win hers, but since Eve was the only puppy bitch entered, my success was pretty much assured. Like her littermate, Eve was under the impression that the show ring had been created expressly for her enjoyment. Though she did, for the most part, keep all four feet on the ground, my Poodle was hard put to contain her enthusiasm for the task at hand.

Those familiar with obedience trials, where dog and handler work as a stolid team and compliance must be immediate and absolute, have been known to say that breed competition is a frivolous exercise, lacking in training and discipline. Nothing could be farther from the truth. By nine months of age, Eve had learned to stand quietly while being examined by a stranger, to keep her attention riveted on me and my cues despite any number of outside distractions, and to trot at my side on a loose leash with her head and tail held high.

What she hadn't yet learned to do was control her natural exuberance. All of which would stand her in good stead as her career proceeded.

Good judges tend to allow youngsters some leeway when it comes to their behavior in the ring. They know that a puppy who shows like a seasoned campaigner often matures into an adult that competes with all the flair of an automaton. Eve took that leeway and ran with it. So no one was more surprised than I when the puppy cavorted all the way to the Winners Bitch award.

"Congratulations!" Aunt Peg crowed, clapping me on the back as I emerged from the ring, clutching my purple ribbon and wearing what I imagine was a somewhat shocked expression.

"How did that happen?" I asked.

"You brought the best bitch on the day, and wonder of wonders, Rachel found you." What Aunt Peg politely didn't mention was that there'd only been two other bitches in the entry, neither one a potential star.

"Eve's first point." I was still somewhat dazed. "From the Puppy Class."

It seemed all the more impressive since I hadn't managed that feat with Faith.

"You'll have to have a picture," Peg pro-nounced. "But first, back you go for Best of Variety."

Sam had already walked Tar into the ring and was setting him up on the mat. The only champion Standard Poodle entered, his was the place of honor at the head of the line. The Winners Dog stood second, and Eve and I brought up the rear.

The judging was over quickly. Faced with a specials dog who looked the part; a sound, if somewhat unexciting Winners Dog; and a puppy who used the BOV class as an opportunity to flip around on the end of her lead like a recently hooked fish, Rachel Lyons wasted no time in giving Tar the top award. Eve, by virtue of being the only bitch in the ring, was Best of Opposite Sex. That meant I now had two nice ribbons to get my picture taken with.

Tar, who had just qualified for the Non-Sporting group, would have his picture taken later. Sam and Aunt Peg headed back to the setup, but I lingered at ringside with Eve until Mrs. Lyons took her next photo break. By then, an assortment of Bichons, Lhasas, and Shibas had shown up for the same reason. Finally, our turn came to pose.

Now that the competition was over, conversation between exhibitor and judge was permitted. As I handed the ribbons back to the judge, who would hold them in the photo, I thanked her for the win.

"She's an adorable puppy," she replied. "I'm sure you'll do very well with her." As I reached down to set Eve's legs, Mrs. Lyons added, "I see you travel with quite an entourage."

"Excuse me?" I straightened, wondering if I'd heard her correctly. Was she making an oblique reference to my connection with Aunt Peg?

The judge nodded toward the other end of the ring. In the rush of showing, and then winning, I'd forgotten all about Jill and Rich. There they were, my own personal camera crew. Legs pressed against the barrier that was meant to keep spectators out, Rich was taping and Jill was speaking into her microphone. Catching my eye, Rich flashed me a thumbs up.

Quickly I looked away. "I'm sorry. They seem to think they're doing a story about me. I hope they didn't get in your way."

"Not at all," Mrs. Lyons said happily. "Are you somebody famous?"

"No."

I was tempted to add that, on the contrary, Jill and Rich were somebody desperate, but the photographer chose that moment to toss his squeaky toy, and instead I braced to hold the puppy in place as the flash popped. I couldn't help but notice that the judge's smile was directed just as much toward Rich as it was toward the still photographer.

Photo session finished, I hustled Eve back to the setup. "Guess what?" I said in annoyance as the puppy hopped back up on her table.

Aunt Peg, who already had Zeke half undone, removed a comb from her mouth and asked, "What?"

"I just found out why Mrs. Lyons put Eve up."

"Why?" Sam was sitting on top of Tar's crate, sipping a soda. Since his Poodle had more showing left to do, he'd merely gathered the dog's long, silky ear hair into rubber bands, then left him, snoozing contentedly, on his table.

"Because she saw Jill and Rich taping from ringside and thought I was somebody famous."

"*You?*" Aunt Peg laughed out loud.

"Yes, me," I grumbled, affronted by her reaction all the same.

"A point's a point," Sam said philosophically. "Take them any way you can get them. There will be plenty you deserve that you don't win."

As any dog show exhibitor will be happy

to tell you, Sam was right about that.

"When's your group?" I asked.

He reached over and consulted the schedule. "Third after Sporting and Terrier. They're about to start any minute."

I went to work getting Eve taken apart. Her topknot had to come down and be brushed out, then replaced with the looser pony tails she wore at home. Her ears needed to be wrapped, and her neck hair sprayed with conditioner to dilute the stickiness of the hair spray that had been holding it in place. That done, I offered her a bowl of cool water, then ran her outside for a quick exercise in the parking lot.

By the time I got back, Sam and Tar were heading up to the ring. I stowed the puppy in her crate next to Zeke's and joined Aunt Peg, who was about to follow. It was hard to ignore the fact that Jill and Rich were still trailing along behind.

"Tar looks good," I said as we found our places at ringside.

Group dogs line up in size order, and Sam had taken the position at the head of the line. A liver spotted Dalmatian was behind him, followed by a red Chow. The black Standard Poodle stood on tight, high feet. His neck arched as he surveyed the competition disdainfully.

"So does Sam," Aunt Peg mentioned.

I knew she was dying for me to respond. So help me, I couldn't think of a thing to say. In the ring, the handlers stood up and the dogs began the first go-round.

"I gather you haven't forgiven him yet."

"Would you?" I asked pointedly. I'd expected a quick answer and was surprised when she hesitated. Sam had never been able to do anything wrong in Aunt Peg's eyes.

"I don't know," she said finally. "But then again, the whole point is that you're not me. You're a kinder person than I am, you always have been. Somehow I expected this would all blow over when Sam came to his senses and returned."

Me? Kind? Only in the comparison, I thought. Next to Aunt Peg, a grizzly bear had softer moments.

"One piece of advice," said Peg. "I know you don't want it, but you're getting it anyway. Someday the two of you are going to get back together. I know it, you know it, and Sam knows it too. Don't make him wait too long."

There's nothing longer than the drive home from a dog show where you've lost. The aura of accomplishment that follows winning, however, makes the miles seem to fly by. Even though it was only one point, Eve was now officially started toward her championship.

Not only that, but I had progressed from being a novice exhibitor, who could — on a lucky day — put points on a beautiful bitch that someone else had bred and coached her to show, to being a fledgling breeder who was capable of presenting her own stock creditably enough to get noticed from the Puppy Class. It felt like quite a coup.

Tar had put the finishing touch on our good day by taking third in the Non-Sporting group. The win was duly recorded from ringside by Rich. I'd fully expected Jill Prescott to lose interest as the dog show day wore on. Instead, she and her cameraman had stuck it out until the very end. Indeed, several times during the trip home I found myself examining the cars behind me in the rearview mirror, checking to make sure I wasn't being followed. There's nothing like a little paranoia to keep you on your toes.

Dusk had already fallen by the time we came to our exit on the Merritt Parkway. Eve was asleep beside me, her body curled comfortably in the bucket seat, her black nose resting on her dainty, shaved front paws. She smelled like hair spray, and conditioner, and very clean dog, an aroma I found as comforting as those nostalgic scents from my youth. As I turned into our neighborhood, Eve lifted her head and blinked her eyes.

"Perfect timing," I told her, reaching over to ruffle through the puppy's thick neck hair. "We're almost home."

I'd figured I'd call Bob when we got in to make arrangements to pick up Davey and Faith. But as we pulled onto our road, my foot eased up off the gas pedal in surprise. Our house, which should have been dark and still, was instead lit up like a neon billboard. Inside and outside, every single light had been turned on. From the end of the street, our small Cape stood out like a beacon.

Frowning, I let the Volvo coast down the block and into the driveway. What the heck was going on? Had Bob and Davey decided to meet us here? If so, where was Bob's car? Eve stood up on the seat beside me and began to bark. The noise bounced around the enclosed car, assaulting my ears.

"Shhh." I reached over and cupped a hand around the puppy's muzzle. "Faith can't hear you yet. You'll have to wait until you get inside to brag about your day."

Because an appearance by Bob and Davey was the only way to explain what I was seeing, I fully expected our arrival to bring Faith racing to the front window of the house. It didn't.

"Curiouser and curiouser," I muttered, gathering up some of our stuff. When I opened the car door, Eve leapt over me and ran to the steps. I followed more slowly. Standing back, I stared, perplexed, at the brightly lit house.

If no one was home, who had turned on all the lights? I was certain I hadn't left things this way. Though we'd started out early that morning, the sun had already been up. Maybe I'd left on one light in the kitchen, but nothing like this. Aside from the fact that it was overkill, this festival of light had to be costing me a small fortune.

I joined Eve at the top of the steps, pulled open the storm door, fitted my key to the lock. And froze.

Maybe it was power of suggestion: Jill and Rich shadowing me all day until I'd begun to feel a little hunted. Or maybe it was the fact that I do seem to stumble over more than my share of mysteries. Or maybe I was just growing a little more cautious in my old age.

I pulled the key out of the door and turned the knob. It was locked, just as I'd left it. Dumping my stuff on the stoop, I hopped down the steps and walked around the back of the house. The gate leading into the fenced yard was latched and closed. The back door was securely locked, too.

Eve, who was happy inside or out as long as she was home and with me, took the opportunity to sniff out a few likely spots and pee. Feeling baffled and more than a little foolish, I surveyed the house from the rear, just as I'd done in front. Everything looked okay.

Aside from the lights, all was just as it had been that morning when we'd set out. I unlocked the back door and let the puppy bound ahead of me into the kitchen. If there were any intruders, Eve wasn't too concerned about their presence. She ran directly to the pantry where I keep the dog biscuits, her tail wagging expectantly.

I stopped just inside the back door and began flipping off switches. Almost immediately, the phone began to ring. Nerves stretched tight, I jumped at the sound and spun around. For no discernible reason, my heart was racing. Breath shuddered in my lungs.

In the time it took me to recover, the machine picked up. I stood very still and listened. My message played, followed by a beep.

"Mel?" said a familiar voice. "It's Bob. We were just checking to see if you were back yet —"

Of course it was Bob. Who else would it be? Feeling like an idiot, I dashed across the kitchen and snatched up the phone.

"Bob? I'm here."

"Is everything okay?" he said after a pause. "You sound a little strange."

"Just out of breath. I ran to get the phone." It was as good an excuse as any. I pressed the receiver to my ear and began to walk through the house, turning off lights as I went. "Did you and Davey stop over here today by any chance?"

"At your house? No, why?"

"All my lights are on. Every one. I'm sure I didn't leave the place like this."

Bob thought for a minute. "You probably left when it was still dark and didn't realize —"

"I didn't."

"Maybe you had a short, or a power failure, or a power surge." Bob's knowledge of electricity was about as nonexistent as my own.

"I guess . . ."

"Everything else all right?"

"Fine." I was upstairs now, checking room by room. Everything, even my unmade bed, looked just as I'd left it. Shoulders finally beginning to relax, I headed back downstairs. "Eve won her first point. How are you guys doing?"

"Davey had a great day. Pam said the kid's a natural rider. I'll let him tell you all about it. We'll be there in ten minutes, okay?"

"Great." I hung up the phone, got Eve her biscuit, filled her bowl with fresh, cold water.

And all the while, my thoughts were spinning. I'd had power outages before; power surges, too. They'd never turned on all the lights. But if that didn't explain what had happened, what did?

6

Having followed Aunt Peg's example and happily devoted the majority of my free time to the sport of dogs, I've often wished there was a way to turn my avocation into a career. Unfortunately, unlike my new sister-in-law, Bertie, I lack the talent to be a professional handler. And though I'm now a pretty decent groomer, I've only worked on Poodles. Give me a Cocker, a terrier, or a Maltese and I wouldn't have a clue. As for dog training . . . well, let's just say, Poodles are easy.

Fortunately for the state of my bank account, however, I don't lack for gainful employment. I'm a former special ed. teacher, currently working as a special needs tutor at Howard Academy, a prestigious private school in Greenwich, Connecticut.

There are many things I love about my job. Among them is the fact that most of the school's classrooms are housed in a turn-of-the-century mansion that once belonged to robber baron, Joshua Howard.

Another is that my students are a lively, intelligent, and highly sophisticated bunch who challenge me every day. But the thing I like best is Howard Academy's lenient policy toward certain aspects of my life — namely the Poodles. Faith has been coming with me to school for more than a year, and now that Eve is old enough to have basic manners, she's been accorded the same privilege.

My students love having the dogs in their classroom. They're also not above using the Poodles as an excuse to try to avoid work. I figure their antics are a small price to pay for the luxury of not having to leave my dogs home alone all day.

On Monday, the school day flew by. With temperatures nearing sixty and spring vacation due to start at the end of the week, nobody's mind was on work. I could hardly blame my students for their inattention. Spring fever was infecting me, too.

When the last bell rang, I was already packed and ready to go. The Poodles scampered ahead of me, down the corridor and out to the back parking lot. By the time I reached the Volvo, Faith had her front paws up on the side door and was gazing in the window. If I'd have given her the keys, she probably could have unlocked the doors and warmed up the car for me.

I know what you're thinking, but Poodles are like that.

I stopped at home long enough to drop off the dogs and make sure Bob had met Davey's school bus. The two of them were due at the pony farm for Davey's second riding lesson. Armed with a list from Pam, Bob and Davey had gone shopping the day before while I'd been in Rhode Island. Upon my return Davey had shown off his new outfit, which included a helmet, paddock boots, and leather chaps.

He spun around the living room, modeling the ensemble like a runway veteran. Bear in mind, this is my child we're talking about, the one who thinks it's okay to wear dirty clothes he finds on the floor if his mother doesn't get them into the hamper fast enough. Davey is not what you would call fashion forward.

"Chaps?" I whispered to Bob out of the side of my mouth. "He looks like a cowboy. I don't know much about horses, but I do know that was an English saddle Willow was wearing the other day."

Having secured our approval of his finery, Davey was chasing Faith and Eve around the room. The Poodles seemed mostly unimpressed — they're not fashion forward either — and Davey's running was severely compromised by the new outfit.

"He's supposed to look like that," Bob whispered back as the trio of ruffians skidded around our legs. "Trust me. Pam's instructions were very explicit. I didn't dare improvise a thing."

Much as I would have liked to watch Davey's riding lesson, I had a prior commitment. A few months earlier, I'd gotten to know a friend of Bertie's who was running a pet-sitting business. When Sarah moved away over the winter, I'd been reluctantly persuaded to cover several of her clients until they could make other arrangements. In time, all but one had.

Phil Dutton lived and worked in Old Greenwich, but his job required him to commute to the city twice a week. Mondays and Thursdays his elderly dogs, Mutt and Maisie, were alone in the house for hours. My job was simply to go and break up the monotony of their long day. I let them out and played with them, tuned the TV to a channel they liked, and checked their water and food supplies.

I'd told Phil several times that he'd be better off with a pet-sitting service that could send someone over earlier in the afternoon. I'd even called around and gotten him some names. But Phil hated to make changes; and he'd decided that Mutt and Maisie were used to me. Since both were sweet old dogs, I couldn't bear to disappoint them.

A note on my kitchen counter confirmed that Bob and Davey had come and gone. I let Eve and Faith in from their run in the backyard, refilled their water bowl, handed out biscuits, and headed out.

My station wagon was sitting in the driveway. A light blue Mazda was parked in front of the house. Rich gave me a cheery wave from the driver's side. Jill smiled her perky smile. I growled under my breath.

I started to get into the Volvo, then changed my mind and strolled down to the street.

"Hey," Rich said as Jill rolled down her window. "Find any dead bodies yet?"

"If I had, I'm sure you'd have heard about it."

Jill made shooing motions with her hands. "Don't mind us. Just go on about your business. We're not going to get in your way."

They were in my way *now*, I thought. Sitting there, watching my house. Watching me. I wondered whether they'd been at school earlier when I'd been too busy to notice. I wondered whether I should alert school security.

Taking such action would probably involve a conversation with Russell Hanover II, the school's headmaster, the kind of conversation I tried to avoid at all costs. Howard Academy was very well known in the right circles, but when it came to the media, the school kept a deliberately low profile. And when it came to Russell Hanover, I tried to keep a low profile as well.

"Have you been following me?" I asked.

I could have sworn Rich started to nod, but when Jill shook her head, he followed her cue. "Not following you," she said firmly. "Just checking in every now and then, and picking up some background shots. You know, for when the story takes off."

"There isn't going to be a story. Nothing's going to take off." Abruptly I frowned. "After the dog show ended yesterday, where did you go?"

"Home," Jill answered. "Just like you."

Right. If they hadn't followed me, how did they know I'd come straight home? And what if, rather than following, they'd been leading the way? Was there a possibility they'd beaten me back and . . .

And what? I wondered. Gotten inside my

84

house and turned on all the lights? What would have been the point? Even to me, the idea sounded pretty far-fetched.

I turned and stalked back to my car. As I backed the Volvo out of my driveway, Rich had the nerve to wave again. As if he wanted me to know he was ready. As if we were friends coordinating our efforts. Deliberately I kept both hands on the steering wheel and stifled the gesture I wanted to give him.

When I started down the street, the Mazda pulled out and fell into place behind me.

Phil Dutton lived in a small, older home on a crowded street near the railroad tracks in Old Greenwich. His was a bachelor's house, a commuter's house; comfortably, if sparsely, furnished and often a little messy. As far as Mutt and Maisie were concerned, however, I'm sure it was heaven on earth.

The two dogs were littermates of an indeterminate breed — Shih Tzu/terrier mix was my best guess — that Phil had rescued from the Stamford pound when they were puppies. Some miserable, coldhearted person had left the pair, small and shivering, in a box by the side of the Post Road. Rescued before they could freeze or starve, they'd been transported to the pound where Phil had found them. Now, eleven years later, Mutt and Maisie ruled Phil's house as if it was their own private kingdom, which, of course, it was.

Over my protests, Phil had given me a key to his house. "If anything ever happens to me," he'd said, "I want to know that someone will be able to get in and take care of my babies." And, having seen pictures of Faith and Eve, he'd offered to take my key and safeguard the Poodles for me. Luckily I knew I could count on Aunt Peg should the need arise. Though I was sure that Phil meant well, his offer wasn't anything I wanted to accept. I was hoping to find a way to sever our relationship, not enhance it.

As I unlocked the front door, I could hear the scramble of eager feet. Two leather leashes hung on a hook by the door. I grabbed them before dropping to my knees to greet the little dogs.

Though they were littermates, Maisie and Mutt didn't have much in common when it came to looks. Mutt had reddish hair that was long and curly, and a tail that flipped up over his back. Maisie's blond coat was shorter and wiry. Her ears stood up on the top of her head, and there was a devilish gleam in her dark eyes.

As always, Maisie greeted me by throwing herself into my arms. Her smooth pink tongue licked my neck, my ears, my face. Mutt was the shyer of the two, hanging back for just a second before allowing me to reach out and scratch under his chin.

"Time to go out," I said. Two tails, one short, one long, whipped back and forth with delight. "Who wants to go for a walk?"

Our routine seldom varied. Mutt had to stop and sniff every bush in his tiny front yard on the way to the street. Maisie, accustomed to the delays, used the time to rub up against my legs like a cat and enjoy the warmth of the sun on her face. Finally we reached the sidewalk and were off, the dogs running at a sprightly gait that belied their age, toward a baseball field at the end of the road.

Forty minutes later, the two hairy monsters dragged me home with as much enthusiasm as they'd pulled me away earlier. If they'd been my dogs, I would have taught them how to walk on a leash properly. But since Phil didn't seem to mind their lack of manners, I simply wrapped one lead around each wrist and jogged along behind.

Back inside the house, both dogs headed purposefully for the kitchen. As I placed the leashes back on their hook, I could hear

Mutt and Maisie slurping at the water bowl. I'd fill it again before I left, but in the meantime I needed to do a quick tour of the downstairs and make sure neither dog had had any accidents before my arrival.

Many of the homes along Phil's road had been remodeled in the last decade to take advantage of soaring real estate values in the area. Not this one. Its small windows and cramped, dark rooms still reflected its 1950s origins. Even the living room, with drapes open and TV on — tuned to *Animal Planet* for Mutt and Maisie's viewing enjoyment — caught little afternoon light. I was staring hard at the patterned rug, trying to pick out any abnormalities in the design when the hair on the back of my neck rose.

Someone was watching me.

Involuntarily, I whipped around. The room behind me was empty. Even Mutt and Maisie, who usually stuck like shadows during my visits, were nowhere to be seen. Frowning, I expelled a shaky breath. My gaze slid to the front window. There was no sign of the blue Mazda.

"Mutt? Maisie?" I lifted a hand and massaged the back of my neck. "Where are you guys?"

Hiding with guilty consciences, no doubt. They knew what I was doing.

I gave myself a mental shake and got back to work. The living room rug looked in need of a good vacuuming but was otherwise fine. On to the dining room, where I headed first for the table. One of the dogs persisted in thinking that if the evidence of a misdeed was hidden I'd never find it.

This room was as dimly lit as the one I'd just left. A light switch on the wall didn't help much, turning on a dusty chandelier over the table but most of the bulbs were out. Muttering under my breath, I pulled out a chair and hunkered down to have a look.

A flashlight would have helped. Failing that, I gave the area the sniff test. Nothing. Mutt and Maisie were in the clear.

"You can come out now," I called, my voice muffled as I backed out from beneath the table. I braced my hands on my knees, rose to my feet, turned in place . . . and screamed.

It took a moment for the face, only inches from mine, to swim into focus. "Oh," I said, heart still fluttering. "It's you."

"Of course it's me," Phil Dutton replied. "This is my house. Who were you expecting?"

"Nobody." I tried to back up. The table, right behind me, prevented a retreat. "I wasn't expecting anybody. That's why you startled me."

"Sorry about that." Phil's thin lips lifted in a smile. "I didn't mean to scare you." He was an unremarkable-looking man, perhaps a decade older than I. The kind of man you'd never pick out of a crowd, or remember the day after a party. He reached out a hand to steady me. "Are you okay?"

"Fine. Absolutely fine."

I hated that my voice was shaking. I'm not a jumpy person, I don't scare easily. My reaction felt all out of proportion.

All I could think was that this had to be Jill and Rich's doing. I wasn't accustomed to being followed, much less spied upon. Knowing they were out there somewhere must have set my nerves on edge.

It wasn't Phil's fault that I was behaving like an idiot. Nevertheless, I wanted his hand off me. I slipped out from between his body and the table and headed for the kitchen.

"What are you doing here?" I asked. "Isn't this one of your New York days?"

"Meetings got cancelled. I came home early. I've been working in my office in the basement. I guess that's why I didn't hear you come in."

I paused in the doorway to the kitchen.

Mutt and Maisie's water bowl was empty, the linoleum floor around it wet. The dogs were sacked out on a rumpled blanket close by. No wonder they hadn't been as desperate for diversion as they usually were.

"You mean you've been here the whole time?"

Phil nodded.

"Why didn't you call and tell me not to come?"

"And deprive Maisie and Mutt of the pleasure of your company?" His voice was smooth, his tone oily. He reminded me of a man sitting on a bar stool and trying out pickup lines by rote. "You know how much they look forward to your visits."

"They're wonderful dogs. I look forward to seeing them, too."

So why was I suddenly feeling so uncomfortable? Looking for distraction, I grabbed a couple of paper towels off the roll and began to mop the floor. Puddle gone, I threw the towels in the garbage, then picked up the water bowl and refilled it in the sink.

Phil had gone over and sat down on the blanket between Mutt and Maisie. He had an arm curled around each. Usually I would take some time to play with the dogs now, maybe brush through their coats or clip their nails. But not unexpectedly, both seemed content to sit with their owner.

"I guess I'm done, then," I said.

"Until Thursday," Phil agreed. "Thanks. From all of us."

"You're welcome."

I could feel his eyes on me as I walked all the way to the front door. Or maybe it was my imagination again. Jill's power of suggestion seemed to be working on me, big time.

On the other hand, I supposed I could look on the bright side.

At least I hadn't found any dead bodies yet.

7

Pam's pony farm turned out to be a delightful piece of property tucked away in a private location just off Old Long Ridge Road. The unpaved driveway slowed my speed, giving me plenty of time to appreciate the pastoral setting. Fields, bound by post-and-rail fencing, flanked the long driveway. Each held a small band of grazing Welsh ponies. The ponies lifted their heads curiously as I drove by, then went back to munching contentedly on the abundant spring grass.

At the end of the driveway, I came to a barn that was long and low. Two rows of stalls opened off a wide, covered center aisle. Painted white with green trim, the stable matched a modest, tree-shaded clapboard house on the other side of a turnaround.

Two tricolor Jack Russell Terriers came zooming outside to bark at my arrival. They raced twice around the driveway, their short legs pumping like pistons, then disappeared back inside the barn. I guessed I'd been officially greeted.

Pulling over to park next to Bob's Trans Am in the shade of a large maple tree, I saw a riding ring out behind the barn. Davey was in the ring on Willow. Bob and Pam were leaning against the rail watching. I got out and went to join them.

"Great," said Bob. "You made it. The lesson was supposed to be over ten minutes ago, but I asked Pam to hang on a little longer so you could see Davey ride."

Pam flashed me a grin. "Bobby can be very persuasive."

"Thanks for waiting," I said. "I hope I didn't inconvenience you too much."

"Not at all. Davey's a great kid."

I found myself warming to Pam. All right, what mother wouldn't?

Coming around the turn at a sedate walk, Davey lifted his reins and steered the palomino pony over to the rail. "Look Mom! I'm riding."

"I can see that. Is it fun?"

"It's great. I can even trot. Want to see me? Pam says someday I'll be able to gallop. Willow knows how to jump, too."

"Not so fast." Pam laughed. "We're going to take things one step at a time." She reached out and corrected the position of Davey's leg. "Heels down, remember?"

"Yup." Davey nodded seriously. "Heels

down. Eyes ahead. If I begin to slip, grab hold of the mane."

"What'd I tell you?" said Bob. "He's a natural."

All right, let's give some credit where it's due. Davey did look good on the pony. Happy, too. Hard as it was for me to admit, there were definite pluses to having Bob back in his son's life. Not just for Davey, but for me as well.

For years I'd wrestled with the pressures of being a single parent. I'd driven myself crazy trying to get everything about Davey's upbringing just right. Now suddenly, with Bob back in the picture, some of the heat was off. Never in my wildest dreams would it have occurred to me to get Davey a pony. But here, sitting right in front of me, was proof of how good the idea had been.

"Take her one more time around, Davey," Pam instructed. "Then it'll be time to go in."

"Okay." Davey turned the pony's head back to the track and pressed his heels to her sides. Obligingly, Willow ambled away.

"What a nice pony," I said. "Is she always that quiet?"

"With beginners, yes. She knows her job and she's very good at it. Some of the other ponies are a little livelier, but from what

Bobby told me about Davey I thought Willow would be the best choice to get him started."

Pam walked over to the gate and opened it, waiting as the palomino completed her circuit of the ring. The pony walked through the opening and headed automatically for the back of the barn. Reins looped on her neck, Davey turned in the saddle and waved.

From where I was standing, it looked as though Willow was the decision-making half of that team. But then again, Davey was having a ball, so who was I to complain?

I glanced over at my ex-husband. He was gazing at his son proudly. *"Bobby?"*

Bob flushed slightly. "Don't ask me. Pam's the one who started it."

"I see." My lips twitched. "I thought maybe that was your cowboy name."

"Smart-ass." He reached over and smacked me on the butt. "That's the last time I confess something about my childhood to you."

"I hope not." It occurred to me that I was getting to know Bob much better now than I had when we were married. For the first time we were forming a real relationship as adults. Better late than never. "Is Davey finished now?"

"Not quite yet. It'll be another twenty

minutes or so. Pam has this theory that it's really important for kids to learn how to take care of their ponies, not just be riders. Davey will help her take Willow's tack off, brush her dry, and pick out her feet. He's not done until the pony is ready to go back in her stall."

It sounded like a good system to me.

"If Pam can make that work," I said, "maybe she can come over sometime and teach Davey how to clean up his room."

"She probably could," said Bob. "Pam's pretty determined. She inherited this place from her parents, but she runs it all by herself. I wouldn't think it would be easy to make a go of it, but she does. Teaching lessons in the spring and fall, camp in the summer. She also sells some of the ponies she breeds to the big show barns in Greenwich and North Salem."

"I have to admit I'm a little envious. I'd love to have this much land and this much privacy. Faith and Eve would love it here."

Speaking of the Poodles, who were waiting for us at home, was impetus enough to make me push away from the fence and head for the barn to collect my child. "I've got a pot roast simmering in the crock pot," I told Bob. "Do you want to join us for dinner?"

"I would but . . ."

I paused and glanced back. Bob's expression was carefully neutral. "But what?"

"Pam and I sort of have plans."

"Pam and you . . . ?"

Oh.

I guessed I should have seen that coming. Pam wasn't just an acquaintance who'd managed to convince Bob that a pony would make a nice present for his son, she was a woman he was interested in. Of course. Willow's unexpected arrival in our lives made much more sense now.

"That's all right, isn't it?"

I looked up. To my surprise, Bob seemed to be waiting for my approval. "Of course it's all right. Why wouldn't it be?"

"Well, you know, you and I . . . You and I, we were . . ."

"Married," I supplied since he seemed to be having trouble getting the word out. "But you've also been married to Jennifer since then. I don't remember you caring what I thought about that at the time."

"Yes, well, things are different now."

He was right; they were. Bob had originally returned to Connecticut hoping to resurrect our relationship in Sam's absence. Things hadn't turned out the way he'd planned, but we'd come through the experience with a friendship that was stronger than ever.

Bob and I would never be partners again in any way except as Davey's parents, but I would always wish him the best. Pam seemed like a nice woman, and I certainly never expected him to live the life of a monk.

"Go for it," I said. "Have a great time. You can have dinner with Davey and me any day."

"Thanks." Bob brushed a quick kiss across my cheek. "I'll hold you to that."

"Feel free." All at once my smile faded. That feeling was back. The one I'd had earlier of being watched.

I shivered slightly and had a look around. On one side, ponies were standing quietly in their pasture. Another held a patch of leafy woods where all seemed still. In the barn's center aisle, Pam was holding Willow while Davey carefully brushed her legs. Bob's and my cars were the only ones in the driveway.

All was just as it had been moments before. Nothing seemed out of the ordinary. Except my back was tingling and I'd begun to sweat.

"What's the matter?" Bob asked.

"Nothing," I said firmly.

As if saying it could make it so.

Wednesday, when school let out, I made one quick stop, then drove directly to Aunt Peg's house in Greenwich.

She and Rose were arguing again. Why on earth either one of them would think *I* would make a good mediator was beyond my comprehension. Nevertheless, I'd apparently been called up to active duty. Luckily for Davey, he had a play date, thus sparing him the spectacle of watching two grown women spar like a pair of WWF wrestlers.

When I got to Aunt Peg's house, Rose was already there. I saw her silver Taurus sitting in the driveway. It wasn't until I'd pulled up beside it, however, that I realized Rose was still sitting behind the wheel. That didn't bode well.

We opened our doors at the same time. Faith and Eve jumped out of the Volvo and immediately ran past me toward the wide steps that led to Aunt Peg's front door.

My aunt has scaled down her kennel considerably over the last few years. At the moment there are only five Cedar Crest Standard Poodles in residence, including Eve's brother Zeke. All of them live in the house; and all but Zeke are retired show champions.

Aunt Peg's Poodles are superb watchdogs. I knew they must have alerted her to Rose's arrival. Even now, I could hear them barking through the front windows of the house.

Faith and Eve went flying up the steps, their voices joining with those of their relatives within.

"Been here long?" I asked Rose.

"Five minutes." She reached back into the car and reemerged holding a small red Dachshund puppy. "I was gathering my thoughts."

"Really? I thought maybe you were waiting for reinforcements."

"That too." Rose's smile was wry.

I held out my hands and she put the puppy into them. He turned his tapered face up to me and gave me a grin. His ears were soft as fine leather; his tail beat back and forth against my hip. What a little charmer.

"Peter and I have been calling him Dox," said Rose. "I think he's beginning to know his name already. I'm trying very hard to stay objective. The last thing I need to do is get attached to him."

"He probably ought to pee before we go inside," I said. "Does he have a collar and leash?"

Rose shook her head. "He's never gone anywhere before. There's never been a need."

Like Pam's pony farm, Aunt Peg's home had ample acreage and was set a distance back from the road. I lowered the puppy to the ground at my feet. "He should be fine, as long as the Poodles don't run over him."

Which of course they did.

Waiting impatiently by the front door, Faith turned around to see what was keeping me. At the sight of Dox, her head flew up. She spun on her hindquarter and came racing back down the stairs.

New puppy! Catching her excitement, if not its cause, Eve wheeled around and galloped in pursuit.

One good thing about being charged by two big, hairy Standard Poodles: it made the little Dachshund pee. Job complete, I whisked Dox back up into my arms. Both Poodles skidded to a stop in front of me, and I performed the introductions with him at eye-level rather than underfoot.

Rose glanced toward the house. If anything, the clamor of barking dogs had intensified. Briefly she closed her eyes.

"He's going to get trampled in there, isn't he?"

"Not if I can help it. I'll hold onto him until Aunt Peg puts the rest of those hooligans out back."

The front door opened before we'd even reached the porch. Aunt Peg had probably been observing from inside for just as long as her dogs had. As the herd of Poodles danced around our legs, she favored Rose and me both with the same stern look.

"That puppy doesn't have fleas, does he?"

"No." Rose sounded like she was guessing.

"Worms?"

"Certainly not!" Another guess.

"Has he had his baby shots?"

Rose shrugged helplessly.

"Why don't you call your friend Marian Firth and ask?" I suggested. "She's the one who ought to know." Before Peg could protest, I thrust the puppy into her arms. "Isn't he sweet?"

You didn't have to be a dog person to be a sucker for a cute puppy. One look at Dox and Aunt Peg would turn to putty. At least that's what I was hoping.

"Adorable," Aunt Peg agreed. Then her tone sharpened. "But then that's his function, isn't it? Quite a tall order for such a little dog. To be endearing enough to bring out the big bidders. To entice someone to plunk down a large sum of money on a thoroughly ill-conceived impulse purchase."

Oops.

I reached out and took the Dachshund back. As I stroked his neck, he sniffed my sweater and curled himself happily against my chest. World War III might rage around us, but Dox was quite content.

"Now, see here," said Aunt Rose. "I know you think that I'm the villain in this drama of yours, but I'm every bit the innocent bystander this puppy is."

"I don't think so." Aunt Peg's shoulders stiffened. "To begin with, you never should have accepted a dog as a donation in the first place. Having done so — once all the reasons why the notion was utter lunacy had been explained to you — you should have wasted no time in giving him back."

Innocent bystander? Utter lunacy? Even for these two, this was a bit much. I heaved a windy sigh and got out the big guns.

"Did I mention I brought cake?"

Aunt Peg, whose sweet tooth was legendary, stopped mid-snarl and peered at my empty hands. "Where is it?"

"Out in the car. I saw Dox and got distracted . . ."

"You see? That's precisely what's going to happen —"

"Oh please," Rose snorted. "Give me some credit —"

I held up a hand. To my surprise, it worked. Both women stopped talking.

"Both of you, take a deep breath," I said.

"And try to remember you're adults. I'll be right back."

Leaving Dox with Rose, I ran back outside and fetched the sacrificial offering. When I returned, Aunt Peg had put the older Poodles out in the backyard. Zeke and Eve, whose coats would suffer in the hair-pulling games that were sure to ensue, remained inside with us.

Peg and Rose had moved into the kitchen, where Dox had joined the big black puppies on the floor. Aunt Peg was brewing tea. Rose and I, who preferred coffee, were, as was usually the case at Peg's house, out of luck.

"I can't imagine what Marian was thinking," Aunt Peg said, when we'd all gotten settled around the table with a drink and a piece of cake. "I'm certain she knows better than to donate a puppy to a charity auction. What on earth would have made her behave that way?"

"Technically, she didn't," Rose answered. "After we spoke, I looked it up in Peter's records. The receipt for the tax write-off was made out to George Firth, not Marian. Presumably that would be her husband?"

"Ex-husband." Aunt Peg was a bottomless well when it came to dog show information of all kinds. "I believe they separated more than a year ago. Marian was the one who showed the Dachshunds, though, not George. They were definitely her dogs. I don't know what he would be doing with one of her puppies now."

"Giving it away." I paused to lick a forkful of mocha icing. "Maybe that's the point."

8

Aunt Peg stared at me thoughtfully. "You know, that's not the dumbest thing you've ever said."

"Thank you." At this point in my life, I take compliments wherever I can find them. "How well do you know Mrs. Firth?"

"Not well," Peg mused. "But I daresay we've crossed paths often enough that I could probably call her on the phone."

Translated, that meant that Aunt Peg had watched Marian's Dachshunds win at prestigious shows and Marian had watched Aunt Peg's Poodles do the same. This had happened on enough occasions that both their credentials were established to everyone's satisfaction. The dog show world really is a very small place.

"Excuse me, would you?" Aunt Peg rose. "I think I'll go see what I can find out."

While she was gone, I cut myself another piece of cake. A sliver, actually, so thin it barely counted at all. Aunt Rose watched me maneuver the skinny slice onto my plate with a benign expression.

"I thought Peg would calm down if she saw for herself that Dox was doing fine," she said. "It doesn't seem to be working."

The Dachshund puppy was lying under the table, a rubber chew toy clutched tightly between his short front legs. Perched outside the circle of chairs, both Poodles were keeping an eye on him, trying to figure out how the smallest dog had ended up with the best toy.

"You're not the home she's worried about," I said. "It's what happens after the auction. Letting a puppy go to the highest bidder is like selling one as a Christmas present. People get so wrapped up in the excitement of the moment that they don't stop to think whether or not what they're doing is a good thing. Bringing a puppy into your house is a major commitment. For some people it involves a whole change of lifestyle."

"Tell me about it," Rose muttered.

I started to speak, then decided to keep eating instead. I was trying hard not to lecture, especially since every time I opened my mouth I heard Aunt Peg's words coming out. Rose and Peter had only recently returned to lower Fairfield County; getting on their case over an issue they clearly didn't understand was no way to welcome them back.

"Nobody invited you to finish the cake while I was gone," Aunt Peg said from the doorway. She eyed our clean plates suspiciously, as if checking for evidence that we'd helped ourselves to seconds. "I've just spoken to Marian, who's apparently been beside herself with worry over little Dox. She was greatly relieved to discover his whereabouts."

"Does she want him back?" I asked.

"Desperately, but he's not hers to take." Peg marched over to the table and began to box the cake. "There's a juicy story there, and my guess is, Marian's dying to tell it. You and I —" this, not unexpectedly, was directed at me "— are expected shortly."

"What about me?" asked Rose.

"What about you?" Peg inquired.

"I hate to bring this up —"

"Then don't."

Rose sighed and continued. "I have to admit I may have had an ulterior motive in coming here today."

I paused in the act of piling our dishes in the sink. If I had to jump between them on a moment's notice, I wanted to have my hands free.

"As Melanie has so graciously pointed out, taking care of a puppy is a big job. One that requires time and commitment, neither of which I happen to have in abundance. I know you're not entirely delighted about the circumstances that brought Dox into my life, but seeing as the auction is such a worthy cause, I was hoping you might be willing to overlook your misgivings. . . ."

It didn't take a genius to see where this was going, nor to realize that Aunt Peg was not going to react favorably.

"Don't tell me you expect me to take care of that puppy for you?" she asked incredulously.

"Only until the auction."

As if that would smooth things over. Rose might as well have poured gasoline directly onto the fire that was smoldering in Aunt Peg's expression.

"You've already got a houseful of dogs. I hardly see how one more would make any difference."

Standing beside the counter, I braced for the explosion. Aunt Peg's Poodles were all quite a bit older than Dox: housebroken, past the teething stage, beyond the need for a special diet and shots. Dox was a project. He was still enough of a baby to require someone to attend to his needs. In his case, one more would make a big difference.

Then I had a thought. Not necessarily a

good one, mind you. But timely enough to keep one small Dachshund puppy from getting caught in the crossfire. I slipped between the two women and scooped Dox up into my arms.

"Why don't I take him home with me?" I suggested.

"What a wonderful idea." Rose looked relieved.

"Have you lost your mind?" asked Peg.

"No." I may have sounded a little defensive.

"You'll have to watch him every minute and make sure he doesn't chew on Eve's coat."

"I can do that."

"Are you going to take him to school with you, too?"

Good question. I had to admit, I hadn't considered that.

"Sure," I said blithely. "Why not?"

There were a dozen good reasons, most of which Aunt Peg was intimately acquainted with, especially since when Eve had been this age, she'd been staying with Peg while I was at work.

"Thank you, dear." Aunt Rose slipped her arms around my shoulders and pulled me into a hug. "You're a lifesaver."

She picked up her purse and hurried from

the room before I could change my mind. A moment later, Peg and I heard the front door slam.

"Lifesaver?" Peg snorted. "I think the word she was looking for was sucker."

Yeah, probably. Times like this remind me of that biblical story about Moses and the bulrushes. The one where his mother put him in a basket and aimed him downstream toward a new family and a better life. I've often thought it was too bad my mother didn't have the same idea. It certainly would have saved on future complications where my relatives are concerned.

Grumbling the whole way, Aunt Peg trudged downstairs and found me a baby-sized crate in her basement. We tucked Dox inside, loaded my two Poodles in the car, and left to go visiting.

Considering the guest we brought with us, our welcome at Marian Firth's home in Ridgefield was all but assured. She opened her front door with a tentative smile, prepared to be gracious if not effusive. But the moment she caught sight of the little Dachshund, all that changed. Marian's face lit up. As if of their own accord, her hands shot forward to touch him.

"May I?" she asked.

"Of course." I delivered the puppy into her arms.

Marian was slender and fragile looking, probably a year or two on either side of forty. Her skin was pale; her features, delicate. She looked like a strong wind would blow her over, but she hugged Dox to her fiercely. Her body seemed to fold in around him; her lower lip was quivering.

"Oh, my sweet boy," she crooned. "I'm so glad you're all right."

"He's been fine," I assured her. "A very nice woman has been keeping him. She calls him Dox."

"Dox?" Marian looked up. "I wouldn't say that's terribly dignified."

"She isn't a dog person," Aunt Peg said. The explanation seemed to satisfy both of them. Peg performed the introductions, and we followed Marian inside.

Her house was small and obviously not new. Its walls and floors had a shabby, neglected look that provided an incongruous backdrop to the good furniture crammed into every available space. Three Dachshunds — Standards like Dox, two smooth, one wire-haired — came galloping out to say hello. They eddied around our legs like a canine whirlpool.

"Welcome to the dump," Marian announced. Her body might have looked frail, but her voice was clear and strong. "As you can see, I got the short end of the stick in the divorce. George kept the Mercedes, the IRA, and most of the stock portfolio. I got my mother's furniture, an alimony payment that wouldn't support a gnat, and the dogs.

"Well," she amended, setting Dox down to play with the other three on the floor, "most of them anyway. Do you mind telling me where the puppy . . . where Dox . . . has been for the last two weeks?"

Aunt Peg and I found seats on a long sofa upholstered in an ornate fabric that would have looked at home in Versailles. The coffee table by our legs was so highly polished I probably could have seen my face in it if it hadn't been piled high with dog books.

"He's been living for part of that time with my Aunt Rose," I said. "Her husband, Peter, runs an Outreach program at the community center in Stamford. The two of them are putting together a benefit auction, and Peter's been soliciting high-ticket items from donors in the area." I paused to let her take that in, then added, "Dox was donated to be one of the prizes."

Aunt Peg harrumphed under her breath. "I'm quite certain you're not the one re-

114

sponsible for turning this lovely puppy into a tax write-off."

Marian's face had blanched. She was shaking her head slowly from side to side as if she couldn't believe what she was hearing. "No, that would be George's doing. My husband . . . my ex-husband. Though even for him, that sounds rather incredible. But then, as I've discovered, divorce does things to people. It twists them around and turns them into monsters you barely even recognize."

She paused and swallowed heavily. It took her a moment to get her emotions back in check. She used the time to glance at the Dachshunds, who were now lying on the floor at our feet. Marian smiled slightly; the sight seemed to give her strength.

"I always knew George was a strong, determined man," she continued. "Tough as nails, you might say. But I never realized how petty, how vindictive, how downright mean he could be until I told him I wanted a separation. We were both adults, of course. And there weren't any children involved. I thought we could manage to keep things civil.

"Imagine, at one point I thought we might even be able to forgo the enormous lawyers' fees and simply go through mediation. Not

George." Marian's laugh was bitter. "He knew right from the start what a slugfest it was going to turn into."

"What did he do?" I asked.

"For one thing, he immediately booked himself consultations with the dozen best divorce attorneys in Fairfield County. Of course, he never had any intention of hiring more than one. But once he'd spoken to each of them, they were unable to take me on as a client. It would have been a conflict, do you see? That was his way of insuring that he'd get topnotch representation and I wouldn't."

One of the Dachshunds got up and came over to sniff my leg, checking out the Poodles' scent. I reached down and ran a hand down the long length of his back. The dog's body was sleek and hard-packed with muscle.

"He sounds like a bum," Aunt Peg said decisively. "I can't say that I remember seeing him at any dog shows. Should I?"

"No, George had no interest in the Dachshunds. If he'd had his way, the Tulip Tree line would have died when my mother did. Weekend dog shows conflicted with his golf game. I don't think he ever came to a single one."

"How did he end up with one of your puppies?" I asked.

"For that you'll have to blame an attorney with more education than morals, a well-meaning judge, and a judicial system that hasn't a clue what's at stake in disputes that involve animals. George didn't want my dogs. He didn't even *like* my dogs. But what he wanted to do was hurt me. So he went after Primadonna."

Aunt Peg nodded. Presumably she'd heard of the dog.

Not me. I had a life.

"Who's Primadonna?" I asked.

"That's her right there." Marian gestured toward the Dachshund who was now sitting beside me. Realizing we were talking about her, the elegant red bitch lifted her head and tipped it to one side. "She's the best dog the Tulip Tree line ever produced, arguably one of the best I've ever seen."

Aunt Peg nodded again. It was all the encouragement Marian needed.

"I never gave her a big career," she said. "Point chasing and year-end awards don't impress me much. But Donna finished her championship with four majors, including one at our national specialty where she was Best of Winners over a huge entry. I might have specialed her more, but she came along just as my marriage was falling apart. George made sure I was too preoccupied to go to many shows. Even so, Donna became a group and specialty Best in Show winner."

"I'm impressed," I said.

"Yes," Marian agreed. "George's attorney was, too. Even though he barely had any idea what it all meant. When it came time to divide our assets, he placed an absurdly high value on Donna and her potential progeny. The whole thing was patently ridiculous. Any responsible breeder will tell you that breeding dogs is more likely to make you broke than rich."

I'd only had one litter so far, but I knew what she was saying was true. Financially speaking, the cost of producing a litter of healthy, happy puppies far outweighs the gain.

"What happened?" Peg prodded. "What did the judge do?"

"After much wrangling on both our parts, he awarded Donna to me." Marian's relief was evident. "But in order to avoid leaving George out in the cold, he gave him pick puppy from Donna's first litter."

"And that would be Dox?"

"Right." Marian grimaced. "Of course, you can see how much George wanted the puppy. He no sooner got custody of him than he gave him away. *Gave* him away!" she repeated, in case we'd failed to pick up on the full extent of her outrage the first time.

"You have no idea how worried I've been. George wanted to strike back at me and the judge handed him the perfect means. Thank goodness I divorced that bastard, otherwise I'd probably have ended up killing him."

Oh Lord, I thought. Don't say that. With my luck, Jill was skulking around outside somewhere, listening. Right this moment, she was probably rubbing her hands with glee.

"I used to be a doormat," Marian announced, "but no more. The next person who gets in my way had better watch out, because I'll run right over their asses like a Mack truck in low gear."

9

It was hard to think of a comeback for that on a moment's notice. Wisely, I opted to say nothing.

Not Aunt Peg. "Good for you!" she cried. At least she stopped short of pumping her fist in the air.

"What will you do about Dox?" I asked.

"Do?" Marian asked. "There's nothing I can do. That puppy doesn't belong to me. There are several pages of legally binding documents to attest to that fact. That's why I've been so upset. I hadn't even been able to get any information about him. All I knew was that he had been given away to some poor people's charity like a bundle of old clothes."

Peter probably would have objected to having his Outreach program and his rather tony auction characterized in such a way, but the point hardly seemed worth arguing. Given away was given away.

At the moment, nobody had any control over Dox's eventual disposition, not even

Peter. When the gavel fell, the Dachshund puppy would be delivered to whoever had placed the last bid. It was that simple.

And all at once, it was just that easy.

"Suppose you could buy him back," I asked. "Would you?"

"Of course," Marian replied immediately. Her eyes skimmed around the small room. "Which is not to say that my finances are unlimited. But yes, I'd give up a great deal to have him returned to me. Considering how much trouble I had getting Donna in whelp, there's a very real chance she may never have another litter. It would mean a tremendous amount to me, and to the Tulip Tree line, to have Dox back."

"Why don't you just go to Peter's auction and bid on him?"

"But —" Marian started to protest, then stopped, looking flummoxed.

For a moment, Aunt Peg looked equally startled. Then she began to smile.

"I can't imagine why I didn't think of that," she said. "You've fulfilled your end of the bargain. You produced a puppy and delivered it to your ex-husband. It was his choice to give the puppy away. Surely there's nothing in the agreement that prevents you from getting involved again after the fact."

"Now that you mention it," Marian said slowly, "I don't believe there is."

Bingo, I thought. It was a great feeling.

"I don't suppose you could leave him with me until the night of the event?"

"I wish I could. But for the moment he belongs to the community center. I've been charged with his care, but I certainly don't have the authority to place him with someone else."

"Don't worry." Aunt Peg leaned over and patted Marian's arm. "Melanie will do right by Dox. And if, after the auction, George's attorney should have occasion to look into the proceedings, he'll find that everything happened in a way that was open and above-board."

So there we were, the three of us, feeling utterly pleased with ourselves. One problem solved, I thought. Or at least nearly so.

Overconfidence; it will get you every time.

I stopped by Joey Brickman's house on the way home to pick up Davey from his play date. Joey's mother and I have been friends since our sons were toddlers; and unlike my meddling relatives, Alice has *not* spent the last few months asking me what I intend to do about Sam. Which was why the first words out of her mouth caught me by surprise.

"So I guess you and Sam have patched things up?" Alice said as Davey ran to find his shoes, his jacket, his backpack, and anything else he might have left lying around the Brickmans' home.

"What makes you say that?"

Her hand waved down the road in the direction of my house. "He's down there waiting for you."

"He is?"

"Yup. I saw that snazzy new SUV he's got parked in your driveway when the kids were out riding their scooters on the sidewalk."

The new SUV was a BMW X-5. Actually, according to Sam, the BMW people call it a sports activity vehicle, though the distinction was lost on me. The summer before, Sam had unexpectedly inherited a bundle of money. As far as I could tell, the only outward manifestation of his new financial status was that he'd traded in his Chevy Blazer for the BMW.

Alice studied my expression. "You weren't expecting him, were you?"

"Not exactly."

Once Sam wouldn't have thought anything of dropping by my house without an invitation. But since he'd taken his six-month sabbatical, things had been more formal between us, perhaps even a bit strained. Granted, I'd been the one responsible for the cooling of our relationship, but Sam had followed my cue.

So what was I to make of this surprise appearance? Only one way to find out.

"Come on, Davey," I called down the hallway in the direction that he and Joey had disappeared. Sometimes Alice and I talked so long that the kids simply went back to playing. "We've got to go."

"Not that I'm doubting Davey's word," she said while we waited for the boys to show up, "but did Bob really buy him a pony?"

"He really did." The Brickmans had been out of town the weekend before and had missed the big arrival. "A palomino Welsh Pony named Willow. She's actually pretty cute, if you're into stuff like that. Does Joey want to come and take a ride?"

"Joey, no. If it doesn't have wheels and an engine, he's not interested. Carly's the one who's horse-crazy. She's been pumping Davey for information all afternoon."

Carly was Joey's little sister, a thoughtful and engaging five-year-old who'd started kindergarten in the fall. Like her mother, she was slightly plump and almost always smiling. I knew she'd fall in love with Willow on sight.

"Consider yourselves invited," I said. "I'm sure Davey would be happy to share his pony. To tell the truth, even though he's having fun, he'd probably prefer something with wheels himself."

The child in question came barreling down the hallway. His shoes were untied, his shirt untucked, his backpack dragging on the floor behind him. Situation normal. It was time to go find out why Sam was sitting in my driveway.

The answer to that turned out to be short and sweet.

"I'm sitting out here," Sam said, "because I don't have a key to your house."

Nothing like a man who takes questions literally.

Once upon a time Sam had had a key. While he was gone, I'd had the locks changed. It didn't take a genius to decipher that message, and Sam had gotten my point loud and clear. Now, presumably, he was hoping I'd get his.

"Would you like one?" I stopped beside the BMW and squinted up at him.

Sam was a good half-foot taller than I, and the setting sun slanted into my eyes. I wanted to see his expression as he thought about all the things the question implied. Maybe the look on his face, rather than his words, would tell me where Sam thought our relationship was going.

His expression gave nothing away, however, and neither did his answer. "Only if you'd feel comfortable with that."

Yada, yada, yada.

Ever since Sam's return, it seemed as though all our conversations were filled with near-misses and evasions. There was much we needed to talk about, yet somehow none of it was getting said.

Sam had stepped back into my life with a wedding ring. As far as he was concerned, a two-carat diamond in a black velvet box expressed everything he wanted to say. Not me. I wanted to hear the words: the excuses, the apologies, all of it. I wanted him to make me understand why he'd needed to leave. So far, it hadn't happened.

"I'll think about it," I told him.

"Do that. In the meantime, I stopped by to see if I could take my two favorite people out to dinner."

"Out?" I turned around and walked back to my car. After greeting Sam, Davey and the Poodles had run on ahead into the house. Dox, however, was still sitting in the Volvo in his crate. "We just got back.

Davey's been at Joey's house, and I've been running around since school got out. Come on in, and we'll eat here instead."

"Sounds good to me." Sam looked at the crate curiously as I lifted it out. "Who's that?"

"Dox, my Aunt Rose's auction puppy. I started telling you about him at the show, remember?"

"Sure. Let me get that." Sam reached over and took the crate out of my hands. "What's he doing here?"

"I'm going to be taking care of him for a few weeks. It's kind of a long story."

"Is anything that involves your family *not* a long story?"

Now that he mentioned it, no.

"I'll fill you in over dinner," I said.

At the foot of the front steps I paused and glanced toward the street. Over the last few days, checking my back had become a habit. And with good reason. A couple houses up, a light blue Mazda was sitting by the curb. This time Jill was in the driver's seat.

"Go on in," I said to Sam. "I'll be there in just a minute."

The reporter rolled down her window as I approached. She offered a tentative smile. "Surely you can't think I'm bothering you. I'm not even parked in front of your house.

I don't know why you can't just ignore me."

"I don't know why you can't just ignore *me*. Where's Rich?" Knowing these two, I figured I'd better check in case he was hiding in the bushes, hoping to shoot some juicy footage through the windows of my house.

"Rich went home." Jill sounded displeased with her partner's lack of dedication. "He got bored."

One down, one to go, I thought happily.

"That's not surprising, considering that I lead a pretty boring life."

"Not all the time," Jill said determinedly.

This whole thing was beginning to feel a touch surreal. Looking past her into the car, I saw that Jill had outfitted herself for a long wait. A well-creased paperback sat open on the front seat, along with a cell phone and a thermos of hot coffee. From the looks of things, she was not about to give up any time soon.

"You can pack it in for tonight," I said. "I'm home, I'm going inside and I'm not coming out again. Trust me, there won't be anything for you to see."

"Thanks for the tip." Jill's smile was sunny. "Run along, then. Don't let me keep you from Sam."

I'd started to turn away, but her casual use of his name brought me up short. "Do you know Sam?"

"Sure. We met Sunday, at the dog show."

As I recalled, she'd asked about Sam but I hadn't introduced them. Nor had I seen them talking. So why did she sound so chummy all of a sudden?

"Have you spoken to him since?"

"Yes." Jill paused, then added, "He's a lot friendlier than you are."

"Is he?" It was hard to talk through teeth that were gritted, but I managed. "How did you know how to get in touch with him?"

"That part was easy. Especially when you're a reporter, like I am. He was showing a Poodle at the dog show, so his name and address were in the catalog. I got his phone number from information."

"And he talked to you on the phone?"

"Why wouldn't he? Not everyone has hangups about the media like you do. Most people want their fifteen minutes of fame, and if I'm the one who can give it to them, so much the better."

Sam wouldn't have talked to her about me, I thought. He couldn't have. He wouldn't betray me like that.

But then again, why should I be so sure? If I'd learned anything in the past year it was that I didn't know Sam nearly as well as I thought I did.

Eve met me at the front door as I walked into the house. I followed the sound of Sam's and Davey's voices to the kitchen. They were debating the merits of spaghetti with meat sauce over macaroni and cheese with hamburger mixed in. My two gourmets.

"Hey," said Sam. "Faith and Dox are out back, and Davey's planning our menu. Want me to cook?"

"Sure." Maybe it would be easier to talk if we were both busy. "Davey, don't you have some homework you ought to be starting?"

"I was going to help Sam make dinner."

"How about if we do that another time?" Sam reached out and ruffled my son's hair. "I wouldn't want you falling behind in your schoolwork on account of me. We'll call you when everything's ready."

"Okay," Davey agreed. He slipped down off his chair, walked down the hall, picked up his backpack, and carried it up the steps to his room.

"Is everything all right?" Sam asked as I went over to the refrigerator and got out a couple of beers. He already had an onion, a green pepper, and a box of fresh mushrooms on the counter. I guessed that meant we were having spaghetti.

"I don't know." I set his bottle of Sam Adams next to the cutting board on the counter. "Did you talk to Jill Prescott about me?"

Sam looked up. "Briefly."

"Why?"

"She called and asked me a couple of questions —"

"And you answered them?" My voice rose.

"Actually, I told her if she wanted information she should call and ask you."

I wanted to believe him. I wasn't sure I did. "She said you were very friendly."

"I was. But that doesn't mean I was going to allow her to invade your privacy. I saw how you felt about her interview idea last weekend at the show. I didn't tell her anything you wouldn't have told her yourself."

"I wouldn't have told her anything!"

"And I pretty much didn't, either," Sam's tone was soothing. "Ask her yourself. Was that who you were talking to outside?"

I nodded. "Ever since Sunday, she and Rich have been following me around. Waiting for me to stumble onto a murder or something. It's really creepy. I feel like people are watching me all the time. The whole thing is making me nuts."

"So I see." Sam got out a frying pan and began to heat some olive oil on the stove. He was as at home in my kitchen as I was. "Do you want me to have a talk with her?"

"No, I'll do that. Don't worry about it."

"You're sure?"

"Positive. I'll be fine."

I would be fine, I told myself firmly. For whatever reason, being shadowed by Jill and Rich was making my imagination work overtime. That was my problem, not Sam's; and I'd solve it myself, without his help.

I'd learned that lesson the hard way. No matter how tempting the notion was, it simply didn't pay to be too dependent on a man who coped with his problems by running away.

10

Davey finished his homework before dinner was on the table; in second grade, you don't get a lot. Sam's spaghetti turned out to be every bit as good as its aroma had forecast. The Dachshund puppy and my two Poodles were already halfway to becoming fast friends. In short, despite the strife that had gotten us off to a somewhat shaky start, the evening managed to pull itself together.

Later, Sam and I tucked Davey into bed together, sharing the routine as we'd done so many times in the past, with each of us reading a chapter from Davey's current favorite, *Charlotte's Web.* The cozy, familiar ritual felt exactly right. It reminded me how much all of us had given up due to my stubborn insistence that Sam and I not slip back into our old relationship without first examining how things had gone awry.

Maybe I was wrong to hold out for something perfect, I thought, standing in the doorway to Davey's semidarkened bedroom and listening to Sam read.

Maybe I was asking too much.

After a few minutes, Sam tucked the book away in Davey's night table. He smoothed the blankets over my already sleeping son. Watching the care with which Sam performed the simple tasks, a sudden, unexpected sheen of tears misted my view. What we shared was something precious and rare — not perfect perhaps, but certainly well worth fighting for.

As Sam headed downstairs, I took a moment to turn off the light and give Faith, who slept at the foot of Davey's bed, a pat. Then I slipped across the hall to my own bedroom. A quick survey revealed at least a semblance of order. Close enough, anyway, for what I had in mind. With luck, Sam wouldn't even notice his surroundings; he'd have other, more important things to concentrate on.

Turning to go, I caught my own reflection in the mirror above the dresser. My cheeks were slightly flushed, my eyes bright with anticipation. I hurried into the hallway and down the steps, only to stop, frowning, at the bottom. I'd expected to find Sam in the living room, or maybe even the kitchen. I hadn't thought to see him standing by the front door with his coat on.

"You're leaving?" I didn't even try to keep

the disappointment from my voice.

"It seemed like a good idea."

I couldn't imagine why. It seemed like a terrible idea to me.

I crossed the short distance between us, reached up, and slid my hands beneath the leather jacket that was already growing warm with his heat. Palms flat against Sam's chest, I nestled my body in close, stood up on my toes, and pressed my lips to his.

I felt Sam's mouth curve in a smile. Then he dipped his head toward mine and returned the kiss. His hands went around my waist, molding my hips hard against his. The first kiss turned into a second. Sam wanted this every bit as much as I did. Yet still, he pulled away.

"I think I'd better go."

"Why?" I sounded breathless and confused, which was pretty much the way I felt. My hands reached for him, even as he stepped back.

"Answer me one question," Sam said softly. "Do you trust me?"

Of all the possible questions in the world, I thought, don't ask me that one. How could I answer what I didn't know? Yes . . . no . . . maybe . . .

I wanted to trust Sam. I wanted to believe that he wouldn't betray my confidences to Jill

Prescott just as I wanted to believe that he would never leave us again, but how could I?

Sam and I had been engaged once; as far as I was concerned, we'd already made a lifetime commitment. And yet when things got tough, he hadn't turned to me. Instead he'd found his only comfort in solitude. Obviously there'd been something lacking in our relationship; and until we found that hole and patched it, I would always wonder what the next rough spot might bring.

Did I trust Sam to always want what was best for us? Yes. Did I trust him to always *do* what was best for us? Maybe not.

"That's not a simple question." I followed Sam's lead and stepped away as well.

"Yes or no, Melanie. That's all I want to know. Do you trust me?"

I knew what Sam wanted me to say. I knew what he needed to hear. And I was as incapable of building our future on a lie as I was of flying to the moon. In the end, my silence spoke for me.

"That's why I have to go." Sam leaned down and brushed one last gentle kiss across my lips. "I love you, Melanie."

"I love you, too." Those words came easily, truthfully, joyously. But I could see by the look in Sam's eyes that they weren't enough.

He reached for the knob and opened the front door. "I'll see you this weekend, right?"

I blinked my eyes and tried to concentrate. After a moment, Saturday swam into focus. There was a dog show Saturday in New Jersey; Aunt Peg was judging Poodles. Sam and I were both planning to go and watch.

"Right," I said. "Saturday."

His gaze raked over my tousled hair and flushed cheeks. The ghost of a smile played across his lips. "Sweet dreams," Sam said.

Like hell. Two could play this game. I drew the tip of my tongue across my lower lip and exhaled softly. "You, too."

The door slammed behind him as Sam let himself out.

I didn't have sweet dreams or any dreams at all that I remembered. Instead, I fell into a light, restless slumber that left me drifting in and out of sleep. I'd finally begun to nod off when my eyes suddenly flew open and I jerked upright in bed.

My heart was racing. My fingers gripped the covers. I had no idea what was wrong.

The room was dark save for a narrow beam of moonlight shining in through the window. The clock on the nightstand read three thirteen a.m. I gulped in air and sat perfectly still, listening. . . .

For what? I wondered. I had no idea.

Next to me on the bed, Eve was awake as well. Her head was up, her ears pricked. I had pushed Dox's crate against the wall in the corner. Now I could hear him moving within. Was that the unaccustomed noise that had awakened us?

No, I realized abruptly, there was something else. The slight but unmistakable sounds of movement from downstairs. A door swished open. A floorboard creaked.

Davey? Not likely. My son slept like a rock. Besides, if he was up, he wouldn't have gone downstairs, he'd have come to me. Then who . . . ?

My heart froze, even as my brain flatly refused to register the implications. My imagination had been running amok lately. This was nothing more than another symptom of the same problem. It couldn't be anything other than that, could it?

For a minute, I strained to hear something else. Anything else.

And then I did.

Someone was moving in the hallway outside my bedroom. Breath lodged painfully in my throat. My hand went to the night table, searching for a weapon. All I came up with was a book. Paperback, not even hardcover. Big help.

All at once, I heard a soft whine. Faith's black muzzle wedged into the crack I'd left in the doorway and pushed the bedroom door open.

"Oh, it's you." Relief made my shoulders sag.

Of course it was Faith. Who else would it have been? The big Poodle was up and prowling around the house, that was all.

She padded quietly into the bedroom. Her tail, usually carried high in the air, was low and still. Her ears were flat against her head. She looked at me uncertainly.

"What's the matter?" I patted the bed beside me. Faith didn't hop up to join us. "What are you doing up?"

She didn't answer. She didn't have to, because both of us heard the next sound at the same time. It was coming from downstairs. My first, hopeful guess had been wrong. It wasn't Faith who'd awakened us. Whatever had gotten us up had roused her as well.

Shaking, shivering, I slipped from beneath the covers. I heard . . . something . . . But what was it? The swish of material being dragged? The hushed whisper of voices?

Was there someone in my house?

Call 911. That was my first thought. Pick up the phone beside the bed and call. And say what? I wondered. That I was hearing noises? That my old house might be creaking in the night? That my dogs were awake and I hoped I wasn't imagining things?

Jill Prescott would get a good laugh out of this, I thought, nervous tension buzzing through my body like a jolt of electricity looking for a fuse to blow. I could see her lead-in now. *Melanie Travis thinks she knows how to solve mysteries. The only mystery last night was why she brought the police racing on an emergency call to her empty home.*

Faith and Eve were watchdogs, weren't they? If someone was downstairs, surely they'd have sounded an alarm. Maybe, I thought. And maybe not. The Poodles were also creatures of habit, accustomed to sleeping through the night, and socialized to look to me for guidance when they were unsure.

I crept past Faith to the bedroom door. Cautiously I peered through the slender opening. And saw nothing. But still . . . I could swear I heard voices. Was that a good sign or a bad sign? Wouldn't intruders at least have the sense to be quiet?

Faith came up beside me, pressing her warm, solid body against my leg. The comfort she offered was tangible and welcome. Whatever was wrong, my Poodle wanted to help. I reached down and stroked her neck and shoulders.

"What *is* that?" I whispered.

Her tail came up and began to wag slowly. Faith didn't care what was happening downstairs. As long as we were together, all was right with her world. Now I needed to make sure that all was right with mine.

"We'd better go see," I said.

I had no idea if the impulse was brave or foolhardy, but I couldn't spend the rest of the night cowering in my bedroom. Looking around, I saw a bud vase sitting on the dresser. It wasn't much but at least I wasn't empty-handed.

Eve hopped off the bed and came to join us in the doorway. Like her dam, she knew what "go" meant. Like Faith, she was always ready to have an adventure, even in the middle of the night. If we were going somewhere, she didn't want to be left behind.

Slipping out into the hallway, I went first to Davey's room. His door was open; I could see his small form curled beneath the comforter, his head resting on the pillow. His breathing was deep and even.

I reached out and pulled the bedroom door closed. Behind me, both Poodles were waiting expectantly, ready for whatever might come next. Even better than letting

141

these two big dogs accompany me down-stairs, I realized suddenly, I could send them on ahead.

"Who wants to go out?" I whispered, my tone urgent, inviting. "Come on, let's go outside!"

Eve yipped and danced her front feet in the air. This was more exciting than she'd hoped. An *outdoors* adventure in the dark!

Together, the Poodles scrambled past me. When I'd only had one dog, the mad dash to the back door had taken place in silence. With two, however, the excitement was mul-tiplied. It had become a competition. Faith and Eve were barking as they ran; the clamor they created seemed to bounce off the walls.

I knew what they were saying. Each was yelling the canine version of "Me first! Me first!" But as I ran along behind them, I could only hope that someone down below would hear their deep-throated bellowing in the darkness and envision a pair of attack-trained Dobermans bearing down upon them.

By the time I reached the bottom of the stairs, the Poodles had already skidded around the banister and headed down the hallway toward the kitchen. I caught my breath, reflecting on the fact that the tone of their barking hadn't changed. That was a good sign. If they'd seen anyone, I would know it by now.

On the other hand, having sent the pair on a single-minded dash to the back door, I'd left the rest of the small house unscouted. Pausing, I reached around and flipped on lights in the living and dining rooms. Both were blessedly empty, just as I'd left them before going to bed.

I was telling myself it was a good thing that I hadn't called the police when I reached the kitchen. Eve was standing by the back door, waiting for me to open it. Faith, however, was in the middle of the room peering curiously at the little television set that was a new addition to my kitchen counter.

The TV was on and its screen cast an eerie glow out into the shadowy room. Shimmering colors reflected off the refrigerator, the sink, the shiny tile floor. The effect was spooky, and at the same time, compelling. Faith stared as though mesmerized.

An infomercial was playing. The participants were talking to each other about the incredible value of the product they were hawking. Theirs were the voices I'd heard from upstairs.

"What on earth . . . ?"

I reached for the wall, found the switch panel and turned on lights inside and out. Eve whined impatiently by the back door. As well she should: I'd told her I was going to let her out.

Automatically I went to flip up the dead bolt. Abruptly, my hand froze in midair. The lever was already upright. The door wasn't locked.

I sucked in a breath and spun around, certain in that instant that I'd felt someone creeping up behind me. There was no one there.

Of course not.

This was ridiculous. I snapped off the TV and the room fell silent. Still, my heart was pounding so powerfully it hurt to breathe. I could feel its rhythm pounding in my ears.

I wasn't an idiot. I was a grown-up with responsibilities. And I always locked my doors at night.

At least I thought I did. Unless the argument I'd had with Sam had been a more potent distraction than I'd realized, which appeared to be the case.

Giving up on the back door, Eve went and slurped a drink from the water bowl. The utter normalcy of her actions began to have a calming effect on my nerves. I crossed the room and opened the basement door.

Lights on, I stuck my head down the steps.

Like the rest of the house, it was empty. Silent. Undisturbed.

Now that the puppy had had a drink, not to mention this burst of nocturnal excitement, there was no way her bladder was going to hold until morning. I opened the back door and let both Poodles briefly outside.

There was a possibility, I admitted to myself, that I'd forgotten to lock the dead bolt. But had I left the TV on? No. No way. Hadn't happened.

I watched that set in the mornings when I was getting Davey ready for school. And sometimes in the evening while I was cooking dinner. But not last night. Sam had been there and we'd been talking. The set had never been on.

I hadn't touched that TV any more than I'd left on all the lights in the house last Sunday. I had no explanation for any of this. What the hell was going on?

11

Figuring out a way to keep me, Dox, *and* Russell Hanover all happy had seemed like an easier task the day before when I'd been well rested and not concentrating too heavily on the details. Thursday morning, as Davey and I raced to get ready for school, I drank two cups of strong dark coffee, struggled not to yawn, and wondered why on earth I'd ever thought that bringing the Dachshund puppy home with me was a good idea.

Not that Dox was hard to take care of: he wasn't. The puppy was bright and eager to please, not to mention cute as a button. Food hadn't been a problem; Eve was still eating puppy kibble herself. And since Dox spent most of his time either with me or in a crate, his lack of housebreaking wasn't an issue either.

What to do with him during the day while I was at work was another matter. Of course, Aunt Peg had pointed that problem out to me at the time. Then, I'd glossed over her objections; now they were coming back to haunt me. Nevertheless, I didn't seem to have much choice. Dox couldn't sit home by himself all day, so he was going to have to come with me to school.

For once, luck was with me. When my canine cohorts and I pulled into the teachers' parking lot, I saw that Mr. Hanover's dark green Jaguar was not yet parked in its customary space beside the back door. The God of Good Intentions was on my side.

Not only that, but my luck held, and the school day passed uneventfully. I stashed Dox's crate in a quiet corner of my classroom and piled Faith's and Eve's beds around it. The three dogs kept each other company, and, to my immense relief, no one even noticed my unauthorized addition.

After school I was due at Phil Dutton's to take care of Mutt and Maisie. Before heading to Old Greenwich, however, I had to drive home, drop off the dogs, and pick up Davey. Usually my son's bus delivers him to my house within minutes of my arrival, but that day the driver must have been running late. I had plenty of time to let the dogs out for a run and fix a snack.

The second time I went to the front door to check if the bus was coming, I saw a light blue Mazda parked on the other side of the street. Jill Prescott, the dogged cable news reporter, had returned. Briefly, I wondered if she was waiting for Davey's bus, too. I recalled that feeling I'd had earlier in the week when I'd sensed someone was watching us at the pony farm.

It was one thing for Jill and Rich to follow me around, or even for them to talk to Sam. But when they started thinking that my child was fair game, things were spinning seriously out of control.

Annoyed, I strode out of the house and across the street. Jill saw me coming and got out of the car. No doubt the expression on my face told her that this was a confrontation she wanted to be standing up for.

"What's the matter now?" she asked as I drew near.

"This has got to stop."

"Actually, it doesn't. It's a free country."

"You're harassing me."

"Don't be ridiculous. I'm not coming anywhere near you." Jill's eyes were wide with innocence. "Ask the police. I'm sure they'll agree. You're getting all bent out of shape over nothing. Sam didn't mind talking to me. Neither did Margaret Turnbull."

Like that was a surprise. Aunt Peg could blab all day when the mood struck her. And there was nothing she liked better than an appreciative audience.

"I want you to stay away from Davey," I said.

"Fine. I have no intention of bothering your child. The story isn't about him. Although I do think the ex-husband desertion angle is going to add drama to the piece, don't you?"

So she'd talked to Bob, too. It figured.

"There isn't going to be any piece," I said firmly. "Look, let's not discuss this out here." In a small neighborhood like mine, residents kept tabs on one another. I'd just as soon not have to explain to my neighbor, Edna Silano, why she'd seen me arguing in the street. "Why don't you come inside for a minute and we'll talk."

"You're asking me in?" Jill's surprised expression had a rehearsed look. If she hoped to make it on network TV she was going to have to brush up on her spontaneous emoting. "Are you sure that wouldn't violate your privacy, or your code of ethics, or something?"

"Probably," I agreed, ignoring her sarcasm. "But I guess I'm just going to have to risk it."

The reporter followed me across the street and into the house. Her head swiveled back and forth as she entered; I got the impression she was storing away mental notes

149

on such things as the décor and my prowess as a housekeeper. Unfortunately, neither one was terribly impressive.

"Have a seat." I waved toward the living room. "I'm just going to go let my dogs in and I'll be right back."

I might as well not even have bothered with the instructions. Jill didn't follow them. Instead she accompanied me out to the kitchen. "Nice place."

"Thanks." I held the door as the Poodles and Dox scrambled up the steps. "I like it."

"I thought you just had two Poodles."

"Dox is a guest." I got three peanut butter biscuits from the pantry and handed them out.

"Dox? What an unusual name. Is that D-O-X?"

I turned and looked at her.

"This isn't an interview."

"Of course not. We're just talking. Just like you said."

Right. And Stonehenge is just a pile of rocks.

I supposed it was too late now to rescind my offer and boot her back out the door. Maybe I could disarm Jill with my hostessing skills, such as they were. "Would you like something to drink?"

"Sure. Diet anything, if you have it. It's

true what they say, the camera really does add ten pounds."

Jill was slender as a stick. She'd have to put on weight to be considered slim. I got a soda out of the refrigerator.

"Getting much on-air time lately?"

Her frown came and went so quickly I almost missed it. "Not really. But that's going to change. As soon as I bring in a big story."

She'd taken a seat at the kitchen table. I placed soda and glass in front of her, then pulled out a chair and joined her. "This big story."

"If I'm lucky."

"What if you're not?"

"Then eventually I guess I'll have to give up and move on. But don't worry about me. My instincts are pretty good. I think I'm in the right place."

Jill pulled her purse into her lap and began to rummage through it. "I'm sorry, my memory is terrible. And of course, I don't want to get anything wrong. Do you mind if I take notes?"

"Yes," I said succinctly. "I do mind. Besides, what I have to say won't be noteworthy. I want you to stop following me around. I don't know how to make myself any clearer than that. Go away and leave me alone."

I'd half hoped Jill might take offense at my tone. It didn't happen. I had to give the woman credit; she didn't even blink.

Instead she looked at me and sighed. "That's pretty clear all right. The only problem is, it isn't going to happen. Let's get something straight. I'm not following you because I think it's fun. I'd rather be just about anywhere else than sitting in that damn car. But it's not like I have a choice.

"Back at the station I'm low man on the totem pole, and trust me, nobody else is going to give me a leg up. The only way to get ahead in this business is to make it happen yourself. I have to find a story that's going to break me out of the pack. For better or for worse, you're it."

"I'm *not* it," I said. I might as well have been talking to one of Faith's chew toys for all the good my objections did.

"You are," she said simply. "You have to be."

"Why?"

"Because you're all I've got!" Her voice rose. "For pity's sake, do you think big stories are a dime a dozen in Fairfield County? I swear this must be the snooze capital of the East Coast."

"Then why don't you go someplace else?"

"Because this is where I have my foot in

152

the door. Maybe what I've accomplished doesn't seem like much to you, but at least it's something. At least I'm working in television."

She wasn't going to listen to logic. Indeed judging by the stubborn set of Jill's shoulders, she wasn't going to listen to anything except what she wanted to hear. I sorted quickly through the alternatives.

"What if we could find a compromise," I proposed.

Jill put down her soda. "I'm listening."

"As you're obviously aware, I do seem to be a bit of a magnet for trouble. I have no idea why." Bad luck probably. Or maybe bad karma from a former life. "For whatever reason, I have had an affinity for being in the wrong place at the right time. Of course, that doesn't mean it's going to happen again. Maybe all the adventures I'm going to have are behind me now."

Fat chance, I thought. But one could always hope. "But if they're not, if I should somehow get involved in another murder . . ."

"Yes?" Jill prompted when I hesitated. I couldn't believe I was about to make this offer.

"I'll call you."

Jill's eyes lit up. I raised a hand, forestalling her enthusiastic outburst.

"Not for an interview. Not for a story about me. But I'll give you the inside scoop on the mystery when it's over."

Jill's enthusiasm died. She frowned and shook her head. "I need something that's breaking news. Something I can report on live."

"You need whatever you can get." Outside, I heard the squeal of air brakes, signaling the arrival of Davey's bus.

"What you're offering isn't good enough."

I pushed back my chair and stood. "Look at it this way. It'll get you out of your car and back to your own life. It will make Rich happy."

"What's he got to do with this?"

"He's the other half of your team, isn't he? It seems to me that one reason why a guy might schlepp a camera all the way to Rhode Island on a wild goose chase is because he wants to humor a pretty coworker. It must be hard for the two of you to get together when you're spending all your spare time shadowing me."

Jill didn't look convinced. "Rich knows how important my career is to me."

The Poodles, hearing Davey's bus, had already run to the front door with Dox scampering happily along behind to see what all the fuss was about. I needed to go with them. But first I needed to get things settled with Jill.

"Look," I said, "What I'm offering you is the best of both worlds. You get your life back, plus, if you're lucky — and I'm unlucky — you'll get your story, too."

"Not the way I want it," Jill said stubbornly.

I threw up my hands. I'm a reasonable person. At least I'd like to think I am. But there was no reasoning with Jill Prescott, Miss Cable News.

"Come on." I spun around and headed for the front door. "Time's up. Out you go. Back to your car."

"Just like that?" Jill asked. At least she was following me. If she refused to leave, I had no idea how I was going to get rid of her. "We're done? We didn't agree on anything."

"We tried." I shrugged. "I guess that's about as close as we're going to come."

With three dogs, two of them pretty big, milling around the door, I could see why Jill would hang back. Not me. I waded through the melee and opened it just as Davey reached the top of the steps.

"Hey!" He shrugged out of his backpack and let it fall to the floor. His sweatshirt followed a moment later. "Only one more day of school until spring break!"

This announcement was accompanied by a victory dance which made up in enthusiasm what it lacked in coordination. Eve, getting into the spirit of the celebration, spun around on her hind legs and knocked Davey over. Giggling, he went down in a heap. Taking their cue, the dogs piled on top of him.

As I reached down to pick up Davey's things, Jill said from behind me, "Cute kid."

"Thanks."

"I won't have time for children." Her voice was firm. "I'll be too busy with my career."

"Oh? You've decided that already?"

"Sure. Why not?" Pressing her back to the wall, Jill inched her way around the pile of bodies in the middle of the floor.

"It just seems like you're a little young to be ruling things out of your life."

"I'm twenty-two years old, and I know what I want. I figure that gives me a head start on most people. Believe me, I have no intention of spending my early work years floundering. I've set my goals and I'm going after them."

She slipped out through the open doorway and left without looking back. Watching her go, I didn't know whether to be impressed by her determination or scared half to death that it was aimed in my direction.

Fortunately, Davey loves to ride in the car. Most days he doesn't even care where we're going as long as we're on the road. This wasn't the first time I'd taken him to Phil Dutton's house when I was pet-sitting. By now, he knew the routine almost as well as I did.

Bearing Monday's experience in mind, I didn't use my key to let us in. Instead, I rang the doorbell, then waited a minute to see if anyone would answer.

"Come on, Mom." Davey tugged at my sleeve, impatiently.

We could hear Maisie and Mutt inside, yapping frantically and throwing themselves against the door. I fitted the key to the lock. As soon as the door was open, Davey slithered through ahead of me. I hung back, using my body to block the space so the two dogs couldn't dash out.

"Hello?" I called. "Anybody home?"

The house looked empty. Then again, it had looked empty on Monday, too. The fact that Phil had been there the whole time without my knowing it seemed kind of strange. He said he'd been working in the basement, but I had no way of knowing if that was true or not. For all I knew, he might have been watching me.

"Of course nobody's home!" Davey snorted with all the disdain a seven-year-old could muster. "That's why we're here."

"Right." I blew out a breath and reached for Mutt's and Maisie's leashes.

I had no intention of telling Davey otherwise. There was no reason that my son needed to know that there'd been nobody in our house the night before either, and yet somehow the door had gotten unlocked and the television set turned on.

Whoever Nobody was, he was beginning to drive me crazy.

12

That night Aunt Peg phoned to ask for a favor.

You might call this familiar territory. As usual, I tried to find out what she wanted before agreeing to get involved. Such reticence on my part is a survival skill of sorts. You wouldn't believe some of the hare-brained ideas Aunt Peg has come up with. Nor the entirely reasonable way she has of explaining what she wants.

"This will only take an hour of your time," she said. "Maybe two, tops."

I carried the phone over to a chair and sat down. When Aunt Peg starts talking about the brevity of her plans, it's time to settle in for the duration.

"What do I need to do?"

"Drive down to Norwalk and have a nice chat with George Firth."

"Why would I want to do that?"

"Because Marian asked me to." Not surprisingly, Aunt Peg hurried on before I could interrupt. "She's still very upset over

159

this whole situation with Dox. Marian is not what you might call a patient woman. She wants things resolved now, right this minute if possible."

Gee, I thought. I guessed that meant that Marian Firth and my Aunt Peg had more in common than their love of dogs.

"Of course, Marian can't talk to George herself. If there was anything at all amicable about their divorce this never would have happened in the first place. She needs somebody objective to intervene, someone who can convince George of the error of his ways."

"Why me?" I asked. I may also have rolled my eyes toward the heavens as I uttered this plaintive cry.

I was speaking rhetorically, but Aunt Peg, who thankfully couldn't see the gesture, chose to answer. "I'd be happy to go see George myself, but there's a problem with that. According to Marian, the man works all week and golfs on Sundays. So the only day there's a hope of catching him when he might be receptive to listening is Saturday. As you well know, this Saturday I'll be judging at the Twin Forks dog show. Of course Marian understood that I couldn't be in two places at once, so she was quite delighted when I volunteered you to take my place."

"Aunt Peg, you're only judging one breed, and Poodles are scheduled for the afternoon. The dog show is an hour away; you'll have your whole morning free."

My aunt's silence rebuked me for pointing out the obvious. "Technically that's true. But you know how I get before an assignment. . . ."

"Nervous?"

"Justifiably concerned about doing a good job." Her tone was prim. "I'd hate to be distracted at a crucial time. And what if I got stuck in traffic on the way to the showground? What if I missed my assignment altogether?"

Not likely, considering that Aunt Peg had made a habit of arriving hours early for the judging assignments she'd performed thus far. Since I suffered similar nerves when I went in the ring, however, I decided not to press the issue.

"I don't know what makes you think I'd be any good at this," I said instead. "I don't even know George Firth. Why would he listen to anything I have to say?"

"Because you'll be the voice of reason. Perhaps he has no idea what a terrible thing he did by throwing poor little Dox out into the world to fend for himself. Once he's been made to understand where he went

161

wrong, I've no doubt you'll be able to convince him to retract his decision."

Hadn't I solved this problem once already? I wondered. Or maybe even twice, considering that the puppy in question, far from fending for himself in the cold, cruel world, was at that moment asleep quite comfortably under my kitchen table.

"Has it occurred to you that that may be a bad idea?" I asked. "The way things stand now, Marian is assured of having a chance to bid on the puppy at the auction. If George changes his mind and takes Dox back, who knows what sort of disposal scheme he'll come up with next?"

"Don't worry about that," said Aunt Peg, "Marian has a plan. I must say, it sounds rather ingenious to me."

Oh Good Lord. Aunt Peg with an idea was bad enough. Peg and Marian hatching up schemes together was definitely more than I could handle.

"Don't tell me," I said. "I don't even want to know."

"But you will go and talk to George?"

I'd been planning to go to the dog show myself. Not to show Eve, of course; with Aunt Peg judging, we were ineligible. But I'd hoped to hook up with Sam and spend the day spectating, watching some of the other interesting breeds we never got a chance to see when we were busy exhibiting.

On the other hand, as I'd pointed out to Peg, the show was not that far away. With luck, I could see George Saturday morning and still be in northern New Jersey by early afternoon.

"I guess I can," I said. "Davey will be with Bob. He's going to have a riding lesson on Willow. Do you happen to have George's phone number? I'll call and see if I can set something up."

Of course she did. Peg was nothing if not always prepared. Boy Scouts could learn volumes by following my aunt around. She read me the number, and I jotted it down.

"There's something else I wanted to talk to you about," I said. "A couple of strange things have been happening around here."

"Strange?" Her voice perked up. Aunt Peg likes strange. "Like what?"

I explained about the lights being on when I got home from the dog show. I told her about Jill Prescott, who apparently had no intention of giving up in her quest to make both of us famous. Lastly, I related the adventure I'd had the night before.

Somehow, laying out the bare facts in the light of day made them seem a good deal less threatening than they had at the time.

Frightened as I'd been in the middle of the night, it was hard to recapture that emotion in the retelling.

Even Aunt Peg, who loves a good spooky story, was singularly unimpressed. "It sounds to me like you need a good electrician. How old is that house anyway? Maybe your wiring has begun to go."

"It was built in the fifties, but I don't think the wiring's the problem. And I don't need an electrician to tell me when my back door's unlocked."

"You said yourself you might have been responsible for that oversight," Aunt Peg pointed out. "And as for Jill Prescott, if she's bothering you, why don't you just tell her to get lost?"

"I have, several times. She doesn't pay any attention."

Aunt Peg harrumphed. When she says something, people sit up and take notice. It's hard for her to understand that that's a gift not all of us share.

"Don't worry," she said briskly. "Sooner or later, Jill will simply get bored with the game she's playing and give up. In the meantime, Dox's dilemma needs to take precedence."

You can see why it's a good thing my aunt never had children.

"How is the puppy doing, by the way? Is he fitting in well?"

"Just fine." Dox wasn't the only one under the table. Actually all three dogs were sacked out on the floor around me. The little Dachshund was curled in a small ball, the curve of his back nestled against Faith's long legs. "The Poodles have accepted him like a long lost brother."

"Excellent. You will let me know how things turn out, won't you?"

Certainly, Herr Generale. Her wish was my command.

Saturday morning, I awoke to the sound of rain lashing against the side of the house. I'd left my bedroom window open a crack, and the sheer curtains billowed inward, propelled by the force of a gusting wind. Around here, April is one of those months where you hope for the best but often end up admitting that it really isn't spring just yet. Though the dog show was being held indoors, I imagined that Davey's plans for the day had probably been placed on hold.

I was due at George Firth's condominium in Norwalk at ten. We'd spoken briefly on the phone, and I'd explained only that I needed some further information regarding his donation to the benefit. I could take

Davey with me if I had to, but first I needed to confirm my son's arrangements — or lack thereof — with Bob. Before I got a chance to call my ex-husband, however, he surprised me by showing up.

"What are you doing here?" I asked as he took off his jacket and shook it out, splattering a spray of raindrops around the hallway.

"Picking up Davey. That was the plan, right?"

"It was. But I thought he was going to have a riding lesson. Surely nobody rides in weather like this."

"No, but Pam said to go ahead and bring him over to the farm, anyway. She says there are plenty of other things he can learn to do to care for his pony. Who knows?" Bob grinned. "Maybe she'll let him muck a few stalls."

With Davey's schedule back in place, my life became a little less complicated. I told Bob I'd stop by and pick Davey up after the show and explained to the dogs that they were going to be in for a tough day as I couldn't take all three of them to either George's condo or the dog show.

Faith looked resigned. Eve did her best to make me feel guilty about the less than perfect arrangement. Dox didn't have a clue.

He was just happy to get the biscuit I gave him when I locked him in his crate. Ah, the innocence of youth.

In contrast to his ex-wife, whose fortunes seemed to have declined with the divorce, George Firth was obviously doing just fine. His careful directions led me to an upscale condominium cluster down by the shore in Norwalk. A guard at the front gate called to check whether I was expected, then waved me in.

The buildings were white stucco, clean and streamlined in appearance. None were more than three stories high, and they wrapped around a colorful harbor, offering views out onto Long Island Sound. Even this early in the year several boats were already out of storage and bobbing in their moorings as the Sound rose and fell, whipped by the driving rain. On a sunny day, the vista must have been magnificent.

Alerted to my arrival by the guard, George was waiting on the third-story landing outside his apartment when I pulled up. He introduced himself as I climbed the stairs and held out a hand when I reached the landing. Marian had seemed wan and fragile; her ex-husband was robust. Not particularly tall, but built on a heavy frame, he had thick features and broad fleshy hands. George's smile was warm and friendly, though, as he ushered me into his home.

I stepped inside the foyer and stopped, staring in rapt surprise at the windows that ran the length of the living room. The view was breathtaking. Sliding glass doors opened out onto a balcony that seemed to hang out over the water. The Sound looked close enough to reach out and touch.

"Great, isn't it?" George took my slicker and hung it over the back of a chair to dry. "That's why I bought the place. First time you see that view, it hits you right between the eyes. I see it every day and it still gets to me."

"It's gorgeous." Drawn irresistibly, I walked over to the window and gazed out. "Do you have a boat?"

"Not yet. I'm hoping to start shopping around this summer. I don't want to seem abrupt, but if you don't mind, I'm in kind of a time crunch here. You said on the phone that you needed some information . . . ?"

"Right." Reluctantly, I turned to face the room. "It's about the Dachshund puppy you donated to Peter Donovan's charity auction to benefit the Stamford Outreach program —"

"Yeah, yeah, yeah." George looked bored.

And impatient. "What do you need to know?"

"We've heard from your ex-wife —"

"Marian?" His interest suddenly returned. "She doesn't have anything to do with this. That puppy is mine, I'm free to do anything I want with it."

"I'm sure you are. But as it happens, auction organizers have become concerned about the viability of offering a live animal as one of the prizes —"

"Mr. Donovan didn't mention any concerns when I spoke with him about my donation. In fact, he seemed to think the whole thing was a rather nifty idea."

Nifty? George Firth didn't look old enough to use words that had last been in vogue in the fifties. I wondered if his vocabulary had had anything to do with the reason Marian had divorced him. Or maybe it was that time crunch thing.

"Yes, well, Mr. Donovan has since been in touch with several dog breeders who have registered an objection to the proceedings —"

"Marian put them up to it, didn't she?" George scowled. With his heavy jowls and wide body, he looked like a Bullmastiff in a serious snit. "That's what this is all about. All those dog people know each other, and they stick together, too." He peered at me from beneath bushy brows. "I guess that means you're one of them?"

"Well, yes, but that's not why I'm here —"

"I assume you've spoken to my ex-wife?" Before I could reply, George was already moving on. "I'm sure she told you her side of the story. I'm not the kind of guy to go airing my dirty laundry in public, but since you're already in the middle of this, let's lay out a few facts.

"Number one, Marian left me. I was perfectly happy with the status quo, she was the one who wanted out. So if she's changed her mind now about the way things turned out, I hardly see how that can be my fault, can you?"

"No, but —"

"Number two, this arrangement with the dogs was perfectly legal. Marian wanted to keep all the dogs, even the ones that were worth money, that might have been considered assets from the marriage."

I'd been in the dog show world long enough to know that very few dogs, even top winning ones, were worth enough money to be viewed as assets. George, however, was on a roll.

"The judge decided to let things go her way. Marian retained sole ownership of all

170

the dogs. All I got . . ." He paused, then repeated the phrase for emphasis, "*All I got* was the promise of one puppy to be delivered sometime in the future."

I glanced around the posh apartment. "I wouldn't say that was *all* you got."

"Hey." George threw up his hands. "So I make good money. I'm not apologizing for that. I work hard for it. Truth be told, that's probably why my marriage fell apart. Maybe I'm a bit of a workaholic. But you know, there are worse things in the world than a guy who spends too much time at the office. Like a wife who's running around with someone else behind the guy's back."

"Oh." Of course, there were two sides to the story. There always were.

"Yeah," George said. "Oh. Now I hear the schmuck she dumped me for has left her high and dry, so I guess there's some poetic justice in that. But if Marian thinks I'm going to give up all this to go back to a house filled with dogs and a wife who did nothing but complain, she'd better think again."

He sounded pretty sure of himself, but as far as I knew, Marian *had* thought again. When Peg and I had spoken with her she hadn't mentioned anything about wanting to get back together with George. Indeed, if

171

I remembered correctly, she'd wished him dead, which hardly sounded like a prelude to reconciliation to me.

"And by the way," said George, "since we're on the subject, did Marian tell you how long it took her to deliver that puppy that I'd been promised?"

"No."

"It was more than a year. First she said that Donna was missing her seasons. Then she said the stud dog she'd picked was unavailable. Okay, maybe I'll let that slide once, but more than that? No way."

A pair of seagulls, gliding past the window in unison, caught my eye. Gracefully buoyant, they swooped down over the Sound, fishing for lunch. I watched their progress for several seconds before turning back to George. "Considering that you gave the puppy away as soon as you got him, I can't say that I see why you were in such a hurry."

"It was the principle of the thing."

"And the Dachshunds were nothing more than an asset from the marriage, like a house or a car."

"Don't put words in my mouth," George grumbled. "And don't go trying to paint me as some sort of dog hater. I always liked the dogs just fine. The dog shows, now, they were pretty stupid. But the dogs and I got along."

"If that's the case, why did you give the puppy away?"

George shrugged. "You get a divorce and your life changes. Even if you think things are mostly going to stay the same, they don't. By the time Donna finally had her litter, I was settled here. And guess what? Everything's all spelled out in the purchase agreement. No dogs allowed. Not little ones, not cute ones, not puppies that don't take up much space. No dogs, period. So what else was I going to do?"

That was easy. "You might have left him with your ex-wife."

"You're kidding me." George stood up. He was shaking his head incredulously. "Tell me you're kidding. After what she put me through? Not a chance. Marian owed me that puppy, and by God, I was going to see that she paid."

13

It was a good thing Aunt Peg hadn't been the one to go see George Firth. Though I'd blithely dismissed her fears of getting stuck in traffic, I ended up sitting on the approach to the George Washington Bridge for nearly an hour. By the time I arrived at the location in Elizabeth, New Jersey, Poodles were nearly due to go in the ring. Aunt Peg would have been having a cow.

And then, of course, I couldn't find a place to park. Kennel clubs devote untold hours debating how best to attract spectators to their shows. Well, I'm here to tell them that the answer is simple: make attending your event an inviting experience. Don't expect that casual sightseers will do what I did, circle the block three times and end up parked in a supermarket lot a quarter mile away. It isn't going to happen.

At least the rain had tapered off. Jogging back to the building where the show was being held, I merely got damp, not soaking wet. I was standing in line waiting to pay admission when a hand grasped my shoulder.

"Hey," said Bertie. "I'm glad I saw you come in. Are you busy?"

Bertie was my new sister-in-law; she and my younger brother, Frank, had gotten married over Christmas. She was also a professional handler with a thriving business and a growing string of good dogs.

"Just waiting to pay." There seemed to be a hold-up at the front of the line.

"Screw that. I'll tell them you're my assistant. Besides, you don't want your hand stamped. That damn ink never washes off."

Since Bertie wasn't much given to profanity, I gathered she wasn't having a good day. This impression was further reinforced when the tall redhead used her hold on my shoulder to yank me out of line. "Come on, let's go. I've got three Bichons due in the ring in five minutes."

Shedding my jacket as I went, I trotted along behind her. The room where the show was being held was small. Rings, grooming, and concessions all battled for the same limited amount of space. Bertie's setup was near the front of the building. No wonder she'd seen me come in.

I tossed my coat on top of a stack of crates and threw my purse inside the bottom one. "What do you want me to do?"

"When I made these entries, I thought I'd have help today. I hired an assistant," Bertie said, frowning. "She lasted a week and a half. I've got three Bichon bitches, one puppy and two in Open. If I pull any of them, I'll break the major."

For dogs that have yet to finish their championships, majors are the Holy Grail of showing. In order to become a champion, each dog must have at least two major wins, meaning that they must beat enough competition to pick up three or more points at a single show. Depending on the time of year and a breed's popularity, finding major entries can be an exercise in extreme frustration. Nobody breaks a major if they can possibly avoid it, especially not a hard-working pro who depends on the goodwill of the other professional handlers to make her life a little easier.

"I need you to hold for me at ringside, then show one of the Open bitches."

Bertie already had all three Bichons groomed and ready to go. She grabbed a rubber band out of her tack box. Automatically I stuck out my arm. Bertie ran the band up over my wrist and elbow then used it to anchor a numbered armband in place. She handed me a comb and stuck several pieces of dried liver in my pocket.

It was all happening so fast I never had a chance to even think of saying no. Pre-ring nerves, however, only took a second to appear, and I did feel obliged to mention one thing. "You know, I've never shown a Bichon before."

"There's nothing to it," Bertie said quickly. "It's just like showing a Poodle, except the tail goes over the back instead of up."

Yeah right. Bichon experts, I was sure, would beg to differ. Every breed has its little idiosyncrasies, its own distinctly different style of presentation. Just from watching at ringside, I'd learned that.

Most sporting dogs have their collars removed while the judge examines them. Working handlers tend to toss their bait until their rings become littered with it. German Shepherds gait at the speed of light, while Pekingese are slow as snails. The variations are endless.

"You'll do fine." Bertie handed me one of the Bichons, then picked up the other two, tucking one under each arm for the trip to the ring. "Just follow me and do what I do."

She made it sound so easy.

That advice might have actually worked if anyone had consulted the Bichon I was showing about the plan. Her name was

Rhonda, and, as I quickly discovered, she had a mind of her own. Rhonda knew Bertie; she'd never seen me before. Within thirty seconds of our acquaintance, she'd decided to make it her mission in life to escape from me and return to the handler with whom she thought she belonged.

I reasoned with Rhonda while Bertie was in the ring showing the puppy. I argued with her as Bertie found someone sitting ringside to hold the puppy while she prepped her bitch for the Open Class. I pleaded for a little cooperation when our class filed into the ring. All to no avail. Rhonda was a small, white, whirling dervish on the end of my leash.

I had no idea how Bertie had decided which of the two bitches she would handle in the class. It's not unusual for pros with large strings to have more than one entry in Open. Often one dog is entered as a backup. One will be shown if the entry draws a major, the other if it doesn't. With a major on the nose, however, everyone has to go in the ring.

In a case like that, the dog with less seniority will usually be handed off to an assistant. Or alternatively the handler will show the dog he thinks is most likely to win under a particular judge. Sometimes he'll opt to stick with the one that belongs to his biggest and most powerful client.

Some show dogs become jaded. They'll go in the ring and perform for anyone. Others need the "human connection" of showing for the person with whom they've bonded. Unfortunately for me, Rhonda belonged to the latter group. We'd been in the ring less than a minute before she'd sized me up and decided I was second string.

Following Bertie's lead was out of the question. Getting anywhere near her was a recipe for disaster. The only thing I could think to do was put as many of the other Open bitches between us as possible while distracting Rhonda with bait from the supply that had been shoved in my pocket.

Bertie went to the front of the line. I aimed for the back. Rhonda spun in circles and nipped at my ankles. Her displeasure couldn't have been made more clear if she'd written a sign and posted it ringside.

Busy with her own entry, Bertie shot me encouraging glances. They turned to worried frowns as the judge made his first pass down the line. I was kneeling on the floor beside Rhonda holding her in place. One hand gripped her firmly beneath the chin, the other supported her hindquarter. Still she managed to wiggle and snort.

The judge looked amused. In case you're wondering, that's not good.

Okay, so I'm not the best handler in the world. Except for those few lucky individuals who seem to possess a magic touch, handling dogs — and especially a dog you've just met — is a skill that can take years to master. Not only had I not yet put in the time, but so far the bulk of my show ring experience had been with my own dogs, dogs I had trained to my specifications. Dogs that wanted to listen to me.

Rhonda was the Brave New World of handling for me, and she was doing her best not to be discovered.

When it was our turn for the individual examination, I led her up to the table. *Just like showing a Poodle,* Bertie had said, obviously overlooking the fact that I showed Standards, not Minis or Toys. I'd never presented a dog on a table before.

I tried to lift Rhonda as I'd seen the other handlers do: grasping her in such a way that the hair was mussed as little as possible. Of course, that method didn't give me the most secure hold. Not only that, but the fluffy white Bichon was a lot heavier than she looked.

Rhonda landed on the table with a thump. The scathing look she sent my way was meant to insult my technique, and quite possibly my heritage. Ignoring the Bichon's fit of pique, I stacked her, placing her short legs squarely under her body in a stance calculated to accentuate her good points.

The pose would have worked to better advantage if Rhonda hadn't taken one look at the approaching judge and launched herself into the air. Fortunately, forewarned by the bitch's earlier antics, I hadn't let my guard down. I leapt around the front of the table and caught her mid-leap, staggering slightly beneath the unexpected load.

"Nice catch." The judge smiled kindly.

"Thanks," I mumbled, hurrying to get Rhonda back into position so she could be examined. Once again the Bichon wasn't cooperating.

"This must be her first show. Don't worry, she'll get used to it." The judge was obviously an old hand at getting the job done. He calmly worked around my restraining hands, performing the examination quickly and gently.

When he was finished, I lowered Rhonda to the floor and attempted the triangle gaiting pattern I'd seen the judge request from the other entries. The only reason the Bichon stayed within three feet of me was because we were attached by a strip of leather and I outweighed her. Even stooping over to dangle a piece of dried liver in front of her nose — the donkey-and-carrot theory — didn't help. Rhonda planted her feet on the rubber mat and dared me to make her move. Short of straying into the realm of highly objectionable show ring behavior, there was nothing I could do but acknowledge defeat.

To no one's surprise, Rhonda didn't get a ribbon. I bent down, picked her up, and scuttled from the ring like the loser I was. Bertie, meanwhile, had won the class. I waited by the gate, watching as the winners of the other bitch classes went back in to vie for Winners Bitch and the coveted major points.

"Give her to me," a voice said from behind me. The man sounded impatient and more than a little annoyed. Before I could respond I was poked, rather rudely, on the shoulder.

"Excuse me?" I turned to find a young couple standing close up behind me.

Husband and wife, from the looks of them; both were scowling ferociously. Dimly, I noted that Rhonda's tail had begun to wag. *Finally* something had made her happy.

The man held out his hands, encircling mine. "I said let me have her."

I tried to step back and found my legs braced against the side of the ring. Rhonda was wiggling again; obviously she recognized the pair. It didn't matter, I couldn't hand her over without permission.

I slid a desperate glance in Bertie's direction. Not unexpectedly she hadn't noticed my dilemma. All her attention was focused on the competition in the ring.

"I'm afraid I can't do that. As soon as Bertie is finished —"

"I'll give her a piece of my mind," the man growled. "In the meantime, she's my dog, and especially after the idiotic display you put on in there, I don't want you holding her. Hand her over."

"I really can't," I said again, trying to angle my body away. Between the spectators, the ring itself, and these two, I was hemmed in on all sides. "Not unless Bertie tells me to."

"Bertie can go to hell," the woman said heatedly. "Right this minute we don't give a damn what she says."

Miraculously, the ring steward materialized beside me, walkie-talkie in hand. "Is there a problem here?"

"Yes, there's a problem!" the man snorted. Then, realizing abruptly who he was addressing, he moderated his tone. The

AKC does not take kindly to displays of bad sportsmanship or nasty behavior of any kind. If the steward had to call the rep, the man would be flirting with sanctions. "This moron won't give me my dog."

The steward inclined her head in my direction, waiting for an explanation. I noted she didn't correct him about the moron part.

"She probably is their dog," I said. We could all see perfectly well that Rhonda's wagging tail backed up their claim. "But their handler gave her to me to hold, and until —"

"Our handler is fired!" the woman interjected hotly. "And you have no right to hold our baby hostage."

Baby? *Hostage?* Was it just me, or were these two people seriously nuts?

"Does she, boopums?" The woman lowered her head and made kissing noises in front of Rhonda's nose.

The Bichon's whole body was vibrating now. Mindful of the way she'd launched herself into the air earlier, I took a firmer hold.

"Where is this handler now?" asked the steward.

I nodded toward the ring. Bertie, thankfully, had just been awarded Winners Bitch. "She'll be out in a second."

And of course, having won Winners, she'd

need to go right back in for Best of Breed. What a mess.

"All three of you," the steward said firmly, "wait right there." She waved the bitch who'd been second in the Open Class back into the ring so that Reserve Winners could be judged.

Tucking the coveted purple ribbon in her pocket, Bertie came and stood by the gate, waiting out of the way until it was her turn again. Obviously she'd been oblivious to our little drama. I sidled her way.

"Help!" I muttered.

"What?" Turning to look, she sized up the problem in an instant. Bertie was no dummy.

"Hi Jean, Mike." Her smile was placating. "I didn't know you were here today."

Dogs that live and travel with professional handlers never see their owners before they go in the ring. A distraction like that would ruin their performance. Socializing, if permitted at all, takes place afterwards.

"That was obvious!" Jean snapped. "Would you please tell your incompetent assistant to give us our dog?"

"It's okay," Bertie said to me.

I handed Rhonda over. Or rather, I didn't resist when Mike snatched her out of my arms.

"It is *not* okay," Mike said loudly. I think

he relished the fact that other spectators at ringside had begun to listen in. "We have to talk. *Right now.*"

"Right now, I'm going back in the ring."

Reserve Winners had just been awarded. The steward was calling the entries for Best of Breed.

"Why don't you let your assistant take her?" Jean gave me a dirty look. "She was good enough for our dog, why not Benton's?"

Benton, I presumed, was the owner of the other Open bitch. Bertie didn't answer. She did roll her eyes. The steward came over and shepherded Bertie to the back of the line where she belonged. Clearly nothing was going to be allowed to disrupt the judge's schedule on her watch.

Judging for Best of Breed was over in a matter of minutes. One of the specials won the Breed, another was Best of Opposite Sex. The Winners Dog was Best of Winners, beating Bertie's bitch and thereby securing the major for himself.

"I guess the judge gave you what he thought you deserved," Jean sneered when Bertie emerged, ribbonless, from the ring.

There was no use pointing out that, thanks to the steward's smooth intervention, the judge had probably never even noticed what was going on. Nor that the outcome had been pretty much what I would have expected anyway.

"Look," Bertie said in a soothing tone, "I can see you're upset. Let's go back to the setup and discuss this, okay?"

"You better believe it." Mike's stance was puffed up and edgy, that of a bully standing on the playground and looking for someone to hit. "You better believe that's exactly what we're going to do."

I collected the Bichon puppy who'd been sitting happily in a spectator's lap, and joined the back of the unhappy procession. The steward watched us remove ourselves from her jurisdiction with evident relief.

Back at the setup, Bertie quickly removed her Bichon's leash and locked the bitch in a crate. I followed suit with the puppy. Not Rhonda; Jean was gripping her so tightly that the Bichon was beginning to look uncomfortable.

Join the crowd, I thought.

I glanced over at Bertie, wondering what she wanted me to do. I was happy to hang around and provide moral support. Then again, as the object of the owners' ire, maybe I was better off making myself scarce.

As I hesitated, Mike poked a finger in my face. "You. Who are you, anyway?"

"Melanie Travis —"

"What the hell did you think you were doing in the ring with our dog?" Jean joined her husband's attack. "You certainly weren't handling her. Have you ever even been to a dog show before? It's obvious you've never seen a Bichon —"

"Enough," Bertie said firmly. "Don't yell at Melanie. I'm the one you're mad at."

"We signed a contract with you." Mike spun in her direction. "We hired *you* to show Rhonda."

"Unless there were extenuating circumstances. It was all spelled out in the papers you signed. We spoke about this, remember? You agreed that there might be times when an assistant would take Rhonda in the ring."

"When she was a puppy, maybe," Jean said hotly. "But not in the Open Class! You might as well have slapped a sign on her that said 'Don't bother with me, I'm only here as filler.' "

"What happened today was unavoidable. Under normal circumstances, I don't show two Open bitches, you know that. But the major was spot on and they both needed it —"

"Except that Benton's bitch got the major and Rhonda didn't!"

"Benton's bitch finished today." Bertie's eyelid was beginning to twitch. Though her tone remained calm, I could see her control starting to fray. "She's been with me since last fall. Rhonda still needs some singles as well as that second major. Benton's bitch had seniority."

"Fine," Mike snapped. "Then you should have pulled Rhonda."

"If I'd done that, the major would have broken."

"Then you could have shown Rhonda for the singles."

And earned the animosity of every other owner or handler who'd brought a Bichon to the show that day, all of them praying that the major would hold. Besides, if Bertie had shown Rhonda for the singles and, presumably, sent me into the ring with the other bitch, the major would have held. Any way you looked at this, it was a no-win situation.

"I'm sorry about the way things turned out," Bertie said gently. "Rhonda has always enjoyed being shown. I had no idea she wouldn't behave for Melanie. I fully expected her to be as competitive for the major as the other bitch was."

"I don't care what your intentions were," Jean said, scowling. "The end result was that you turned Rhonda into a laughing-stock. Nobody who saw her show today will ever be able to take her seriously again. Did you hear what the judge said? He asked if this was her first show. Her *first* show! My God, this bitch has been to the national specialty!"

Oh, for Pete's sake, I thought. These two really needed to get a grip. Nobody was going to penalize Rhonda in the future for the way she'd behaved today. Chances were, nobody was even going to remember. Jean and Mike had so much emotion invested in Rhonda's career they weren't even thinking clearly.

"Look at it this way," said Bertie. "Now that Benton's bitch is finished, Rhonda will be my number one project. And with Bucks County and Trenton coming up —"

"You can't be serious," said Mike. "After the display you allowed today, you can't think we're going to let you continue showing Rhonda. You're lucky we're not considering a lawsuit."

"I'm sorry you feel that way," Bertie said. There wasn't much else she could do.

"Yeah, you'll be sorry, all right," Jean snapped. "You better believe we're not going to take this lying down. We'll get even, just see if we don't."

Clasping Rhonda to her bosom, she spun around and stormed away. Mike was glowering at us, his hands clenching and unclenching at his sides. He still looked as if he wanted to hit somebody, but after a moment, he turned and followed his wife.

"Oh, crap," said Bertie.

My sentiments exactly.

14

"I'm sorry," I said when Jean and Mike had disappeared from view. "I guess I cost you a client."

"Don't apologize." Bertie's tone was firm: steel, edged with anger. "None of that was your fault. And clients like that I can do without. Rhonda's a good bitch, but that doesn't mean I can leapfrog her ahead of everyone else in my string.

"Besides, I have a responsibility to Benton, too. I've been showing his Bichons for three years. Those two just showed up in January. They'll take Rhonda to another handler and he'll treat them exactly the same way I did. I didn't do anything wrong and neither did you."

I looked at my watch. It was already after two. Aunt Peg had been judging for half an hour. "Are you okay now? Because if you are, I want to get over to the Poodle ring —"

"That's right, I forgot. Peg's judging, isn't she? Go watch and have fun."

Still I hesitated. "They won't come back

and do something awful, will they?"

"There's nothing they can do. So their dog lost. It happens. The worst Jean and Mike Azaria can do is fire me, and they've already done that."

The Poodle ring was at the other end of the room. As is often the case with indoor events where space is at a premium, the show's planners had placed all three Poodle varieties in a ring that was sized for smaller dogs. That wasn't a problem for the Toys and Minis, but any Standard Poodle class with an entry of more than three or four was going to feel pretty cramped.

By the time I got to the ring, Aunt Peg had finished judging Toys and was midway through her Minis. Sam was sitting ringside in a folding chair. His jacket was slung over the seat beside him, saving it for me. I picked up the jacket and sat down.

"I was beginning to wonder about you." Sam leaned over and kissed my cheek. "I thought you'd be here a while ago."

Though I have a cell phone in my car, I almost never turn it on. In this age of instant access, I must be the only person who actually enjoys being out of touch. Sam, who keeps his phone clipped to his belt, can't understand my reluctance to be ever available.

Mostly we avoid a lot of friction by ignoring the issue.

"Traffic," I said. "And then Bertie grabbed me to help out with Bichons as soon as I came in. How's Aunt Peg doing?"

"Guess." Sam grinned.

I didn't have to. This was my aunt's sixth judging assignment since she'd gotten her license the previous November. Each time, she'd drawn a good-sized entry and done a careful, considerate job of examining the Poodles brought before her.

No judge manages to please every exhibitor (the winners obviously go home in a happier frame of mind than the losers), but the fact that Aunt Peg was willing to discuss her judging after she was finished went a long way toward placating those who'd been hoping for a purple ribbon and left with something less. The losers might not agree with her assessment on that day, but at least they were assured that they hadn't been the victims of politics or ignorance.

"Ooh." I gazed into the ring as the Miniature Dog class winners came back to be judged for Winners Dog. "I like that puppy."

Sam nodded. "Peg did, too. I wouldn't be surprised if she gives him the points."

Second guessing the judge from ringside

is a favorite spectator sport. Never mind the fact that only the judge gets to actually handle the entries, feeling for correct bone structure and opening the mouth to check the teeth and bite. Everyone sitting outside the ring has an opinion, and most are only too happy to voice it aloud.

Aunt Peg agreed with my choice and put up the Mini puppy I'd been admiring. Not surprising, really, when you consider that she'd been the one to teach me most of what I knew. As her bitches began to file into the ring, Sam and I caught up on what had been happening since we'd last seen each other midweek.

I told him about taking Dox with me to school, about my conversation with Jill Prescott, and about the visit I'd paid that morning to George Firth. Keeping one eye on the action in the ring, Sam nevertheless managed to listen attentively and make appropriate noises in all the right places. Even so, I found myself reluctant to talk about the disturbance on Wednesday night after he'd left.

For one thing, maybe Aunt Peg was right. Maybe all I needed was a good electrician. For another, I didn't want Sam feeling guilty that he hadn't spent the night. Our relationship needed to get mended on its own terms, not nudged into place by outside considerations.

The afternoon passed quickly. Sam laughed at my description of Rhonda, the show-beast from hell, and commiserated with me over her owners' reaction. We argued the merits of the Standard entry, promising ourselves we'd find out later why Aunt Peg hadn't used an elegant white bitch who looked like a winner from our vantage point. We ate hot dogs smothered in sauerkraut and washed them down with big cups of soda. It was nice not to have to set a good example for a change.

By the time Aunt Peg finished judging Standards, the groups had already started. Three rings near the front of the room had been opened up and joined together to accommodate their needs. Exhibitors and handlers whose dogs hadn't won their respective breeds were packing up to go home. As Sam and Aunt Peg headed for the big ring where the Sporting Group was in progress, I made a small detour.

Bertie was loading a stack of crates onto a dolly when I reached her setup. "I'm glad I caught you," I said. "When you handed me that Bichon earlier, I threw my purse into one of your crates."

Bertie nodded, not surprised. This was a

commonplace occurrence, the exhibitor's version of a low-tech security system. Half the dogs at any given show are snoozing in crates that hold handbags or wallets.

"Which one?"

I had a look, then reached inside a crate that held a Finnish Spitz. My leather purse was tucked beneath the quilted pad he was lying on.

"You're lucky Gunner didn't know it was there." Bertie grinned. "He likes to chew."

"Thanks. I'll bear that in mind the next time you give me two and a half seconds to get ready to go in the ring."

Bertie knew better than to rise to *that* bait. "I see Sam's here," she said instead. "Are you two going out tonight?"

"Not that I know of. We don't have any plans. Actually I'm leaving here to pick up Davey at Bob's house."

"Let me see." Bertie held her hands out in front of her, palms up, as though she were a scale weighing the options. "Dinner with Sam." One hand shot up in the air. "Time with the ex." Her voice, and the other hand, dropped. "Doesn't look like too hard a decision to me."

"I knew I shouldn't have let Frank marry you. You were never this critical before you became my sister-in-law."

"Sure I was. I just didn't say so out loud."

"You're forgetting something," I pointed out. "Sam hasn't asked me to dinner."

"So ask him."

"I asked him the other night." An edge crept into my tone. I hadn't been offering dinner at the time, but Bertie didn't need to hear the specifics. "Now it's his turn."

"Fine by me," Bertie said with all the complacency of a newlywed who was very much in love. "You're on your own with that mess."

Apparently so; and I wasn't getting very far, either. Not only had Sam not brought up the subject of plans for the evening, he continued not to bring it up. As the Sporting group gave way to the Working dogs, I mentioned that I'd be going to Bob's to pick up Davey after the show. Sam merely grunted in reply.

That mess, indeed. If I hadn't been too much of a lady, I might have grunted myself. Instead, I moved over to stand beside Aunt Peg and filled her in on my visit with George Firth that morning.

"It doesn't sound as though he's about to change his mind," she said at the end.

"They may have separated a while ago, but he's still quite angry with Marian. Not entirely without cause, I might add."

"Oh, pish. That doesn't give him an excuse to vent his emotions on a poor, helpless puppy. George Firth is an adult, he ought to try acting like one."

"There's another problem," I said. "Even if he did take Dox back, he wouldn't have any place to keep him. The policy at his condo is no dogs allowed."

In the ring, the judge moved a Bernese Mountain Dog to the head of the line. Beside me, Aunt Peg frowned. For a moment, I wasn't sure if the grimace was in response to the judging or George's lack of responsibility.

"If he doesn't want the puppy and he won't sell him back to Marian, then he ought to place him in a good home," Peg said firmly.

Where the welfare of dogs is concerned, her feelings tend to be black and white. Aunt Peg's determination to do the best for every canine she comes in contact with doesn't allow for shades of gray. In any given situation she would opt for happy dogs over happy humans every time.

"At any rate," I said, "Dox is fine for the time being. And if the problem doesn't get resolved between now and the auction, Marian can still go and bid on him."

I turned to have a word with Sam, only to

find myself talking to empty space. While I'd been busy with Peg, Sam had disappeared.

"Over there." Aunt Peg nodded toward the other side of the ring where the dogs eligible for the Toy group had begun to assemble outside the gate. "He's talking to Terry and Crawford."

So he was. Terry's boss, Crawford Langley, had won the variety in Toy Poodles. He and his exquisite silver entry, both groomed to the nines, were awaiting their turn in the ring. Standing next to Crawford, blocking the ebb and flow of the crowd so that the delicate Toy wouldn't get jostled, Sam and Terry were conferring about something.

No doubt something vitally important, I thought irritably. Like Rangers' scores or Japanese scissors or the price of shredded wheat. Something so important that Sam couldn't even be bothered to tell me he was leaving.

"I'm done," I said.

"Pardon?" Aunt Peg's glance flickered my way, then back into the ring.

The Working dogs had left. The Toys were beginning to come in. With a Poodle in this group — especially one she'd put there — I knew I'd lost Aunt Peg's attention for the duration.

"I'm going home now."

"Don't you want to see what happens?" Peg's tone was distracted; her eyes trained straight ahead. "That Toy of Crawford's is a good one. I think he's got a shot."

"You can tell me how it turns out. Tell Sam I said good-bye, okay?"

The man in question was still on the other side of the ring. He and Terry had merged into a larger group of interested bystanders, many of them like Terry, handlers' assistants who had a stake in the outcome. It didn't look as if he were planning to return any time soon.

"Sure," Peg said. Ten to one she had no idea what she'd just agreed to do.

Somehow the ride home from a dog show always seems much longer than the ride there. On the way, anticipation eats away the miles, while driving home is a bit of a letdown. The excitement is over, and it's time to return to real life, at least for another week.

Thankfully, the traffic wasn't bad. The heavy rains from earlier had tapered off, leaving only a fine mist that coated the pavement with a slick, dark sheen. In just under an hour, I was back in Stamford, pulling up in front of Bob's house.

His Trans Am wasn't in the driveway, but

considering how my ex-husband doted over his car, he'd probably put it in the garage. What was parked there was a truck: a white dually pickup that looked vaguely familiar. After a moment, it came to me. That was Pam's truck; she'd been driving it when she brought Willow to our house.

Interesting. I knew Bob and Davey were spending the day at the pony farm, but Bob hadn't mentioned anything about bringing Pam home with them. Then again, it was really none of my business. If Bob wanted to devote a chunk of his time to an attractive young horse trainer he'd just met, well, why not?

Though my ex-husband lives by himself, the house he'd purchased over the winter was twice the size of Davey's and mine. In a former life, Bob was an accountant, and he's never been able to pass up a good investment. With the strength of the Fairfield County real estate market, he'd had no qualms about purchasing a lovely two story colonial on a secluded two acre lot. The place had resale value written all over it.

Of course, that was the view from the curb. Once you went inside, the jig was up. Like the bachelor he was, Bob owned only a couple rooms of furniture. So far the front hall and dining room were empty. The spacious living room held only a couch, a big-screen TV, a leather recliner, and an entertainment unit with an assortment of electronics that looked capable of launching rockets for NASA.

"Hello?" I called out. The front door had been unlocked, and I'd let myself in.

"In the kitchen," Bob called back. "Come on back."

"Hey, Mom, look!"

It was a good thing I stopped in my tracks. The excitement in Davey's voice was matched by the speed with which he came flying through the dining room and into the front hall. The scooter he was piloting skidded on the hardwood floor, spun out of control, and deposited my son in a heap at my feet.

Davey looked up at me delightedly. "Pretty cool, huh?"

"Very cool." I reached down and hauled him to his feet. "Are you sure you shouldn't be wearing a helmet when you ride that thing?"

"That's what I told him," Pam said, coming around the corner. She was casually dressed in a pair of pleated slacks and a linen shirt. Her long, dark hair, braided the other two times I'd seen her, hung loose and shiny around her shoulders. Looking very much at home, she sipped at a bottle of light beer. "I make all my kids wear helmets when they ride, and that scooter looks more dangerous than any pony at my farm."

"Don't be silly." Bob came up behind her, holding two amber beer bottles by their long necks. He reached out and offered one to me. "It's a toy. There's nothing risky about it. Right, sport?"

"Right!" Davey agreed happily.

You had to love it. Father and son were like children at play, operating on the same wavelength, and perhaps even the same maturity level. The mother was probably the only one who noticed the fresh rip in Davey's jeans and the smear of dirt across his cheek.

"Do you let him ride it in the house often?" I asked.

"Only when it's raining," Bob said blithely. As if that made everything okay. "How was your dog show? Did Peg tick off lots of exhibitors?"

Bob and Aunt Peg have never gotten along. She and I became close during the time when Bob had disappeared from Davey's and my lives and I was struggling to raise my young son as a single parent. Even now that my ex is back, Peg has never managed to forgive him for his past lapses.

"Not that I saw. My aunt was judging today," I explained for Pam's benefit. "I just went over to the show to watch."

She nodded. "Bob tells me you're very involved in all that dog stuff. Standard Poodles, the big ones, right? He says it takes up tons of your time."

"Not that much," I said, uncertain how I felt about the fact that Bob had been discussing me with Pam. "Probably less than you spend with your ponies."

"Yes, but they're my career as well as my avocation, so it makes sense for me. Besides, I don't have a family yet." She smiled sweetly. "When I do, *my* priorities will change."

Was it my imagination, or was I hearing my life criticized by someone I barely knew?

Pam lifted her head and sniffed the air. "Oops. Be right back. I've got to go stir. Come with me, Davey. You can help." The two of them strode off in the direction of the kitchen.

I stared after them, bemused. "Pam is cooking you dinner?"

"Yeah. Isn't she great? It's amazing how quickly she and I have gotten comfortable with one another. I feel like we've known each other for months, instead of just days."

"Are you sure that's a good thing?"

"Why not? She's really terrific. Wait till you've had a chance to get to know her better. You'll see what I mean."

He was either the biggest optimist or else the biggest sucker around. I supposed we'd find out which one soon enough.

15

"Why are we standing out here in the hallway? Come on in, sit down, get comfortable."

"I only have a minute," I said, even as I followed Bob through to the kitchen.

I'd already left the dogs home alone for most of the day. And though they were probably sleeping, unaware of the extra time I might steal at their expense, I couldn't help feeling guilty.

Bob's kitchen was a showplace, newly remodeled before the house had been put on the market. There were Corian countertops, glass-fronted cabinets, a subzero refrigerator, and a collection of copper pots hanging from a rack above the center island. Most of the luxurious appointments were lost on my ex-husband, but Pam seemed to be putting everything to good use. Several pots were simmering on the gas-powered range, and something that smelled delicious was baking in the oven.

"You should stay for dinner," Bob said expansively. "I'm sure Pam's making plenty."

Busy at the stove, Pam didn't turn around, but she did shoot me a look out of the corner of her eye. There wasn't anything welcoming about it. Putting myself in her place, I could understand her feelings; it wasn't as though Sam's ex-wife and I hadn't had our difficulties.

Woman's intuition told me that Pam had more than dinner brewing. Bob might not have realized it yet, but there was romance in the air. Neither one of them would thank me for ruining their chances.

"Another time," I said. "I've been out all day, and I need to get back to the dogs. Are you about ready, Davey?"

"Sure." My son jumped up. Oh, to have the effortless energy of a seven-year-old. "But first you have to come up and see my room. Dad and I hung up some great new posters."

Bob accompanied us on the trek upstairs; Pam remained behind in the kitchen. The first month Bob had been in his new house, Davey's sleepovers had involved air mattresses, sleeping bags, and a pillow carried from home. Somehow, the barren accommodations had made the whole thing easier to take emotionally. At least in my mind, the situation had seemed temporary. I wasn't giving up my son, I was simply adding another experience to his life.

But bit by bit a little boy's bedroom had taken shape in a spacious corner room on the second floor of Bob's house. Over time, I'd had to accept the fact that Davey loved his home away from home. Now there were bunk beds, homemade bookshelves, and a ceiling fan painted to look like an airplane propeller.

The latest addition, apparently, was wall covering. Posters that catered to my son's car fetish now adorned much of what had been blank space. I saw a Hummer, a Porsche, and a racy looking T-bird. The two of them had even managed to find a poster of a Volvo station wagon, my current mode of transportation.

Bob leaned against the doorjamb. "What do you think?"

"It looks great. You've done a lot of work in here."

"Yeah, well, I guess I had a lot of time to make up for." Bob slipped an arm around his son's shoulders. "And Davey helped, too, right?"

"Right!" He ran into the room and launched himself toward the bunk beds, grabbing the upper frame with both hands so he could swing into the lower berth. "Dad said we did such a good job on the bookshelves that we can build a tree house next."

"Wonderful." I forced myself to smile, holding back the multitude of warnings about hammers, and branch strength, and falling from high places that I wanted desperately to issue.

"Don't worry," Bob said gently. It was as though he were reading my mind. "We're saving that project until summer when it's warmer. You'll be out of school then; you can come and help if you want."

"I'd like that." And if Pam didn't — assuming she was still around — she could just learn to deal with it.

Back in the kitchen, I rinsed the beer bottles for recycling, gathered up purse and car keys, and shepherded my procrastinating son toward the door. Though he and Bob were busy debating the merits of taking the scooter home or leaving it there, Pam had turned off the oven and had the door sitting cocked open. It wasn't hard to see she was growing impatient for us to move this party along.

"Leave it here," I said, deciding for them. "That way it will be a special treat for when you're visiting your dad."

"Like Willow," Davey said.

"Right. Like Willow."

I hadn't had a chance to ask how their day at the pony farm had gone, but that oversight was rectified on the trip home. Davey treated me to a blow-by-blow description of stall mucking, tack polishing, and pony grooming. By the time we reached our house I felt incredibly well versed on the topic of equine cleanliness.

All three dogs were, of course, absolutely delighted to see us. The first twenty minutes after our return were devoted to taking them outside, telling them how wonderful they were to put up with us, apologizing for the neglect we'd visited upon them, and bribing them with peanut butter biscuits to make ourselves feel better about the unfortunate way their day had gone.

When things finally settled down, I got around to listening to the three messages on my answering machine. The first one was from George Firth.

"Yeah, hi," he said. "We met this morning. I've been thinking about what you said about the dog and all. It looks like this whole thing isn't working out too well. I called Peter Donovan and told him I want the puppy back. He said you've got it, so now I'm calling you. It might have been nice if you would have come clean this morning and told me that. Anyway, I've changed my mind and I want my dog. Call me back."

He left a phone number, which I duly noted on the pad by the phone. I supposed I would have to call him; there didn't seem to be any way around it. But that didn't mean I had to hurry.

Our conversation had made it clear that George had no concept of the puppy as a living, breathing animal. Like the children who ended up as pawns in a battle between their parents, Dox was a tool he was hoping to manipulate to his own advantage. Tomorrow would be a fine time to talk to Mr. Firth about returning Dox. Maybe even the day after.

The second message was from Jill Prescott. "Hi Melanie!" she said cheerfully. "I just wanted to check in and see how things were going. You did promise to keep me posted on any new and interesting developments in your life."

No, I hadn't, I thought. *Had I?*

Not that it made any difference, since Jill's idea of interesting involved police sirens, dead bodies, and camera-friendly sound bytes. Luckily, I hadn't even come close to anything like that.

Her chirpy voice continued. "I'm doing what you asked and giving you plenty of space, so I trust you'll live up to your end of the bargain and keep me informed. Here's my cell phone number, call anytime. Talk to you soon!"

Jill's phone number joined George's on the pad. Another call I'd put off making for as long as possible.

The answering machine beeped again, signaling the third message. Maybe this would be the one from Ed McMahon telling me that I'd won the Publisher's Clearing-house Sweepstakes?

No such luck. It was Aunt Rose.

"Melanie, dear," she said, "I just wanted to see how you were doing. I know Peter and I have taken tremendous advantage of your good nature, thrusting you into the middle of this situation with Dox. We'd like to try and make it up to you. This week is your spring break, right? Would you and Davey like to come to dinner, maybe Monday night? Let me know, when you get a chance."

Rose's number got added to those I'd already written down, an unnecessary gesture since I knew the phone number by heart. Until his marriage to Bertie just before Christmas, the number had belonged to my brother, Frank, as had the apartment where Peter and Rose were now living. At that point, Frank had moved to Bertie's place in

Wilton, which had room for the dogs she boarded and handled. Frank's apartment — actually one floor of a remodeled Victorian house in Cos Cob — where my brother had performed odd jobs for the elderly owner in exchange for a reduction in his rent, was now Rose and Peter's new abode.

After checking to find out where Davey, Dox, and the Poodles had disappeared to — all four turned out to be happily ensconced on a couch in the living room, Davey playing Nintendo, the dogs cheering on his efforts — I picked up the phone and called Rose back. She answered on the second ring, proof that her prospects for an exciting social life on Saturday night were as dismal as my own.

Then again, I thought, Aunt Rose was in her fifties, married, settled, happy with her life. I was thirty-three and single, sitting home on a Saturday night and watching my dogs play Nintendo. What was wrong with *that* picture?

"Thanks for the invitation," I said to Rose, perhaps a little more heartily than necessary. At least I wasn't a total social outcast. "Monday sounds great. Davey and I would love to come."

"Excellent. I just heard back from Sam. He's going to be joining us as well."

"Sam?" My voice squeaked. Aunt Rose hadn't mentioned that in her message. Probably on purpose. Apparently Aunt Peg wasn't the only closet matchmaker among my relatives.

"Yes, of course, Sam. After all, dear, the three of you are almost a family, aren't you? I couldn't very well leave him out."

Of course she could have, and she damn well knew it. In one fell swoop, Rose had turned what could have been a pleasant evening into yet another opportunity for people-whose-business-it-was-not to engage in an unsubtle attempt to pummel Sam's and my sputtering relationship into acceptable shape.

"Does Sam know that Davey and I are coming, too?"

"Don't be silly. I could hardly invite him over without giving him all the particulars, could I?"

Why not? She'd pulled that trick on me.

"Did you say you just talked to him?"

I wondered if Sam had called her from home. I wondered if he was feeling as lonely as I was.

"That's right. Frankly, I hadn't expected to hear back from either one of you until tomorrow, but Sam said something about you running out on him at a dog show . . . ?"

Aunt Rose let the thought dangle for a moment, before adding, "He seemed to think you were spending the evening with Bob."

"Bob has a date." I was sure I sounded annoyed; I didn't care.

I'd told Sam quite clearly that I was only stopping by Bob's place to pick up Davey. I'd given him every opportunity to ask what I'd be doing after that. The only thing I hadn't done was follow Bertie's advice and ask him out myself.

Idiot, I thought belatedly. Of course Bertie had been right. Chances were *she* hadn't spent many Saturday nights sitting home feeling sorry for herself.

"Good for Bob," Aunt Rose said heartily. My aunt, the former nun, tends to wish the best for everyone. Except, perhaps, Aunt Peg. "Isn't it nice that he's settling in so well. Maybe I should add him to the guest list for Monday, too?"

Only if she wanted her dinner party to turn into a free-for-all. Spending any length of time with Bob and Sam together left me feeling like the monkey in the middle. "I think not," I said firmly.

I spent the next few minutes assuring Aunt Rose that Dox was well, mentioning briefly that I'd met with both Marian and George Firth. Rose, not the ever curious dog person Aunt Peg was, let my judicious omissions slide and asked about Davey's progress with his new pony.

When I got off the phone, I fixed supper for Davey and me, fed the dogs, cleaned everything up, brushed out Eve's topknot and ears, then played a rousing game of Scrabble with my son. Just another exciting, fun-filled night at the Travis house.

Of course, everything felt brighter the next morning. A new day, filled with new possibilities. I could deal with Jill Prescott and George Firth; and I resolved to give Sam a call just as soon as I'd gotten some chores out of the way. I had the whole next week off from work, and life was looking grand.

I managed to hold that thought for most of the morning until I was standing in line at the supermarket, with Davey munching on a cruller, a week's worth of groceries being bagged, and their total rung up on the cash register. I reached in my pocketbook to pay.

Everything was grand, all right. Except for the fact that my wallet was missing.

16

Frowning, I reached in and had another look.

My purse isn't that big, and I don't carry a whole lot of stuff. Once I'd pushed aside sunglasses, checkbook, and an assortment of old lipsticks, there wasn't anyplace left for my wallet to be hiding.

Still, my brain refused to process the obvious conclusion. The enormity of the problem was simply too big to grasp. I'd left my wallet in my purse — I *always* leave my wallet in my purse. Therefore it had to be there.

"Uh, ma'am?" The cashier was a teenage boy with skinny shoulders and pimples on his chin. He'd already bagged the groceries and put them in my cart. A line was beginning to form behind me. "That'll be seventy-two, eighty-six."

"Yes, I know." I was tempted to take the purse and upend it onto the counter. I knew it wouldn't do any good, but it was the only idea I could come up with. "I just can't seem to find my wallet."

"You can pay by debit card if you want."

Like that was an option. If I'd had my debit card — which had been in my wallet — would I have been looking so frantic?

"Or check if you have some I.D."

I looked up. "My I.D. is in my wallet, along with all my cash and credit cards. It's missing. It should be here and it's not."

The boy glanced at the line growing at his register and looked aggrieved. I could hardly blame him. I was feeling much the same way.

"I'm going to have to call the manager," he said.

The store manager listened to my tale of woe, but the expression on his face made it perfectly clear that he was skeptical of patrons who expected to shop in his store when they didn't have the money to pay.

"You don't understand," I said. "I thought I had my wallet when I came in, but it's not in my purse where it should be. It's gone."

Along with my cash, my driver's license, and several credit cards, I thought miserably. Not to mention Triple A and insurance cards, a library card with a book charged against it, and a selection of Davey's baby pictures.

"I'm afraid I can't help you." The manager was already motioning a stock boy over to reshelf the items I'd gathered.

"My checkbook's here. Can I pay by check?"

"You got identification?"

Back to that again. "No, it's in my wallet."

"Look," the manager said, not unkindly. "You probably just misplaced your wallet. Go home and have a look. Maybe you used a credit card to order something online, and you'll find it sitting next to your computer. I've done that."

He might have, but I hadn't. Last time I'd seen my wallet, it had been in my purse. I was sure of it.

The manager nodded toward Davey, who was finishing up the doughnut we hadn't paid for. "Maybe the kid took it out and was playing with it."

Davey looked at me and shook his head. Though he hadn't said much, I knew he was listening to every word. Besides, he'd stopped playing with my pocketbook when he was four.

"Yeah," I said, without much hope. "I'll go home and have a look."

"Does this mean we're not going to have any food?" Davey asked as we left the store. He was trying to sound brave, but his brow was furrowed with concern.

"No, of course not." I reached out and took his hand. Usually my son considers himself too old for hand-holding, but right then he didn't mind. "We still have money, we just don't have it with us. As soon as we figure out what happened to my wallet, we'll come back and buy lots of food."

"You didn't pay for my doughnut," Davey reminded me gravely. "That's stealing. Are we going to go to jail?"

The question brought me up short. There I was, consumed with worry, feeling frustrated and half-crazy over the loss of my cash and credit cards, and my son was concerned about inadvertently shoplifting a thirty-cent doughnut. Motherhood is like that. Just when you think nothing could be more dire than the problem you're facing, it sneaks up, slaps you on the side of the head, and reminds you that the little things are important too.

I gave Davey's small hand a reassuring squeeze. "We were planning to pay for it," I said. Not that good intentions were any excuse. "We would have paid for it if we could. Next time we go shopping at that store, I'll tell them what happened and we can pay then."

"Are you sure?"

I wasn't, but I nodded anyway. One of us

being worried sick about the situation seemed like plenty to me.

We got in the car and I found myself doing what I usually do in times of stress and confusion. I drove to Aunt Peg's house. One thing you have to say for my aunt, give her a problem to gnaw on and chances are she'll either solve it or magnify it tenfold. Maybe I'm a gambler at heart and it's the uncertainty that keeps me coming back.

Worst case, I knew she'd have plenty of food on hand to reassure my hungry child.

Aunt Peg wasn't expecting us, but her Poodles let her know the moment we turned in the driveway. She met us at the door. "This is an unexpected pleasure. Did you come to see how I was holding up after my strenuous day of judging?"

"No," Davey informed her. "Mom's in trouble again."

Peg's smile faded. Holding her dogs at bay with a well placed leg, she ushered us inside. "Are Faith and Eve all right?"

Note my aunt's propensity to inquire after the Poodles' well-being first. In fairness, though, it was unusual for me to stop by without bringing the dogs to visit, and I was sure she'd noted their absence.

"They're fine. Davey and I went to the supermarket. That's why we left them home."

"You were at the market," Aunt Peg repeated. I supposed she was wondering if I had groceries defrosting in the car. "And you decided to come here? Whatever for? What's the matter?"

"Mom lost her wallet." Davey, now rolling on the floor with the Poodles, took time out from his revels to deliver the bad news. "The guy at the store wouldn't let us buy any food because we didn't have any money."

"That *is* trouble," Peg agreed. Above Davey's head, she sent me a questioning look. "I was just working on Zeke when you came in. Maybe you'd like to come and explain what happened while I finish up."

Now that she mentioned it, I noticed that the puppy's ears were unwrapped. His topknot, only partially banded, listed to one side.

At one time Aunt Peg had done her grooming in a well-appointed room in the kennel building out back. The number of Poodles she kept, however, had decreased over the last several years; and in recent months, expediency had brought most of the grooming supplies into the house. A guest room on the ground floor had been transformed into a state-of-the-art hair salon, and overnight guests were now advised to find accommodations elsewhere.

"As for you," Peg said to Davey. "I enjoyed a rather delicious crumb cake with my morning coffee. Perhaps you'd like to go out to the kitchen and help yourself to a piece?"

"I could do that," my son allowed.

"Splendid." Aunt Peg cupped her hand around Zeke's muzzle, holding the big puppy in place as Davey headed off to the kitchen followed by the rest of the herd. Show Poodles never wear collars except when they're in the ring and nearly all are taught to lead by hand. Fingers wrapped gently around his muzzle, Peg escorted the puppy in the other direction.

I followed them down the hallway and found a stool to perch on as she hopped Zeke back up onto the rubber-matted grooming table. The tools for the job — a greyhound comb and pin brush, tiny colored rubber bands, knitting needle for making parts, and spray bottle of water for taming frizzies — were already out on the counter. Aunt Peg picked up the comb and deftly hooked one tooth under one of the remaining bands in Zeke's topknot. A sharp flick of her wrist popped the band and sent it flying.

"Now then," she said pleasantly, "what sort of scrape have you gotten yourself into this time?"

Ignoring the implication that whatever

had gone wrong must have been my fault, I said, "My wallet's missing. When I went to pay at the supermarket, I discovered that it wasn't in my purse."

"Any chance you left it at home?"

"Slight. Minimal, really. I always keep it in my pocketbook."

Remaining bands now gone, Aunt Peg picked up the pin brush and began to stroke though the long silky hair on the top of Zeke's head. "All right, let's backtrack then. When was the last time you remember having it?"

"Thursday," I said after a minute's thought. "I got gas and used a credit card."

"Not since Thursday? That's three days! Surely you've had to pay for something since then."

"I don't think so. Friday, I was at school all day —"

"Pocketbook with you?"

I nodded.

Aunt Peg now had a fresh supply of bright blue rubber bands clenched between her lips. It didn't stop her from talking around them. A talented woman, my aunt. "Where does your purse stay while you're working?"

"In my classroom, in a desk drawer. I throw it there every morning and take it out at night."

"So in theory, any number of people had access to it."

"Yes, but —"

"Someone could have taken your wallet from your purse and you never would have noticed."

"Not at the time, no." My classroom wasn't locked. Kids were in and out all day long. I'd never worried about security at Howard Academy. I'd never had to. "Do you actually think someone at school stole my wallet?"

"Not necessarily." Aunt Peg paused. "I'm just trying out the options. How likely is it that you simply misplaced it?"

"Not very. I've certainly never done it before. I'm not a careless person."

"Precisely. So someone has been in your purse. Let's try to figure out when. Friday at school is one possibility."

I frowned at the thought. This was my second year at Howard Academy and I loved it there. The kids I taught were really good kids, the other teachers were cheerful and generous, the administration was mostly supportive of my efforts. It hurt to think that the theft could have taken place there.

I shook my head but before I could speak, Aunt Peg was already arguing the opposing view. I hate it when she does that.

"I know what you're going to say, that Howard Academy isn't that kind of place. Need I remind you that last year your school was the kind of place where a murder could occur?"

"That was different." It was a lame argument, and we both knew it. Aunt Peg didn't bother to dignify my claim with a response.

"Friday night you were where?" she asked.

"Home." Just like Saturday night, now that I thought about it. Thank goodness this inquisition had nothing to do with the deficiencies of my social life.

"Assuming you still had your wallet with you, where was it?"

"In my bag, on the counter in the kitchen. I always put it there when I come in."

"So, locked inside your house, right?"

"Right. . . ." My thoughts flew back to the middle of the week when I'd thought there was someone in the house, when I'd gone downstairs to find the television on and the back door unlocked.

"What?" asked Aunt Peg.

"I told you what happened Wednesday night."

Eyes lowering to the job at hand, Peg used the long knitting needle to make a part in the dense black hair. "You also just said that you paid for gas on Thursday, so your wallet couldn't have disappeared then."

"That's not what I mean." Despite the room's warmth, I shivered slightly. "What if someone did get into in my house Wednesday night? And what if they came back on Friday?"

"You didn't hear anything?"

"No. . . ."

"Were your doors unlocked Saturday morning when you got up?"

"No, but —"

Aunt Peg glanced up, waiting to hear my objection. Unfortunately, I didn't have one, at least not one that she would find credible. Just a vague, nagging sense of unease that things weren't right, that there was more going on than I knew.

"Yesterday morning you went to see George Firth," she continued. "You don't suppose he stole your wallet, do you?" Her tone perked up. "Marian would love to hear that."

"I doubt it. My bag was sitting with me on the couch the whole time I was there."

"Too bad." Aunt Peg went back to brushing. "Then you went to the show. Pay any tolls on the way?"

"I have E-Z Pass."

"Me, too." Peg grinned. She gets a real kick out of modern technology.

"Admission?"

"No. I was waiting in line to pay, but Bertie came and grabbed me to show a Bichon . . ." My voice trailed off.

"And?" Zeke was now sporting a new top-knot; it was time to wrap his ears. The wraps Aunt Peg had chosen were bright blue to match the rubber bands.

"I threw my purse in the first crate I saw, ran to the ring, went in the Open Class, and proceeded to totally piss off the Bichon's owners, costing Bertie a client in the process."

"You don't lead a dull life," Aunt Peg said mildly. "I'll give you that."

Nor a charmed one either, apparently.

But now that I thought about it, the most likely time for my wallet to have disappeared was the day before, when I'd left it unguarded — not counting the protective ability of a rather cute Finnish Spitz — for several hours at the dog show. And if that was when the deed had been done, it wasn't hard to come up with a pair of possible suspects: Mike and Jean Azaria, Bertie's disgruntled clients who had vowed to get even.

"Phooey," I said.

"Care to tell me the story, or are you just

going to sit there looking disgusted with yourself?"

So I told her the story. Aunt Peg has handled her share of fractious puppies in the ring. She's also been around the dog show world long enough to know the ins and outs of handler contracts, broken majors, and days when all the good luck simply falls someone else's way.

"Good riddance," she said when I was done. "Bertie's better off without clients like that."

No matter, I was still feeling guilty about the way things had turned out. "Well, yes, except that they helped to pay her bills."

"That's not as big a concern as it might have been once. Bertie has Frank to help with that now."

Aunt Peg can be rather old-fashioned about such things. On the other hand, I thought, reconsidering, maybe I was the one who hadn't kept up with the times. My little brother had been a liability for so long that it was hard for me to think of him as an adult who was capable of pulling his own weight. I had to admit his continuing success with the Bean Counter was steadily proving me wrong.

"Okay, so the Azarias are another possibility," I said. It seemed extreme to think that the couple might have resorted to theft in retaliation for a missed major, but I'd long since learned not to dismiss any possibility, however outlandish, where exhibitors and their dogs were concerned.

"What came next?" Aunt Peg asked. "Where did you go after the show? And by the way, Sam was wondering about that too."

"Sam was *not* wondering." Annoyed, I slid off my stool and walked over to the window. "He knew where I was going because I told him. I stopped at Bob's to pick up Davey. Not that Sam seemed even remotely interested in my plans."

"Maybe he didn't want you to think that he cared about the fact that you were spending time with your ex-husband."

How had my love life — muddled as it was — become such a source of interest and discussion for my two aunts? And why did I get the impression that Sam had been lobbying to get both those conniving old ladies on his side?

"I wasn't spending time with Bob. I was in and out in ten minutes. The only person who spent time with Bob last night was Davey's riding teacher, Pam. She was there cooking him dinner."

"Isn't that nice?" said Peg. "The cowboy

has found himself a cowgirl, leaving you perfectly free to —"

"To do what?" I snapped, spinning around to face her. Of course, the fact that I stand five six to Aunt Peg's six feet meant I didn't look nearly as intimidating as I might have hoped.

Instead of backing down, Aunt Peg came at me with both barrels. "To pull your head out of your rear end, stop dancing around what you know you both want, and go make things right with Sam. I swear, Melanie, if you don't get this mess sorted out soon I'm going to find a pair of handcuffs and shackle the two of you together until you do. Am I making myself clear?"

Was there ever a moment, however brief, when she didn't?

Advice, Aunt Peg style. You had to love it.

Either that or slit your wrists.

17

My son had not only helped himself to one piece of coffee cake, he'd helped himself to two. Or possibly three. At any rate, all the remaining crumb cake had vanished. The box was sitting empty on the kitchen table.

I figured there was an outside chance that the Poodles might have played a part in its disappearance.

"First things first," said Aunt Peg, unperturbed by the fact that, between them, one child and four Standard Poodles had disposed of more than a pound of coffee cake. "Let me give you some cash to tide you over until you can get things sorted out. How many credit cards were you carrying?"

"Only two or three, thankfully. I'll call and cancel them as soon as I get home. They all have limits on how much I'm at risk for. Plus I had about forty dollars in cash. It's not so much the financial loss as the inconvenience. I'll be standing in lines and making phone calls all week, trying to get everything replaced."

"Are you going to file a police report?"

"Where?" I asked. "Greenwich? Stamford? New Jersey? I wouldn't have the slightest idea what to tell them. Besides, you know as well as I do, this stuff is gone for good."

"I suppose you're right." Aunt Peg left the room briefly. Upon her return, she handed me a more than generous sum of money.

"Aunt Peg, what are you doing keeping this much cash around the house?"

"Preparing for emergencies, what do you think?"

Sad to say, the biggest emergencies in my aunt's life were probably due to the misadventures of her chronically unpredictable relatives.

"Are we going back to the supermarket now?" Davey asked when we were once again in the car.

"No, we'll go later. I have some phone calls I need to make first." I glanced at him across the seat. "You're not still hungry, are you?"

My son's cheeks colored slightly, but he didn't answer. Considering the amount of starch that had crept into his diet lately, I was lucky he burned calories with the dispatch of a Whippet.

Davey was gazing out the window when

we turned onto our road. I figured he was probably looking for Joey Brickman. Maybe I'd try to get the two of them together for a couple of hours that afternoon.

"Hey!" he said, pointing. "Why is that lady waving at you?"

The lady in question was Jill Prescott. She'd jumped out of her car when she saw us coming and was now standing in the street, waving her arms above her head. As if the sight of a woman in the middle of the road wasn't arresting enough.

"Melanie, stop!" she called. "I have to talk to you."

I knew Jill was desperate for a scoop, but this was carrying things way too far. What could possibly be so important that she had to flag us down in the street? I rolled to a stop beside her and opened my window.

"What's up?" Maybe my tone wasn't as friendly as it might have been. So sue me for wanting a private life.

"Look." Jill gestured toward her car.

The blue Mazda was parked in the shade. It took me a minute to figure out what I was seeing in the car's semi-dark interior. When I did, I gasped.

Two black noses were pressed up against the mostly closed windows. Two black, pom-ponned tails were wagging furiously.

Faith and Eve were hopping up and down on the back seat of Jill's car.

My stomach plummeted, even as I went cold all over. Quickly I shifted the Volvo into park. "Davey, stay right here. Don't move."

"Right, Mom." He was staring too.

Luckily our road gets little traffic. I didn't bother pulling over. I simply got out of the Volvo and left it where it was. "What are my dogs doing in your car? What happened? Where did you get them from?"

In two quick strides, I reached the door and yanked it open. The Poodles came tumbling out. Eve's greeting was unrestrained; she twirled in place, delighted to see me.

Faith's reaction was more reserved. Her tail was up, but she pressed her nose into my hand and whined softly. The older Poodle knew what the puppy hadn't grasped yet: that the two of them were never supposed to be loose when I wasn't with them. Somehow Faith had broken a cardinal rule; this was her way of apologizing. Too bad she couldn't offer an explanation.

I gave my Poodle a reassuring pat, then spun around to face Jill. "What the hell is going on?"

"Hey, don't yell at me. I was just trying to help."

"Help what? How did you get my dogs?" I

walked back to the Volvo and put both Poodles inside. "When I left this morning, they were locked in my house."

"Well when I got here, they were running in the road."

My heart sputtered at the thought. "That's not possible."

"Ask your neighbors if you don't believe me," Jill said. "Instead of yelling at me, you ought to be thanking me. If I hadn't caught them, who knows where they might be by now."

The answer to that was chilling, horrifying. Even faced with unexpected freedom, I was almost positive that Faith wouldn't have run away. She knew better. But Eve? With a puppy her age anything was possible. Not only that, but neither one of the Poodles knew the first thing about cars. Their survival skills in traffic were nil.

This was every responsible dog owner's worst nightmare. And somehow — for reasons I couldn't yet begin to fathom — it was happening to me.

"You're right," I said. "I'm sorry. I'm just . . ."

Just what? I wondered. Confused? Shaken? Scared half to death? All of the above?

Behind the Volvo, a car horn tooted gently, asking for my attention. I was blocking the street and someone needed to get by. I waved to the driver and opened my car door.

"Jill, would you come inside with me so we can talk?"

"Sure. Let me just lock my car."

In my quiet neighborhood, the thought had probably never occurred to her before. Now it seemed like a very good idea.

I pulled the Volvo into my driveway and parked. Davey reached for his door handle, but I stopped him. "Hang on a minute, okay? I'm still trying to figure out what's going on. Why don't you keep Faith and Eve company out here while I check out the house. As soon as I'm sure everything's okay, I'll be right back out to get you."

Jill joined me by the front steps. The door was closed and locked, just as I'd left it. The Poodles hadn't gotten out this way.

I hopped down and started around the back.

"You might want to wait," said Jill. "Rich should be here any minute. He can go inside with us."

"Rich?"

"I called him when I got here. As soon as I saw that the dogs were loose and realized you weren't home. That's when I began to think maybe something was wrong."

I frowned. "And you called for a camera so you could document the problem?"

"Sure, why not? I'm a reporter, you know that. That's what I do." Her gaze shifted past me and down the street, settling on an old Volkswagen Beetle that was going at least twenty miles an hour over the speed limit. "Good, here he comes now."

Rich pulled the VW along the curb in front of the house and hopped out, camera in tow. "Hey guys, what's up?"

"We don't know," Jill told him. "We were just about to go inside."

Leaving them to discuss the issue, I headed around back. I wanted action, not talk. The only way my Poodles could have gotten loose was if someone had been inside my house and let them out. I shuddered at the thought.

What would burglars want with my small Cape? It was just a little house, like all the other little houses in the neighborhood. If anything, I'd have thought that the sight of two big dogs inside would have made it the least attractive target on the block.

The gate to the tall cedar fencing around the backyard was open. That was hardly surprising. If it had been shut, the Poodles would still have been inside.

I walked through the gate and rounded

the corner of the house. My back screen door was standing open. The inner door was wood on the bottom, with a multipaned window on top. One of the small, square panes of glass near the dead bolt was missing. There was no doubt now, if indeed there'd ever been any. Someone had broken in.

Drawn forward on reluctant feet, I climbed the steps and had a closer look. The door had been closed, but it wasn't latched. A shove of my hand pushed it open.

I hesitated a moment, then stepped inside the kitchen. Shards of glass from the missing pane crunched beneath my feet. Other than that, the kitchen looked undisturbed.

"Hey, wait!" Rich came scrambling up the outside steps. "Let me go first." The camera was up on his shoulder. Presumably he'd turned it on. "You don't know what's in there."

I reached out and placed my hand over the lens. "Whatever we find, you don't need a picture of it."

"Yes, he does." Jill joined Rich on the step. "What if somebody's been murdered in there? The police will want Rich's tape for evidence." Her eyes were glowing with excitement. No doubt she was already envisioning Rich's footage with her lead-in on the evening news.

As for me, I was beginning to get annoyed. It was one thing to want company walking into a house where I knew an invasion had taken place. It was another for Jill to start suggesting all sorts of horrible possibilities in that hopeful, breathy tone. Thank God Davey wasn't there to hear her.

"Nobody's been murdered," I snapped. "There wasn't anybody home. That's probably why whoever was here thought this looked like a good place to hit. Besides, if there was a dead body in there, the police wouldn't want your tape, they'd want us to wait outside and not contaminate anything."

"You would know," Rich said. He lowered the camera.

As if I were the expert. As if I discovered dead bodies every day of the week. What was wrong with these two? Did they actually believe my life was *that* exciting? I wondered if I should tell them I'd picked up most of my expertise watching *Law & Order*.

"Turn that back on." Jill gave Rich a poke. "We're reporters. We have freedom of the press and First Amendment rights."

"Not in my house, you don't." I pulled the door around and began to close it between us.

241

My initial concern that someone might still be inside was fading. Any burglars foolish enough to hang around until I got home had probably climbed out a window while we'd been arguing. Now I just wanted to look around and assess the damage.

"Jill, cool down." Rich set the camera on a counter. "If she doesn't want me to film in here I'm not going to." His gaze shifted over to me. "But you still shouldn't be alone, just in case . . . you know."

Unfortunately, I did. "Thanks. Let's go have a look."

I strode through the kitchen and into the hallway, checking the living and dining rooms as I passed. I'd always found the quiet solitude of my little house comforting. Now it seemed eerily still.

I saw no one, and yet someone else's presence seemed to permeate the space. My space. Nothing looked different, but I couldn't help wonder what had been touched, handled. The thought of some unknown person walking through my rooms, going through my things, made my skin crawl.

"Someone messed this place up pretty good," Rich said, pausing by the living room.

I went back and had another look. A collection of toys — human and canine — were strewn around the floor. Magazines and books were piled haphazardly on tabletops. Two chairs were overturned in one corner. Davey had made them into a fort the night before.

"Nope." My small smile came as a relief. "That's pretty much normal for us. Try living with two dogs and a seven-year-old —" I broke off suddenly, spun away from the living room and sprinted for the stairs.

"What?" Rich was quick, I had to give him that. Even caught unaware, he didn't lose a step. "What's the matter?"

"I don't have two dogs right now, I have three."

Poor Dox. In all the excitement of finding Faith and Eve outside, I'd forgotten all about him. When Davey and I had left to go shopping that morning, I'd left the Dachshund puppy locked inside his crate in the corner of my bedroom.

It wasn't the first time he'd been left crated in the four days he'd been living with us. It was, however, the first time he hadn't begun to bark impatiently upon my arrival home. Usually he'd be scratching at the wire-mesh door, clamoring to be let out immediately.

I reached the top step, grabbed the newel

post, swung a U-turn, and headed for my bedroom. "Dox?" I called. "Hey buddy, what's up?"

There was no answering whine, no sound of scrambling feet. I reached the door to my bedroom and immediately saw why. The corner was empty. Only a slight indentation in the rug marked the spot where Dox's crate had been.

Now I knew what my intruder had been after.

The Dachshund puppy was gone.

18

"Oh no," I breathed softly.

Momentum carried me into the room. I walked over to the corner where Dox's crate had been and stared at the empty space longingly, as if hopeful desperation could bring the Dachshund puppy back.

"What's wrong?" Jill asked. She and Rich crowded up beside me. "What are you looking at? I don't see anything."

"That's the problem. There should be a crate sitting there with a puppy inside. It's gone."

Rich's eyes widened. "You mean he's been dognapped?"

"It looks that way."

Jill was scribbling on her pad. "Dox, that was his name, wasn't it?"

It annoyed me to see her looking so happy about this unexpected development, and I didn't bother to answer. Instead I turned away and checked out the rest of the room. My jewelry box hadn't been touched. The drawers in dresser and night table didn't appear to have been opened. Not that I had a lot that was worth stealing, but most burglars would have at least had a look.

Jill followed me around, pen poised to make more notes. "How much was the puppy worth? Lots of money, right? Was it a show dog like your other two? And how come the thief took only the one dog and not all three?"

Good question.

"Let's all go back downstairs," I said. "I'll answer your questions, and you can answer some of mine. But first I want to go get Davey and the Poodles."

I'd told my son to wait in the car. He hadn't exactly obeyed me, but at least he'd come close. He was shooting hoops in the driveway. Faith and Eve were his appreciative audience sitting side by side on the front seat of the Volvo. Nose prints were smeared everywhere; I could see I was going to have some serious window cleaning to do.

"That took long enough," Davey said when I reappeared. He tossed the ball to me, and I shot it through the hoop.

Before going out to fetch him, I'd stopped in the kitchen to sweep up the glass and make a call to the Stamford police. They'd promised to send somebody by, but since the break-in had already occurred and the robbers were long gone, I wasn't counting on a particularly timely arrival.

"Sorry about that. You can come inside now."

I opened the car, released the dogs, and brought them into the house, too. Not unexpectedly, both Poodles made a dash for the water bowl.

"I need you to do something for me," I told Davey. "Can you go upstairs to my bedroom, call Aunt Peg, and ask her to come over?"

"We just saw Aunt Peg." No flies on this kid.

"I know, but I need to see her again. Tell her it's important."

"Okay," Davey said cheerfully. There's nothing he likes more than being trusted with a mission.

When Davey had gone upstairs, I beckoned the two reporters toward the living room. Jill was quivering with excitement.

"Isn't this great?" she asked. "All right, so it isn't a murder, but it's not your usual, run-of-the-mill burglary, either. Remember that important stallion that got stolen in Ireland? That was big news for weeks. Maybe we can build up the glamor angle of the dog show world in the report. That ought to be good for some bonus points in the ratings. . . ."

Oh brother. Was it just me, I wondered, or

did everyone who knew her wish that Jill had an off switch?

"What time did you arrive at my house this morning?"

My question interrupted her flow of words. She sputtered to a stop, then considered for a moment. "I don't know. Ten-thirty, maybe eleven? I mean, it's Sunday for Pete's sake. I have a life, too."

Rich raised a brow at that. It wasn't hard to guess what he was wondering. I ignored him and followed up with another question. "And what were you planning to do here?"

"You know, keep an eye on things. Just in case."

"Like you've been doing for the last week?"

Jill's head tilted to one side. I took that as an assent.

"Except that I haven't seen you around since Thursday." Faith came trotting into the living room. I patted the couch beside me. The big Poodle hopped up on the cushion, turned twice, lay down, and rested her head in my lap. "Last time we talked, I told you I'd call you if there was anything you needed to know."

"All well and good," Jill said defensively, "except that you didn't call, did you? You didn't even get back to me after I left you a message last night. So I figured it was time for me to stop by and have a look around."

"The reason I didn't call you," I said, keeping my tone carefully neutral, "was because I didn't have anything to say. Just because you want my life to be some big exciting story doesn't mean it actually is one."

"I don't know." Rich hazarded a grin. "Suddenly things are beginning to look a whole lot more interesting."

Yes, they were. Now that Jill was back in the picture.

"My point exactly." I stared hard at both of them.

Jill's cheeks flushed pink. Her eyes grew angry. "Wait a minute. You can't think that I had something to do with your dog's disappearance."

"I don't know, did you?"

"That's crazy. Why would I want to do something like that?"

The answer to that was pretty obvious. I was interested to see that even Rich didn't look as though he entirely discounted the possibility.

"Supposing I did take your stupid dog," Jill snapped. "Where would I have put him?"

"I don't know," I said again. It was depressing the number of answers I didn't have. "Davey and I were gone for almost two hours. Maybe you watched us leave. That would have given you enough time to take Dox, stash him somewhere else, come back and pretend to rescue the Poodles."

Even to me, the theory sounded like a stretch. Which was a shame, because right about then I was looking for someone convenient to blame for all the recent turmoil in my life, and Jill was awfully handy.

After a moment, I sighed and blew out a breath. "All right, scratch that. You got here between ten-thirty and eleven. Did you see anything unusual?"

"You mean aside from the fact that there were two big, black hairy Poodles running around outside your house?"

I supposed I deserved the snippy tone. "Yes. Aside from that."

She shook her head. "Whoever was in here must have been gone by the time I arrived. All I saw were your two dogs outside by themselves. That seemed pretty strange to me because I didn't think you'd be that careless. So right away I began to wonder if maybe something was wrong."

She would, I thought. It was just the way her mind worked. And probably mine as well, I admitted grudgingly.

"What did you do then?"

"I got out of my car, walked up to your house, and rang the doorbell. When nobody answered, I looked in the window."

There wasn't much I could say to that. I'd have done the same thing myself.

"Then I rounded up the dogs, which took a while. They're not very well trained, you know. A little basic obedience would work wonders for those two."

Faith lifted her head. I think she knew she'd just been insulted. Actually my Poodles were quite well trained. They just didn't take commands from strangers.

"It turns out your puppy likes Egg McMuffins." Jill looked quite pleased with her ingenuity. "I had one with me that was supposed to be my breakfast, but I ended up using it as a bribe. Once I got hold of the puppy, the other dog gave up and came along too. After I had both of them stashed in the car, I called Rich."

"I grabbed my stuff and got over here as soon as I could." He picked up the story. "We were both worried about you. I was thinking we might have to break into the house to make sure you were all right."

Much as I could fault Jill for her macabre brand of enthusiasm, it sounded as though their intentions had been good. Not only that, but Jill had gone out of her way to catch my dogs and put them in a safe place, even donating her breakfast to the cause in the process. If nothing else, I had to be intensely grateful for that.

"Now it's my turn to ask questions," she said eagerly. "Tell me about the missing puppy. Is he some kind of super show dog or something?"

"Sorry to disappoint you," I replied. "But no. Dox might be a show dog someday, but right now he's only a baby. He won't even be eligible for the show ring for another several months."

"Then why take that dog?" Rich asked. "Why not one of the others? Why not all three?"

The first answer that came to mind was that whoever had broken in had been specifically looking for Dox. If that was the case, I was placing my bet on the culprit being one or the other of the battling Firths. I had no intention, however, of telling their story to KZBN Cable News. So I offered a couple other possibilities.

"Maybe whoever was here couldn't catch the Poodles," I said, thinking out loud. "Jill saw for herself that's not easy to do when I'm not around. Or maybe they were intimidated by the bigger dogs. Could be they simply thought the little Dachshund was cute. For Pete's sake, he was sitting right there in a crate, I might as well have packaged him to go."

"Do you think they took anything else?" Jill asked.

"Not that I've noticed so far." My gaze swept around the room. "There's not much in here to steal."

"TV and VCR," Rich pointed out. "Most burglars would rather have that than a puppy."

All too true. But then, why should I expect to be robbed by normal burglars? Was there ever anything in my life that proceeded along even remotely normal lines?

Jill's pad was still open, though she hadn't written anything for a few minutes. "What will you do now?"

"Talk to the police, for one thing. Tell the people whom I was keeping the puppy for that he's gone."

"What are their names?" she asked. "Maybe I should talk to them, too."

"You shouldn't."

"You don't know that. Maybe they want us to run a picture of the missing puppy on the news. Maybe they have videos —"

"Maybe you're dreaming," said Rich, sounding ready to wrap things up.

My sentiments, exactly.

Aunt Peg arrived while I was next door talking to my neighbor, Edna Silano. The tall wooden security fence around my backyard blocked its view from almost every direction, a fact which I was sure had not been lost on my intruder. The gate to the fence, however, was beside my garage on a little grassy strip of land between my house and the one next to it.

Mrs. Silano was an older woman who'd been born in the mountains of Italy and now lived alone in the house she'd come to as a war bride just after World War II. In her years in the United States, she'd raised a family, buried a husband, forged a new life, and never traveled more than fifty miles from the little neighborhood where she'd originally settled with her G.I. sweetheart.

Mrs. Silano was addicted to soap operas, trashy talk shows, national public radio, and looking out her front windows. I was sure there were days when the goings-on at my house added gray strands to her suspiciously dark hair. Which seemed to make her the perfect person to ask if she'd seen anything odd that morning. Unfortunately, Mrs. Silano had nothing to add to the little I already knew.

"I'm so sorry to hear about your troubles," she told me. Her voice was scratchy from years of smoking and still accented with the language of her youth. "But Sunday mornings I'm on my knees in church. I go over to St. Michael's in Greenwich."

She leaned closer as if confiding a great secret. "They're a little more progressive over there than some of the local parishes. At my age, I want to get the best information available, you know? Any new tips they have on getting into heaven, I figure I should take note."

Considering Mrs. Silano had been to confession more times in the previous month than I had in the last five years, I doubted she was going to have any trouble on that score. I thanked her for her time and walked back across the yard to my driveway, where Aunt Peg was just pulling in.

She stepped out of her van and let her gaze sweep up and down imperiously. "I'm glad to see the house isn't on fire."

"Did you expect it to be?"

"Considering what little Davey told me, I thought I should be prepared for the worst."

Aunt Peg had made good time on the trip from Greenwich. Having dropped whatever she was doing to rush to my aid, she'd obviously expected to be confronted by severed limbs, mass mayhem, or aliens on the front lawn. You know, the usual stuff I get involved in.

She was scowling by the time her eyes came to rest on me. "What on earth is so important that you needed to see me immediately, especially since you left my house no more than an hour ago?"

"Someone broke into my house while Davey and I were with you. Dox is missing."

That got her attention. It probably made her feel better, too. "Faith and Eve?"

"They're both fine." We headed inside. "Though they were left outside running loose in the neighborhood."

Aunt Peg stopped abruptly. "You mean Dox is still out there somewhere, and you just haven't found him yet?"

"No, Dox was crated." I kept walking. "He couldn't have gotten away. I'd left both Poodles loose in the house. I assume they slipped out the back door."

Out of habit, we headed for the kitchen. I would have offered to fix us a couple of sandwiches except that the cold cuts I'd intended to buy were still at the supermarket. Which reminded me that I still hadn't called to cancel my credit cards.

"Tuna?" I suggested weakly. I figured there had to be at least a can or two in the cupboard.

"Don't be ridiculous," Aunt Peg snapped. "We don't need food. What we need is to figure out what's going on around here. Pardon me for being blunt, but is *everything* in your life going haywire?"

"Since you asked," I said, equally blunt. "Pretty much so, yes."

"Tell me what's happened since I saw you last."

Ten minutes of talking brought her up to speed. During that time, Eve and Faith wandered by to say hello. Davey dribbled through the kitchen with his basketball and got sent outside. And Aunt Peg helped herself to a kitchen chair and began to eat the tuna sandwiches I'd made because I didn't have anything else to do with my hands.

"George Firth," she said when I was finished. "It had to be."

"Or Marian."

Aunt Peg shook her head. "Marian's a dog person. She never would have left your Poodles at risk like that. While from what I've heard of George, he wouldn't have given it a moment's thought."

"Maybe the Poodles were turned loose as a diversion. Something to keep me busy so I wouldn't have time to go looking for Dox right away. By the way, George left a message on my answering machine last night demanding that I give Dox back."

"There you go, then," Aunt Peg said, as if that settled things to her satisfaction. "He must have decided to take matters into his own hands."

I wasn't so sure. "Why would he? I'd told him that I thought the donation was a bad idea. As far as he knew, I might have been happy to return Dox to him. Whereas your friend Marian struck me as someone who's not terribly patient, maybe just the kind of person who might be capable of doing something desperate."

Aunt Peg sat and thought for a minute. Her fingers drummed idly on the table. "Marian didn't have to do anything desperate," she said finally. "She had a plan."

Ah yes, the plan. Aunt Peg had mentioned it the other day.

"I'm not saying it was a good plan."

My eyes narrowed. "Did it involve any felonious activities?"

"Not that I'm aware of," Peg said blithely.

As if that were reassuring.

I dumped our empty plates in the sink and rejoined her at the table. There didn't seem to be anything else to do.

"You might as well tell me about it," I said.

19

"You needn't look so huffy," Aunt Peg said sharply. "It's not as if I was expecting something like this to happen. Marian's plan was quite innocent and really rather clever."

"Did it have anything to do with her wanting to reconcile with George?"

"Not at all." Aunt Peg looked surprised. "What would make you think that?"

"When I saw George yesterday, he seemed to be under the impression that she wanted him back."

"Oh, pish," said Peg. "That's nothing but George's ego speaking. Marian is better off without him and she knows it. Since their separation, he has apparently filled his need for female companionship by dating several acquaintances of Marian's, women he already knew, through her, during the course of his marriage. The divorce rate being as high as it is, and single women always seeming to outnumber single men . . ."

I pictured the luxurious condominium and hazarded a guess. "Good old George is probably doing pretty well for himself."

"Just so. As you might imagine, Marian has not been exactly thrilled by this turn of events. Recently, however, she came up with a way to make the situation work to her advantage. George's current lady friend is a woman named Lynda French, another friend of Marian's who is also recently divorced. She and Marian are in firm agreement that neither one's relationship with George will be allowed to break up their friendship."

"Good for them." I thought I had a pretty good idea where she was going. "Is Lynda a dog lover, by any chance?"

Aunt Peg nodded as though that was a given. Perhaps in her world it was.

"Marian's plan is really very simple and it hinges on George getting Dox back. Once that happens, Lynda is going to arrange to see the puppy and fall head over heels in love. George, Marian thinks, will be persuaded to give Dox to Lynda as a present. She, of course, will then be happy to pass the puppy back to Marian."

I lifted a brow. "And they think George will fall for that?"

"George doesn't have to fall for anything. He only has to close his eyes and cooperate. Men have been willing to 'fall for' things for centuries where a pretty woman is concerned."

Sad, but true. Not only that, but we all knew that George didn't want Dox. He'd tried to get rid of the puppy once; there was probably no reason to think he wouldn't jump at the chance to do so again.

"However," Aunt Peg continued, "just because George and Marian have been arguing over Dox doesn't mean we should narrow our options. Perhaps neither one of them took him. You told me just this morning there was a possibility your wallet had been lifted by some disgruntled clients of Bertie's. Maybe they were your mysterious visitors."

"To what end?" I asked. "Dox wouldn't mean anything to them."

"How do you know?" Aunt Peg snorted. "Cute as he is, we have yet to come across anyone who thinks of that poor little puppy as anything other than a means to an end. In the Azarias' case, I suppose we're still talking about revenge. They are dog people, after all. Who better to think of taking a dog? On one level, it makes perfect sense."

Right. The dog level. Aunt Peg's preferred context for almost any situation.

I, however, had other ideas, including the one I'd tried out earlier. Perhaps I'd find a more receptive audience in Aunt Peg. "What about that reporter, Jill Prescott?"

"What about her?"

"She's been following me around for days, hoping something horrible would happen that she could turn into a story for the evening news. Well now something has. Maybe it's not as exciting as she was hoping for, but it's better than nothing. She and Rich were here earlier asking questions and trying to shoot some footage. I have to say I found it awfully convenient that she just happened to be on the spot when the break-in occurred, yet somehow managed not to see a thing."

"I suppose we shouldn't rule her out," Aunt Peg agreed. "It's a pity that woman thinks you're going to be the one to earn her her fifteen minutes of fame."

"Jill isn't looking for fifteen minutes. She wants a whole career. And she's in a great tearing hurry to get started. It wouldn't bother her one bit to get her big break at my expense."

"What do you suppose Jill Prescott would do with a Dachshund puppy?" Peg mused.

"I haven't a clue. She doesn't strike me as someone who's terribly savvy about dogs. Hopefully, if Jill does have Dox, she'll keep him somewhere safe until we get this whole mess sorted out. Ditto for Jean and Mike. Also Marian and/or George. Beyond that, I'm pretty well stumped. So if you have any bright ideas about what to do next, feel free to speak up."

The last time Aunt Peg and I had needed to find a missing dog, she'd been brimming with good suggestions. My aunt thrived on problems like this. Surely she wouldn't disappoint me.

I held on to that thought — rather desperately — as the silence between us lengthened.

"If Dox were simply lost," she said finally, "I'd tell you to make flyers, offer a reward, call the local vets and obedience classes, and visit all the pounds in the area. But presumably whoever has the puppy took him on purpose and will take pains to keep him out of sight."

"Rather like Beau," I mentioned, just in case her memory needed jogging.

Beau was one of Aunt Peg's champion Poodles. At one time, he'd been her premier stud dog, the kingpin of the Cedar Crest line. Three years earlier, he'd been taken from her kennel in the middle of the night. The search we'd launched to find him had brought Aunt Peg and me together and ended up changing both our lives.

"Quite so," Aunt Peg said dryly. "However, as you may recall, it did take me more than ten minutes' notice to devise a proper plan. Let me think about it. I'm sure between the two of us we'll come up with something. Now in the meantime, about Sam . . ."

The alacrity with which she changed subjects was enough to give a listener whiplash. What meantime? What *about* Sam? Wasn't Dox the one we were supposed to be helping? And how was it that we were seemingly incapable of holding a conversation that didn't include my one-time fiancé?

"What does he think of this rather incredible run of bad luck you seem to be having?"

"He doesn't," I said firmly. "We haven't spoken about it."

"Whyever not?"

"In case you haven't noticed, there are a lot of things Sam and I don't talk about." Like why he'd felt it was all right to pick up and leave for five months in the midst of the wedding plans that I, his intended bride, had been making.

"In case I haven't noticed?" Aunt Peg repeated incredulously. "Everyone around you would have to be blind, deaf, and dumb not to notice that. You may not like what Sam did, but eventually you're going to have to unbend enough to forgive him. You know how much he cares about you —"

Somewhere in the front of the house the Poodles began to bark. The interruption was a godsend. When the front door banged open and shut and Davey came racing into the kitchen, I was already on my feet. His face was pink with excitement.

"Hey, Mom, there's a policeman outside! He came in a real patrol car and everything. He let me sit in the front seat and he even showed me the button that makes the siren work." My son smiled blissfully. "Oh yeah, he wants to talk to you."

"Did you ask him to come inside?"

"Why would he want to come in here when he can sit outside in his car?"

Sometimes you just have to love the way a seven-year-old boy's mind works. I hurried outside to remedy my son's rudeness. Aunt Peg left while I was talking to Officer Collins, saving me from the rest of her lecture. Unfortunately, that was the only good that came of the officer's visit. He took some notes, exhibited sympathy for my loss, and offered the name of a glass man who might be willing to come on Sunday, albeit at over-time rates.

As Peg and I had discovered in the past, missing dogs, even ones that have been stolen, don't rank very high on the police priority list. Indeed, Officer Collins seemed to think I should be grateful that nothing else had been taken. Since evidence of the break-in — the shattered window in back door — hadn't impressed him much, I declined to mention my earlier problems, with the exception of the missing wallet, which he dutifully noted.

"I'll write out a report," he said. "You can come down and pick up a copy at the station. You'll need it if you want to file an insurance claim."

I thanked him for his time and watched him drive away. Then I went inside and called the glass man. At least he might be able to make himself useful.

As it turned out, Joey Brickman was home, and Davey spent Sunday afternoon playing at his friend's house. I used the time to try to get my life back in order: repairing the broken window on the back door, closing my credit card accounts, and going back to the supermarket to shop for the week's food.

I also left a message on the answering machine of a local locksmith, saying I was in need of a consultation. The notion that a stranger could come into my house at will was more than a little unnerving. If my current locks weren't up to the job of keeping people out, then I'd better find a new system that was.

Before leaving, Aunt Peg had promised to contact Rose and tell her what had happened — sparing me, at least until the following evening, the necessity of making what was sure to be a painful explanation. Rose had entrusted me with Dox. All I'd had to do was keep an eye on the puppy for a month. Hardly an arduous task. So what did it say for the state of my life that I hadn't even been able to manage that?

The two people I didn't call were George and Marian Firth, and you may feel free to file that omission under the heading of "Taking the Coward's Way Out." If either one of them had Dox, then the puppy was probably in good hands. If neither did — and consider that I had no other particularly hot leads on where else to look for him — well, think about it, what did we really have to discuss?

Davey came home just in time for dinner. I'd made his favorite meal, hamburgers and macaroni and cheese, and we ate together in the kitchen as the sun set outside. Before it was fully dark, I'd already leapt up twice to check the locks and turn on more lights. By Davey's bedtime, I had every room in the house brightly lit. All the outdoor flood-lights were on as well.

From the road, I was sure the house looked much the same as it had a week earlier when we'd returned from the dog show in Rhode Island. I wondered if that fact was significant or simply ironic. There was always the slight possibility that I was being stalked by someone who worked for the power company.

After Davey was in bed, I sat in the living room and tried to read. Usually that's a favorite pastime; that night, nothing could hold my attention for long. Every noise, from a car driving by on the road outside to the wind rattling against a shutter, had me leaping to my feet and looking out the window.

I am not by nature a jumpy person. That night I couldn't seem to sit still. Even the Poodles felt my uneasiness. Faith, who most evenings would have been asleep on Davey's bed, kept prowling around the house. The faint click of her toenails on the hardwood floors was a reassuring sound when the quiet began to feel oppressive.

Though I'd been involved in solving several mysteries, this was the first time trouble had followed me home. In the past, finding a murderer had been an intellectual exercise.

I'd followed the leads, put the clues together, and eventually come up with an answer.

The problems I'd investigated had belonged to other people. And much as I might have cared about the outcome, I had not, for the most part, felt personally threatened. I had not become a target. Now, for reasons I couldn't begin to fathom, that had changed. Someone was coming after me, and I had no idea why.

The sudden ring of the telephone sounded like a clarion call in the silent house. I shot up off the couch. The phone was only one room away, sitting on the kitchen counter. Even so, my breathing was short and jerky when I picked it up and heard Sam's voice.

"Melanie? I was just talking to Peg. Are you all right?"

"Fine," I said brightly. Models use that same tone to sell laundry detergent.

"I see." No doubt he did. His next words confirmed it. "Do you want me to come over?"

Now there was a loaded question. Of course the answer was yes . . . and no. Would I have felt more comfortable if Davey and I weren't alone in the house? Yes, definitely. Did I want Sam feeling that he had to rush to my side out of some misplaced sense of duty? Unequivocally no.

"Davey and I are fine. Really. You don't have to worry about us."

"I *do* worry about you." Sam sounded frustrated. "Peg said someone broke into your house this morning."

"I've already had the back door repaired. And I'll get a locksmith out in the morning. There's nothing more you could do. . . ."

Except perhaps keep the nightmares at bay, I added silently.

Sam didn't say anything. For a long moment — wavering — neither did I. Then he spoke again, and my chance slipped away.

"If you don't want me to come, I won't. But you know you can call me any time. I'll be here. I'll answer. Even if you just feel like talking in the middle of the night. Call me, okay?"

"Okay," I whispered. It was all the sound I could seem to manage. "I will."

Unexpectedly, tears stung the corners of my eyes as I replaced the phone. I wondered if I'd made the wrong decision, given the wrong answer. Why did things always have to be so complicated? Would a little simplicity in my love life be too much to ask?

I put the dogs out, brought them back in and turned off most of the downstairs lights.

Then I took my book upstairs to read in bed. Davey was, of course, sleeping like an angel. Faith hopped up and found her usual place beside him on his bed. Without waking, Davey reached out an arm and curled it around trustingly the big Poodle's neck.

For this one moment at least, all was right with the world. If only I didn't have such a hard time keeping things that way.

20

I woke up Monday morning in a bed that was unexpectedly full. At some point during the night two big Poodles, plus my seven-year-old son, had joined me under the covers. So much for thinking that I had things under control.

"Hey!" Davey's eyes opened as I gazed at him.

"Hey, yourself. What are you doing here?"

"Sleeping." He rolled over and yawned. "Until you woke me up."

"Yes, but how did you get here?" I couldn't remember Davey spending a night in my bed since the time when he was four years old and Joey Brickman had told him a ghost story.

"You don't know?" My son began to giggle.

"Should I?"

"You came in my room and got me. It was the middle of the night."

Oh Good Lord, I thought suddenly. He was right. I'm not at my best first thing in the morning, pre-coffee; and it took a moment for the memory to surface. When it did, it had the hazy, indistinct quality of a dream.

The phone had rung, I remembered that. The clock by the bed read two a.m. when the sound had pulled me from a restless slumber. I'd reached across the bed to the nightstand, lifted the receiver to my ear, and heard . . . nothing.

Groggy, barely half awake, I'd grumbled about a wrong number and gone back to sleep. Until ten minutes later, when the phone rang again. That time, I'd waited a beat before picking it up. I'd briefly heard breathing before the caller hung up again.

I'd slammed the phone back down and dialed *69 with shaking fingers. The readout appeared all too quickly. "Access Blocked." As if I couldn't have predicted that. So I'd opted for some low-tech access blocking of my own. I took the phone off the hook and left it off.

Then I'd gotten up and walked restlessly around the house. One by one, I'd checked all the doors and windows, performing the task with the compulsive fervor of someone who wasn't sure where to feel safe anymore. When that was done, I'd gone to get my son.

"You said you wanted company," Davey reminded me now as I reached over and hung the phone back up. "You said it would be like camping out with all four of us in the same bed."

That I had. Luckily Davey hadn't asked any questions, and I hadn't needed to admit that I didn't want company so much as I wanted the complete and utter reassurance that my son was safe. In the dark hours of the early morning, keeping him tucked close in beside me had seemed the best way to insure that.

"Uh-oh," said Davey.

"What?"

"I think Eve needs to pee."

My head whipped around. Of course, Davey was right. The Poodle puppy had hopped down off the bed and was dancing in the doorway, trying desperately to get my attention. I need to go outside, she was telling me. *Right now.*

Speaking Poodle is really only one step away from speaking English. The syntax is pretty clear.

I tossed back the covers and went to do as the puppy had requested. Bladder control is tough for young puppies, but once they reach the age of six months or so, they should be able to make it through the night.

Usually Eve didn't have any problem waiting until I got up.

As I passed the clock in the kitchen, however, I saw why she'd been so anxious. To my amazement, it was nearly nine o'clock. Thank goodness Davey and I were on spring break, or we'd have both been missing our first classes.

Upstairs, I heard the shower begin to run. While that didn't guarantee that Davey was actually standing beneath the spray of water, I decided to hope for the best. The Poodles were busy romping in the backyard. I turned on the coffeemaker, then picked up the phone and dialed Bob.

"I need help," I said when my ex-husband answered. Even to my own ears, my voice sounded tired, defeated. Any why not? I'd hardly gotten any sleep and my life was disintegrating around me. The decision to make this call didn't thrill me, but neither did I seem to have any choice.

"Anything. What's up?"

"I've been having some problems over here and I was wondering if you might be able to take Davey for a couple of days. He's on spring break right now so you won't have to manage getting him to school. Although, of course, that means you'll have him with you all day. But you know what he's like, he's pretty easy, and he gets along with everybody —"

Bob chuckled into the phone. "You don't have to sell me on my own son, Mel. Sure, he can come and stay with me. I'd be happy to have him. But first, tell me what's going on. What kind of problems are you having?"

"Ummm . . ." I wasn't sure how much I wanted to tell him; the last thing I needed was for Bob to start feeling protective. On the other hand, Davey was bound to blurt out the whole story as soon as he saw his father.

I decided to start in the middle, rather than the beginning. "My wallet was stolen over the weekend, and somebody broke into my house yesterday while Davey and I were out —"

"Holy smokes, are you all right?"

"We're fine. Both of us. We weren't even here. The only thing that was taken was a Dachshund puppy I was keeping for my Aunt Rose. Still, I think I'd feel a lot safer if Davey was somewhere else for a little while."

"What about you?" asked Bob.

"What about me?"

"Who's going to be keeping you safe? You're welcome to come and stay too, if you want."

I appreciated the offer, especially since Bob hadn't even hesitated to make it and I knew how much my presence would cramp his budding relationship with Pam. Where ex-wives are concerned, I believes that's called going above and beyond the call of duty.

"Thanks," I said. "But running away isn't going to help. If I don't figure out what's going on, the same problems will still be here when I get back."

Instead Bob and I agreed that I would drop Davey off at the Bean Counter around noon. He and Frank were thinking of extending the coffeehouse menu to include a few specialty sandwiches. With Mondays being the closest thing dog handlers get to a day off, Bertie would be stopping there for lunch.

Not unexpectedly, Bob figured I'd make a good guinea pig, too. My family; what would I do without them?

The Bean Counter is located in a vintage building that had once served as a general store for a North Stamford neighborhood near Old Long Ridge Road. In the eighteen months it had been open, the coffee bar had become a popular gathering place, frequented by businessmen, soccer moms, and local teens.

Though it was barely lunchtime when Davey and I arrived, the small parking lot was nearly full. From the looks of things, Bob's idea to expand the menu was a good one. Inside, there was a line at the counter. Luckily, Bertie had already staked out a small table near the front window and gotten coffees for both of us. As I went to join her, Davey scooted beneath the partition and ran into the kitchen to look for his dad.

"I went ahead and ordered," Bertie told me. "I'm having a Reuben. You're trying something called a Mongolian chicken sandwich."

I slid into my seat. "Did I want that?"

Her green eyes glinted wickedly. "Frank assured me it was terrific."

"Then why aren't you having it?"

"I wasn't sure what Mongols ate, and I wanted to play it safe."

"Thanks a lot."

"Don't mention it. Hey, did I understand Bob correctly? Are you really sending Davey to his house for spring vacation?"

"Sort of." I reached for my coffee. Cream, no sugar; just the way I liked it. "At least that's the end result. Though Bob probably won't find it to be much of a vacation."

I told Bertie about my missing wallet, the

Dachshund puppy I'd managed to lose, the hang-up phone calls in the middle of the night, and the television and lights that I'd never turned on. By the time I was finished, our sandwiches had arrived. It turned out that Mongols ate coconut, raisins, peanuts, and pineapples with their chicken. At least in Frank's and Bob's world, they did.

I looked at Bertie's Reuben longingly. She caught my glance and curled her arm protectively around her plate. Like maybe she thought I was going to reach over and try to steal something from it.

Good call.

"You left your purse in one of my crates Saturday afternoon, didn't you?" Bertie asked, thinking back.

I nodded as I turned my plate from side to side, studying my sandwich from several angles, none of which improved the view. No doubt about it, if I picked that sucker up, everything was going to fall out.

"Jean and Mike were awfully pissed at the show," Bertie mused. "Although it seems pretty far-fetched to think that they'd stoop to stealing your wallet."

"I thought so, too. Unfortunately, I haven't come up with any better ideas." My teeth crunched down hard on a peanut. I sighed and reached for a sip of coffee.

"Though that doesn't explain what happened to Dox. I'm hoping one of the Firths has him. Or possibly Jill Prescott."

Since Bertie didn't know about my connection to the Firths, or who Jill Prescott was, I continued with the explanations. Every so often, she'd let down her guard and I'd sneak a hand across the table. The third time I almost succeeded in making off with the other half of her Reuben.

Bertie slapped my hand sharply. "Cut it out. In my condition, I need all the nutritious food I can get."

"Your condition?" I scoffed. Like a Reuben was going to help maintain that perfect-ten figure.

Bertie smirked.

After a moment, I stopped chewing. "What condition are we talking about?"

The smirk widened into a grin. Bertie just looked at me, waiting for me to figure it out. Then all at once I did. "Oh my God, don't tell me you're pregnant!"

"Why not? You've done it. So have millions of other women. Now it's my turn."

"But, but —"

"But what?"

I blurted out the first thing that came to mind. "You just got married. It seems so fast."

"Hey." She shrugged. "What can I tell you? Sex happens."

Considering the way she and my brother looked at one another, that was no surprise. I'd always figured they'd have kids eventually, I just hadn't expected things to happen so quickly. At times Frank still seemed like a baby to me; it was hard to imagine him with a baby of his own.

"Congratulations," I sputtered. "When?"

"Not for months yet." Bertie munched happily on her sandwich. "I just found out myself a couple of days ago. By the way, it's not public knowledge yet. You're the first person we've told."

I attacked my lunch with renewed enthusiasm. "I think I'm going to like being an aunt. I'm sure it's a lot less complicated than being a mother." Another thought hit me. "And Davey's going to have a cousin to play with. He'll be thrilled."

Frank came over to stand behind Bertie's chair. He placed a hand on her shoulder and beamed at his bride. "She told you, didn't she?"

I nodded. "It's great, Frank. Really great." I'd never seen my brother look so happy, so exuberantly, over-the-moon, blissfully joyous. His smile could have lit the whole room.

Then he glanced down at the table and his smile faded. "Is that a Reuben? Are you sure . . . ?"

Bertie didn't let him finish. "This baby likes corned beef. Besides, I felt like having sauerkraut. I've read the manuals. For the next eight months, I get to eat all sorts of things. I'm entitled."

"Of course, you're entitled . . ." Frank struggled manfully not to say the wrong thing.

"When I was pregnant, all I wanted was tomatoes," I told him. "Dozens and dozens of tomatoes."

"At least tomatoes are a vegetable," Frank began. One look at his wife's face and he knew better than to continue.

Bertie winked at me across the table. "Frank's already gone down to the library and checked out a whole stack of books on parenting. Imagine how prepared he'll be by December."

Either that or we'd all be ready to strangle him. My little brother was going to be a daddy; it was still a little much to take in. I hoped Bob wouldn't feel compelled to offer too much advice. On the other hand, if he did, I was sure Bertie wouldn't feel any compunction about setting him straight.

"Oh look." Frank glanced toward the door. "There's . . ."

My brother's voice faded. He looked suddenly flustered. I turned in my chair and looked to see who had caused such a reaction. Pam Donnelly was entering the coffeehouse.

"Bob's new girlfriend?" I supplied.

Frank looked relieved. "You've met Pam?"

"Sure. A couple of times. I've even been over to her farm with Davey."

"Good." My brother smiled uncertainly. "I mean, that *is* good, isn't it? I just didn't know . . ."

"If Bob and I were adult enough to be able to handle meeting each other's new lovers?"

"Something like that."

"Of course they are," said Bertie. "After all, Bob's known Sam for a while now. They're even getting to like each other."

Frank shot me a meaningful look. "*Everybody* likes Sam."

"Don't start," I warned.

"Hey, Frank!" Pam caught sight of my brother and waved at him exuberantly from across the room. "I just stopped by to pick up a cup of coffee. Is Bobby here?"

Even in the busy, lunchtime crowd, the pitch of Pam's voice carried easily above the babble of conversation. I couldn't help but notice that several people turned to stare.

"He's working in back." Frank began to move toward her through the crush of tables. There was a small office off the kitchen where Bob did most of the paperwork that pertained to running the coffeehouse. "I'll tell him you're here."

Pam's gaze left Frank and slid briefly in Bertie's and my direction. Her eyes narrowed at the sight of Bertie — no doubt the beautiful redhead was accustomed to receiving such looks from other women — then skimmed past me without acknowledgment.

I probably shouldn't have felt miffed, but I did. Hadn't I just told my brother that Bob and I were mature enough to deal with each other's new relationships in a suitably adult fashion? I hoped I hadn't spoken too soon.

Before Frank could reach the other side of the room, Bob came out of the kitchen. Maybe someone behind the counter had told him Pam was there. Or maybe her voice had carried even better than I'd imagined.

At the sight of him, Pam's face lit up like a child's on Christmas morning. "Bobby!" she shrieked. Pushing her way past the line of patrons who were waiting to place an order, she reached Bob just as he circled out from behind a high glass counter that held an assortment of pastries.

Bob held out both hands. To a casual observer — yes, me, thank you very much — it looked as though he intended to give her a hug.

Pam wasn't having any of it. Instead she stepped into his arms, rose up on her toes and kissed him quite thoroughly on the mouth. My eyebrows rose so far I could feel my forehead wrinkling all the way up to my hairline.

I wasn't the only one who was interested. From somewhere in the room, a wolf whistle sounded. It was followed by a small burst of self-conscious laughter.

"That's a bit much," said Bertie. I was glad she'd offered the opinion, thereby saving me from doing so and looking like a shrew. "I haven't met Pam before. Is she always so demonstrative?"

"I don't know. I've only seen her a few times myself."

By now the kissing couple had broken apart. Bob looked more than a little embarrassed by the scene they'd caused. Not Pam; she looked thoroughly satisfied.

I watched as Bob leaned down and said something to her. Pam shook her head. Bob tried again. This time, she glanced in our direction.

"Uh-oh," said Bertie. "Brace yourself."

"He wouldn't," I said.

Why did I even bother? It was obvious he already had. Bob's source of consternation was about to become ours.

It figured.

21

"Hi," Pam said brightly. She'd wound her way to us across the crowded room. Her hips, clad in tight, faded blue jeans, swayed seductively from side to side as she skirted through the maze of tables. "You must be Frank's wife."

"I must be," Bertie agreed. "Bertie Kennedy."

Having already established a professional presence in the dog world, Bertie had kept her maiden name when she and Frank married. Oddly enough, the only relative who'd quibbled about that was my Aunt Rose, who for the majority of her life had been known as Sister Anne Marie. Go figure.

"Pam Donnelly. Nice to meet you." The horsewoman tossed an off-hand smile my way. "Do you mind if I join you two? Bobby's going to fix me a cappuccino to go. I can only stay for a minute."

"Sure," I said. A minute sounded good to me. "Pull up a seat."

Pam snagged an empty, ladder-backed

chair from another table. Setting it face-out, she threw a leg over the seat like she was mounting one of her ponies and straddled the chair backwards. Her arms folded across the back's top rung.

"Bobby's been telling me all about his family," she said to Bertie. "You and Frank just got married, right?"

Bob's family — his parents and an older sister — lived in Florida. If he'd been telling Pam about relatives in the area, he had been talking about *my* family. Maybe it was churlish of me, but I wasn't sure I wanted my life to be fodder for conversation between my ex-husband and his new girlfriend.

"At Christmas," Bertie replied.

"You are so lucky." Pam sighed. "I'll bet it was beautiful. I can't wait to get married. That's every girl's dream, isn't it, to be a bride? I already have my wedding dress picked out."

It seemed to me that she'd do better to find a groom first, but what do I know? I never was one of those little girls who'd dreamt of the perfect wedding day.

Bertie sat back in her chair and grinned. "Does Bob know that?"

"No," said Pam. "And believe me, I have no intention of telling him. Guys these days, it's amazing how little it takes to scare them off. I've found you've gotta be really careful about stuff like that. Besides, Bobby and I have only known each other a couple of weeks. There's no need for either one of us to rush into anything."

"Good point." As Davey's mother, I felt obliged to speak up. "Especially since Bob's been married twice already, I'm sure he'd like to get things right the third time. If there is a third time."

Pam cocked her head in my direction. "I don't mean to be rude . . ." she said.

In my experience, a statement like that is inevitably followed by rudeness. Pam didn't disappoint.

"I don't happen to think that whether or not Bobby marries again is any of your business. You had your chance with him and you blew it."

The expression on Bertie's face was priceless. I wondered if I looked equally flummoxed. Yes, I'd had my chance with Bob, two in fact, which was one more than I'd needed. But no matter what Bob might have told Pam, *I* hadn't blown anything.

"Besides," she continued blithely. "So what if Bobby's made a few mistakes in the past? We all have, haven't we? I'm certainly not the kind of woman who would hold it against him."

By now, Bertie had begun to bounce up and down in her seat. Either she was suffering from a monster bout of hiccups, or she was trying very hard not to laugh. As for me, having found myself reduced to the dubious status of a mistake from the past, I was simply speechless. Compared to this conversation, that Mongolian sandwich was beginning to look like a winner.

Pam stood up as Bob headed our way. He was holding an oversized cup; steam escaped through a vent in the plastic top. "That looks like my cue," she said. "Nice to meet you, Bertie. Good to see you again, Melanie. Davey's off of school this week, right? Will you be bringing him out to ride Willow?"

"I'm not sure yet. Davey's going to be spending the next few days with Bob, so we'll have to see how things work out."

A look of surprise flickered across Pam's face. "Davey's going to be staying with Bob? I didn't know that. What fun!"

"What fun indeed," Bertie muttered as Bob walked Pam to the door. "Shadowed all week by a seven-year-old chaperone. I think you just seriously deflated that woman's balloon."

I pushed aside my plate and joined Bertie in watching Pam leave. "I'm sure you'll understand when I say that I don't think I'll lose any sleep over it."

"I can't imagine why not. I thought it was rather big of her, the way she was willing to overlook your ex-husband's mistakes."

"Actually, I don't think she was willing to overlook them so much as she was willing to blame them on me."

"That, too," Bertie said agreeably. "You don't suppose she and Bob are serious about each other, do you?"

I thought about that for a minute and finally shrugged. "Like Pam said, it's only been a couple of weeks. They're both still in love with the being-in-love stage. Once that wears off, I guess we'll have to see."

Bertie had dogs to look after at home and I had dogs to attend to at Phil Dutton's house in Old Greenwich. Mutt and Maisie would be waiting for their regular Monday visit. Since I was going to Rose and Peter's later, I'd decided to do my hour of pet-sitting on the way home from the Bean Counter. Bertie and I parted at the door.

Davey came out and helped me unload his small suitcase from the back of the Volvo. He'd spent the night at his father's house before, but this was the first time we'd be separated for a couple of days. I set the suitcase on the ground and gathered him into my arms for a big hug.

"You have fun with your Dad, okay?"

"Sure, Mom."

My son thinks he's too old for public displays of affection, but he managed to suffer through. I tried not to sniffle and really embarrass him.

"Do everything he tells you to, right?"

"Right."

That promise came easily. Even I knew it wasn't a hardship. It wasn't as though Bob was going to make Davey eat his vegetables or go to bed on time.

"Call me anytime you want, okay? Or stop by. Or I'll come and see you. . . ."

Davey had stepped back out of my arms, but I hadn't released his hand. "You have to let go, Mom," he pointed out with implacable seven-year-old logic.

"I know." I sighed. "You be good, okay?"

"You told me that already."

I picked up his bag and walked him into the coffeehouse. Bob was waiting just inside the door.

"Everything will be fine," he said. "And don't forget, if you need anything — anything at all — I'm just around the corner."

"Thanks."

"Don't mention it." Bob turned to his

son. "Hey, Davey, want to go back in the kitchen and taste-test the whipped cream?"

Kids. What are you going to do?

A light blue Mazda followed me from the Bean Counter to Old Greenwich. Like that was a surprise. I wondered if Jill had Rich with her today. I speculated as to whether or not they'd gotten any heartwarming footage of me saying good-bye to my son. And my temper rose to a slow boil.

I parked by the curb outside Phil Dutton's house and waited for Jill to pull in behind me. She was alone in the car. The day was warm enough that her window was already down. She offered a tentative smile as I approached.

"I'll be here an hour," I said. "You can time it if you like. Or drive into town and get an ice cream cone. I'm sure you'd enjoy that more than sitting out here on the street."

"I don't mind waiting. Actually, I'm getting rather used to it." Jill's face assumed a look of concern that might have looked genuine to someone who wasn't familiar with the rest of her repertoire. "Did you find your poor little Dachshund yet?"

"No." I bent down, leaned my arms on the car door, and looked in through the open window. "If you were going to hide a Dachshund puppy, where would you put him?"

"I don't have your dog," Jill grumbled. At least her annoyance seemed real. "How many times do I have to tell you that?"

"I'm just asking a simple question."

Like *you've* been doing for the last week, I might have added. Why should Jill Prescott be the only one who got to grill innocent people who only wanted to be left alone?

"I guess I'd give him to Rich," she said after a minute. "He likes dogs."

Frowning, I straightened and stepped away. Yet another pass-along. Poor Dox. In his brief life he'd already had four temporary "homes," not including wherever he was right now, and wherever he might eventually end up. It was a deplorable record for a cute, healthy, AKC-registered puppy. So far, every person he'd come in contact with — with the possible exception of his breeder, Marian Firth — had failed him in some way.

"Do you have any leads?"

Jill's question broke into my thoughts. It was probably just as well. "No," I admitted.

"Too bad." She shaded her eyes and squinted up at Phil Dutton's house. "I was hoping you were here to chase down some bad guys."

Yeah, sure. I did that every day.

"No bad guys here," I said. "Just a couple of lonely old dogs that I pet-sit for a couple of days a week while their owner's at work."

"That doesn't sound too exciting. Still, the way I figure it, something ought to break soon. Now that your house has been robbed, some sort of violence might be the next step, don't you think?"

To my dismay, I felt a whispery shiver of dread slide up and down my spine. "Who says there's going to be a next step?"

Jill just smiled sweetly. "Who says there isn't?"

As always, Mutt and Maisie were delighted to see me. I didn't take it personally. I mean, really, what else did these two old dogs have going on in their lives?

"Walks first," I said, scooping their leashes off the hook. "We'll play when we get back."

I thought Jill might follow me to the base-ball field, but she remained inside her car. I glanced in as we walked by and saw that she was reading a book. Jill didn't even look up. I guessed she figured as long as I was outside in plain view of plenty of people, not too much could go wrong.

Good thought, that.

Mutt and Maisie made short work of our

spin around the park. Sometimes when we were there in the late afternoon, there might be a game or practice session in progress. The two elderly dogs adored that. The crowds and the cheering got them dancing on their toes at the ends of their leashes.

That day, however, all was quiet. I supposed that since it was spring break, many families were out of town. The baseball diamond was deserted; the park around it nearly empty.

Mutt finished his walk by lifting his leg on each of the holly bushes that flanked his front door. Maisie watched this demonstration of macho dominance with a look of bored resignation that was almost human and certainly laughable. Once inside, she led the merry charge to the water bowl.

I was closing the door behind us when a car pulled into the driveway. Phil Dutton parked and got out. Walking over to the house, he looked just as surprised to see me as I was to see him.

"You're early." Phil didn't sound pleased. "I didn't expect you for several hours yet."

"It's spring break. I'm not working this week so I figured I'd come by a bit earlier. You know, so it would break up the day better for Mutt and Maisie?"

I knew I was babbling, but something felt

off. Why did Phil look so flustered? And what was he doing home in the middle of the day? If he was going to be there, what did he need me for?

"Is everything all right?" I asked, stepping aside as he strode into the house.

"Of course." Phil gave the front door a shove. Closed, it blocked off much of the light that had been in the room. He turned to face me with a smile. His teeth, small and even, were stained as though he'd once been a heavy smoker. "What could possibly be wrong?"

"I don't know." Intuition told me to take a step back, so I did. "I just didn't think you'd be here today. Like I said last week, if you're going to be home anyway, it's silly to pay me to come and play with your dogs."

"Don't be so sure of that." Phil's arm brushed mine as he walked past me and headed toward the kitchen. "Can I get you something to drink?"

"No." That sounded too abrupt. I tried again. "No, I'm not thirsty, thank you." Unfortunately, I had to go to the kitchen, too, to check the dogs' food and water bowls. I trailed reluctantly behind him. "Don't mind me. I'll try not to make any noise. I'm sure you have work you want to get back to in your office —"

"As it happens, I don't." Phil pulled a pair of long-necked beers out of the refrigerator. "Sit down with me for a minute. Let's talk."

Maybe he was going to fire me, I thought hopefully. Maybe offering me a beer was his way of letting me down gently. Instead of sitting, I went over, picked up the dogs' water bowl, and carried it to the sink. It was half filled with cloudy water and the bottom was brown and scummy. Didn't he ever wash their things out?

"I can listen and work at the same time," I said. Mutt and Maisie, sprawled side by side on the cool linoleum floor, were waiting for a fresh drink. "Go ahead and talk."

"But that's just it, I don't want you to work. That's not why you're here."

"It isn't?" Thinking he was joking, I flashed him a smile over my shoulder. Phil didn't smile back.

Uh-oh.

"Well, yes, of course it *is*." He was fumbling now, trying to cover what he'd just blurted out. "But not entirely. I mean, you're here because Mutt and Maisie enjoy your company. And so do I."

The almost full bowl fell from my hands and clattered into the sink. Its heavy load of water spilled over the sides, sloshing up onto the counter. I hoped like crazy that I'd misheard him, but I didn't think so.

Back still turned to Phil, I hastily righted the bowl and began to refill it. My face was flaming; my stomach clenched. Maybe I was reading something into his words that wasn't there.

Oh, the heck with it, I thought. Maybe I should just run screaming out the front door and never look back.

Barring that, I definitely needed to say something to defuse the situation. I turned off the water and wiped my hands on a towel. "You know I like spending time with Mutt and Maisie. They're great dogs."

Hearing their names, the two pooches looked up and wagged their tails. I carried the bowl over and put it down beside them. Mutt levered himself up and went to get a drink.

Feeling a compulsive need to fill the silence, I began to babble again. "Of course, you and I usually don't see each other. That's the whole point, isn't it? I mean, if you were here —"

Something, the merest flicker in Phil's expression, made me hesitate. "Well, aside from last week, that is. And then again today . . ."

Why didn't he say something? Why did he

just keep looking at me with that strange expression on his face?

Then finally Phil spoke. His voice was low, his tone soothing. The sound of it set my teeth on edge.

"I guess I have a confession to make," he said. "I wasn't going to tell you this, but I figure you and I are friends now, and friends shouldn't keep secrets from one another."

Phil patted the chair beside him. "Come on," he said again. "Come over and sit by me."

22

I didn't *think* so.

Of all the things that were not about to happen, accepting that invitation ranked very near the top of the list. Instead, I turned to face Phil and remained right where I was. My back was pressed against the lip of the sink; nearly the width of the room was between us. And that was exactly the way I wanted it.

I couldn't imagine what Phil might have to confess. Bearing recent events in mind, however, my thoughts flew immediately to the missing Dachshund puppy. Not to mention my wallet.

I'd been at Phil's last Thursday; Davey and I had stopped for gas on the way over. That was the last time I'd known for sure where my wallet was. And although I'd never given Phil my address, he knew I lived in Stamford. I was listed in the phone book; my house wouldn't have been hard to track down.

"A confession?" I asked, and heard my

voice wobble. "How interesting. I'm listening."

"I thought you might." Now Phil was smiling, looking more sure of himself. He liked having the attention focused his way. "Are you sure you don't want a beer?"

I didn't bother to answer again, I simply shook my head.

"Okay, your choice. I guess I'll just get to it then. I know you'll understand that I was only looking out for Mutt and Maisie's best interests. Any parent, any dog owner, would have done the same."

He paused so long — his fingers fiddling with the salt and pepper shakers on the table, his gaze skittering in several directions around the room — that I began to wonder if he was going to continue. "Would have done what, exactly?" I finally prompted.

Phil hesitated another minute, then pushed back his chair and stood. "Maybe it would be easier to show you."

He walked into the living room. I followed several steps behind. Phil stopped in front of a tall wooden cabinet I'd never paid much attention to.

"Look up there," he said. "What do you see?"

"A potted plant. The leaves look like

they're made of plastic, and they're badly in need of dusting."

"Perfect," Phil chortled. "That's just what you're supposed to see. But that innocent looking plant is actually a hidden video camera."

I sucked in a shocked breath. He didn't seem to notice. His voice, his stance, were growing bolder. "You've probably heard of something like this. The stores call them nannycams. It records everything that goes on in this room."

Phil was proud of the way he'd duped me. He was enjoying the opportunity to show off his toy. A toy that had apparently had me under surveillance for the last four months.

Bile was rising in the back of my throat. "I can't believe this," I choked out. "You've been *spying* on me?"

"I wouldn't put it like that —"

"No?" I spun around, searching the room. I didn't see a television, maybe it was inside the cabinet. "What would you call it?"

"Insurance," Phil said quickly. He was beginning to realize he might have miscalculated. "Protection for my home and my animals."

I'd have called it rampant paranoia, but what was the point? Phil had interviewed me; he'd checked my references. He'd professed to be satisfied with my services. So why had he felt the need to record my every move?

"How many cameras are there in the house? Just that one?"

"Actually three," he admitted. "There's one in the dining room that covers the hall."

And the powder room, I realized, wondering if I'd ever used the facilities. Trying to remember if I'd bothered to shut the door. What else might I have done when I'd assumed I was alone that I should now regret?

"That's two," I said.

Phil flushed slightly. "The third one is upstairs, in my bedroom."

At least I didn't have to worry about that camera. I wondered if there were other women who did, women who hadn't been fortunate enough to be privy to Phil's confessions.

I strode over to the cabinet and yanked it open. As I'd suspected, it contained a TV set. A collection of homemade video tapes was stacked on a shelf below. Each was neatly labeled. As I skimmed over the selection, my horror grew. They were dated twice a week since January, and my name was on every one.

I was beyond outrage now. For a moment, I was afraid I might throw up. There weren't any other women. Just me.

Oh, crap.

I reached into the cabinet and grabbed as many tapes as I could hold.

"Wait a minute," said Phil. "What are you doing?"

To tell the truth, I wasn't sure. All I knew was that I had to get out of there, and I was taking the collection with me. I felt violated, exposed, in a way I'd never before imagined. Not knowing what was on the tapes only made the situation worse.

Watching me, Phil was growing visibly agitated. I wondered if he'd try to stop me. I wondered what I would do if he did.

"Those tapes are my property," he said. "You can't have them."

"No? What do you intend to do with them?"

"Look at them. That's all I do, I just look at them. They make me feel closer to you —"

I yelped slightly and began to back away. If there was one thing I didn't need it was Phil Dutton feeling any closer to me.

"I don't know why you're so upset," he whined. "Maybe it's me, maybe I'm explaining things badly. This is all very innocent. The guy at the store told me that employers do this all the time. I was just making a record of what went on in my house on the days you came when I wasn't here. Surely you can't think there's anything wrong with that."

Arms filled with tapes, I turned slowly to face him. "What do you mean, on the days I came when you weren't here? I thought you were always gone on Mondays and Thursdays. Isn't that why you hired me?"

Phil blinked several times, like an animal caught in the glare of an unexpected light. "Initially, yes. I was working in the city on those days, just as I said."

"And then?" My voice rose ominously.

"Then after a couple months, the project ended. It happens all the time, that's the way freelancers work . . . ."

I didn't give a damn how freelancers worked. I wanted to know why, once Phil had stopped being away twice a week, he continued to use my services. And I was very much beginning to suspect that I wouldn't like his answer.

"When did you stop working in New York?" I asked.

"I'm not sure. Maybe last month? Look, it really isn't important —"

"It is to me." I cast a look in Mutt and Maisie's direction. I was going to miss those little dogs. Too bad they had such a creepy owner.

"The only thing that matters," Phil said, "is that you're here now. And I'm here. I know you always give Mutt and Maisie their full hour, I've seen that on the tapes. So there's no need for you to rush off. I thought we might spend some time getting to know one another."

He had to be nuts, I thought. Or at least seriously deluded. Could Phil Dutton honestly believe any woman would feel that being spied upon was an appropriate prelude to beginning some sort of relationship?

"Look at all the tapes I made of you." He gestured toward the collection in my arms. His eyes were large and liquid. "Isn't that proof of the way I feel?"

Sheesh, I thought. Nuts, it was.

"Did you ever stop to think about my feelings?" I demanded. "Did you ever consider the fact that what you were doing was an invasion of my privacy?"

"No."

Well, then. In his mind, I guessed that made everything all right.

"Tell me something," I said.

"Of course."

His glib answer annoyed me. Of course.

After all, we were buddies now, weren't we? I tried not to snap when I spoke.

"Have you ever been to my house?"

Phil didn't answer right away. Instead he smiled slightly, like a man enjoying a private joke. He turned and gazed out the window. When he finally spoke, I couldn't see his face.

"Why would I want to go to your house when you were already coming here?"

"No reason," I said softly. All at once, I was very glad I'd arranged to have Davey spend the week with Bob.

Phil followed me to the door. It was all I could do not to run. He reached out a hand and his palm rested briefly on my shoulder before I shrugged it off.

"This is turning out all wrong," he said. "It wasn't supposed to be like this. I just wanted us to talk. I thought maybe we could be friends."

He sounded sad, and more than a little lonely. It didn't matter. I couldn't bring myself to care.

"I guess I probably should have told you when I stopped working, but I was still paying you for your time, so what was the harm in that? I figured you were probably glad to have the job. After all, you wouldn't be working if you didn't need the money.

But now everything's out in the open, and that's good, right? We can go back to things being the way they were."

"No," I said firmly. "We can't. For one thing, I was coming here for Mutt and Maisie's sake, and they don't need me anymore. For another, I could never be friends with a man who thinks it's all right to spy on people."

Juggling the tapes, I reached into the pocket of my jeans and fished out the door key he'd given me in January. I left it on the table near the door on my way out.

On my way home, I stopped by the locksmith with whom I'd left a message the day before. What he had to say wasn't encouraging.

"I'll be happy to come over to your house and change every lock you've got," Peter Stiles told me. "Dead bolts are your best bet, but nothing I'm gonna do is foolproof. Let me be honest, Ms. Travis, unless you go to putting bars on your windows, if someone really wants to get into your house, they're gonna come in."

"What about a security system?"

"Same thing." Stiles shrugged. "There's a bunch of good companies out there. Call one of them, get them to rig something up.

What you're going to get for your money is an alarm that makes a whole lotta noise and a direct link to the police station. What's the response time for emergencies in your neighborhood?"

I had no idea. Thankfully, it had never come up.

"Ten, fifteen minutes would be considered pretty good in most areas," Stiles told me. "Whole lotta stuff can happen in fifteen minutes, you know what I mean? You really want some protection, you ought to think about getting yourself a guard dog. Something big and scary like a Doberman or a Rottweiler. Something with lots of teeth. Plenty of burglars think twice about taking on a house with a big dog inside."

My house had two big dogs inside, and as far as I could tell, their presence hadn't deterred the intruder at all. I thanked Stiles for his advice and drove home.

When I got there, my two watchdogs were waiting for me by the front door. At least they were inside the house this time. I squatted down and opened my arms wide to encompass both wriggling bodies. Faith looked past me, out the door. Her body language was easy to read. She was looking for Davey.

"I know." I sighed. It had only been two hours. "I miss him, too."

Aunt Peg called while the two Poodles were chasing each other like maniacs around the backyard. Her sixth sense for my behavioral lapses is uncanny. Poodles in show coat aren't supposed to play chasing games. Chasing inevitably leads to hair pulling, which results in saliva-encrusted mats.

It was no use wondering how Aunt Peg always knew when I was being remiss in my duties as Keeper Of The Coat. The way things had been going recently, I was perfectly willing to believe that she had the place wired.

"So?" she demanded. Not hello. Not how are you. Just, *so?*

And people say the younger generation has no manners.

"So what?" I inquired pleasantly.

"Really, Melanie, don't be fresh. Have you found Dox yet?"

Oh, that. I should have known. And probably would have if I hadn't had eight million other things to think about in the meantime.

"No."

"Where have you looked so far?"

I wondered briefly how to put this. There didn't seem to be a way to sugarcoat it. "Ummm . . . nowhere."

"Nowhere? It's been nearly an entire day. What *have* you been doing?"

"Let's see." I thought back. "I talked to the police. I got the glass fixed in my back door. I talked to Sam, I talked to Bob. I had lunch at the Bean Counter with Bertie —"

"And how was any of that supposed to help Dox?"

"Maybe I misunderstood," I said. "Weren't you the one who was supposed to be coming up with a plan?"

"Not all by myself." Aunt Peg sounded rather huffy. "While you were off gallivanting, however, I did talk to Marian."

That was interesting. "And?"

"She called earlier to ask a favor. She'd like you to bring Dox by her house for another visit."

Perfect, I thought. Just perfect.

"I don't suppose you told her that wouldn't be possible?"

"Not exactly," Peg hedged. "After all, you were the one who thought of her as one of your better suspects. I figured you'd want to tell her about the puppy's disappearance in person and see what kind of response you get."

Considering that Marian was allegedly expecting me to show up with the Dachshund puppy, her reaction would be pretty predictable. On the other hand, there were still several discrepancies between what

George had to say about their divorce and the story Marian was promoting. I supposed it wouldn't hurt to ask a few questions.

"Since you're going out this evening anyway," Peg continued, "I thought you could stop by and see her on your way over to Rose's."

Anyone who thinks that a stop in Ridgefield is on the way from Stamford to Cos Cob has never consulted a map of Connecticut. Not that Aunt Peg lets such simple logistics get in her way.

"Should I take that to mean that Marian is expecting me?"

"She will be." Aunt Peg sounded satisfied. "Just as soon as I call and let her know you're coming."

Maybe Aunt Peg hadn't been childless, I thought as I hung up the phone. Maybe she'd eaten her young.

It would explain a lot.

23

On the way to Marian Firth's house, the thought crossed my mind that perhaps Aunt Peg, in her own sneaky, underhanded fashion, was actually trying to sabotage my evening with Aunt Rose. I mean, really. Why else would she send me all the way up to Ridgefield when I was supposed to be heading to Cos Cob?

My two aunts have always been competitive with one another. And since Rose and Peter moved back to the area, it's taken a great deal of diplomacy on my part not to get caught in the middle. Or maybe I was just being paranoid. On the other hand, I reflected — and the long drive offered me plenty of time for reflection — given the current state of my life, a little paranoia didn't seem entirely out of line.

As Aunt Peg had promised, Marian was expecting me. She opened the door with an expectant smile. Almost immediately her face fell.

"Oh," she said. "When Peg told me you

were coming to see me I just assumed you'd bring my puppy with you."

Either Marian Firth was a wonderful actress, I decided, or she had no idea that Dox was missing.

"Sorry," I said. "I do need to talk to you about him, though."

"Of course." She stepped aside. "Please come in."

The three Dachshunds I'd met on my last visit, two smooths and a wirehair, came tumbling into the hall like a troupe of circus acrobats. At least they looked like the same ones to me. It's taken me several years to reach the point where I can tell several black Poodles apart with total assurance. Sorting out Dachshunds was a skill still in my future.

"Tell me all about my puppy," Marian said. "I want to hear everything."

Tough assignment, that. I decided to wait until we were seated opposite one another in the living room before trying to explain.

"Dox was doing very well," I said. "As you know, I've been keeping him at my house. He and my Poodles were getting along beautifully."

"Were?" Immediately Marian picked up on my use of the past tense. If anything, the woman looked even more fragile than she had on my last visit. "Has something happened?"

"I'm sorry to have to tell you this," I said, "but Dox has disappeared."

Marian's fingers, slender, long, impossibly white, flew to her throat. "He's gone? How is that possible?"

"My house was broken into yesterday —"

"You *lost* my puppy?"

"No," I corrected. "I didn't lose him. He was taken from inside my house." I paused to let that sink in, then added, "It crossed my mind that you might have had something to do with his disappearance."

"You must be joking." Marian stared at me for a long moment. She seemed to be gathering her strength, and when she spoke again her voice had hardened. "Why would you think something like that?"

"Why wouldn't I? You've made no secret of your desire to get Dox back by whatever means possible. Aunt Peg told me about your scheme to try to trick your ex-husband into giving the puppy away."

"You needn't make it sound as though that's something shameful," Marian snapped. "If anyone deserves to be tricked, it's George. Of course I want the puppy back. But it has to be done through the proper channels. I need his registration papers, with everything signed and aboveboard. Dox's value to me lies in his potential as a show dog and stud. Without his papers, he's just another cute Dachshund puppy."

And here I'd thought Marian's major concern had been for Dox's welfare. Considering the show she'd put on last time we'd met, maybe I needed to reconsider my assessment of her acting skills.

"So, then, you don't have any idea where Dox might be?"

"Certainly not."

Marian's fingers had begun to drum on the arm of the sofa. I wondered what she was thinking.

"Do you think George might have had something to do with Dox's disappearance?"

"I wouldn't put it past him. Then again, I wouldn't put anything past my ex-husband."

"He called and left a message for me Saturday night," I said. "He told me he wanted Dox returned. But before I had a chance to get back to him, the puppy was gone."

"Serves him right," Marian muttered. "What did George say when you told him the puppy was missing?"

"As it happens, I haven't told him."

"May I ask why not?"

I could have said that I hadn't had the

chance, but that was an evasion, at best. It was bad enough that I was on my way to offer explanations and apologies to Peter and Rose. At the moment, George was just one more complication I didn't want to deal with. Besides, there was always the possibility that with luck, and perhaps a little judicious sleuthing on my part, Dox might turn up.

All of which was more than I wanted to explain to Marian. "Because it seems unlikely to me that he'd resort to stealing a puppy he already owns," I said instead.

Her back stiffened. "And yet you thought to come and question me."

I glanced around the cluttered living room. It was hard not to compare Marian's small, shabby house with George's sumptuous condo. If she thought she'd been offended before, wait until she heard this.

"Your ex-husband is under the impression that you'd like to get back together with him," I said. "And it has occurred to me that the biggest bone of contention between you is Dox. Removing that source of friction might go a long way toward smoothing the path to reconciliation."

"Reconcile with George?" Marian's brow lifted. "Are you mad? I was lucky to get out when I did. I'm only sorry I didn't divorce the bum sooner."

"That's not what he said."

"You're a fool if you believe everything that George told you."

Abruptly Marian stood. The red Dachshund who'd been lying in her lap jumped nimbly to the ground. When she strode toward the door, I had no choice but to get up and follow.

"I have only one more thing to say." Marian's voice was firm as she held the door open for me to walk through. "If that puppy were a child, and I rescued him, I'd be hailed as a hero. There ought to be laws to protect innocent animals from self-serving schemers like George. Thank goodness there are still people in the world who abhor cruelty and aren't afraid to step forward and do something about it."

I was outside on the step before the full import of her words sank in. Immediately I spun around. "Does that mean — ?"

The door slammed shut in my face.

Considering the week I'd been having, it figured.

It was with decidedly mixed emotions that I finally got myself on the road and heading in the direction of Cos Cob. Maybe

Aunt Peg wasn't the only one who'd used my visit to Marian Firth as a delaying tactic. Much as I enjoyed Rose and Peter's company, I couldn't help but feel that I was being shanghaied into a situation they were intending to manipulate to their own ends.

Frank's former abode, now Rose and Peter's home, was located in a spacious Victorian house that had been remodeled in the middle of the last century to form three good-sized apartments. Traffic on the quiet side street was almost nonexistent, and the Long Island Sound was only a ten-minute walk away. The apartment was a find, and Rose and Peter had been delighted to inherit the lease from their nephew.

By the time I arrived, Sam's silver BMW was already parked out front. That's what I got for running late. I'd lost my opportunity to speak with my aunt and uncle in private and warn them of dire consequences if they so much as alluded to Sam's and my troubled relationship. My only consolation was the knowledge that it probably wouldn't have done much good anyway.

"It's about time you got here!" Peter threw open the front door and drew me inside.

He gathered me into his arms for a spontaneous embrace and I hugged him back warmly. Peter Donovan is one of my favorite relatives. Of course, he wasn't born into my family — we had to grab him by marriage — which is probably why he seems so blessedly normal.

Peter was a former priest who'd left his vocation at the same time Aunt Rose had stopped being Sister Anne Marie. In the three years since they'd made those life-altering decisions, I'd never heard either express a moment's regret for the cloistered lives they'd left behind. Instead, both my aunt and uncle had devoted themselves to continuing on as their faith dictated, doing good works and trying to make the world a better place for those they came in contact with.

"I'm not that late, am I?" I handed Peter a bottle of merlot and followed him toward the back of the apartment. "Where are Sam and Rose?"

"Out on the porch. Rose and I got the idea this would be the perfect opportunity to hold the first barbeque of the year. Last I saw, she and Sam were leaning over the grill. They're probably still negotiating the charcoal briquette to lighter fluid coefficient."

"No, we've solved that problem," Sam announced as Peter and I joined them. Bright orange flames, leaping high into the air out of the open grill behind him, didn't exactly support his claim. "Now we're talking about you."

"Me?" I said with all the innocence I could muster. "I can't imagine why."

"Of course you can," Rose said briskly. One holdover from her convent days was a marked distaste for prevarication. "Where's Davey? Weren't we expecting him, too?"

Now that she mentioned it, yes. I'd forgotten all about the fact that he'd been included in the invitation. "We had a change of plan. Sorry, I should have called and told you about it. Davey's spending the week with Bob."

"The whole week?" Sam sounded surprised. He knew I'd never let Davey out of my sight for that long before. "How did that come about?"

"Oh, you know," I said lightly. "It's spring break." I wondered if I was fooling anyone. They didn't look convinced.

Peter caught my eye and winked. "I'm sure he's having a marvelous time with his new pony. Much better than he'd have here, hanging around with us old fogies." He slipped an arm around his wife's shoulders. "Rose, Melanie brought us a lovely merlot. Come inside and help me pour, won't you?"

Judging by the disgruntled expression on

my aunt's face, Peter's intervention had saved me, at least temporarily, from an inquisition. Of course, their departure also left me standing on the porch alone with Sam. My ex-fiancé was looking more than a little disgruntled himself.

He folded his arms over his chest and leaned back against the porch railing. His long, blue jeans–clad legs were thrust straight out in front of him. His feet were encased in a pair of battered topsiders worn, as always, without socks. I found myself mesmerized by the tiny blond hairs that curled over the top of his feet. Or maybe I just didn't want to meet his gaze.

"What's going on, Mel?" Sam asked.

"What do you mean?"

"I get the feeling you're avoiding me. I'd like to know why. I'm thinking maybe it's because of Bob."

"Bob?" The single shocked word simply slipped out. Sam had to be kidding. He was so far off base it was almost laughable. "What does Bob have to do with anything?"

"That's what I'd like to know." Sam unfolded his arms. He reached up and ran a hand through his already mussed hair. "Look, I'd have to be an idiot not to realize that leaving last year might not have been the best decision I ever made. At the time, I thought — no, let's say I hoped — you'd understand why I felt it was something I had to do. But obviously my not being here gave your ex-husband the opening he was looking for. By the time I got back, he'd all but moved in —"

"He had not," I interrupted hotly.

Maybe I'd briefly entertained the notion of reconnecting with my ex. Emphasis on *briefly*. Bob had arrived in Connecticut at a time when I was feeling particularly adrift. Particularly vulnerable. He'd capitalized on my fragile state, and I hadn't moved as quickly as I might have to stop him. But in the end, I'd said no, firmly and unequivocally. And Bob had never been led to believe, for even a moment, that he might be returning to live with Davey and me.

"All right, maybe I don't mean that literally," Sam said. "But figuratively, it's true. The guy moved in on a relationship I thought was pretty solid. One that should have been able to withstand a small separation."

"A *small* separation?" I echoed incredulously. "Is that what you call it? To me it felt as though a chasm had opened up and swallowed me whole. You turned your back on me and walked out of my life."

Sam looked as though he wanted to say

something. I didn't give him a chance to speak. "I hate to admit it, but if you'd given me the opportunity to beg you to stay, I probably would have done it. But you didn't even do that, because my opinion didn't matter to you. You just left. And all I did — all I *could* do — was stand there and watch you go."

24

Sam didn't answer right away. I felt the full weight of my accusing words, hanging in the air between us. Where were Peter and Rose with that wine anyway? Lord knew I could use a swig of alcohol right about then. Not to mention an interruption.

As if, I thought irritably. My aunt and uncle were probably inside the house, listening to every word we said through the screen door. I couldn't count on either one of them for a timely intervention.

"I realize you're angry," Sam said quietly. "Maybe I didn't realize how angry. But I'm back now. That should count for something."

I stared past him, out into the small yard with its detached one-car garage. In the next yard, pastel sheets hung on a clothesline, wafting gently in the evening breeze. "It means a lot. But it doesn't change the course of my life. You had the power to do that once, and you gave it up. I'm glad you're back, Sam. I hope we can rebuild what we had, but unlike you I can't just erase what happened and slide back to where we were."

Sam frowned. Now his hands were braced on the railing. His fingers flexed open and shut. I guessed I wasn't the only one wishing for that drink.

"I understand what you're saying. There's an element of trust that has to be re-earned. But I can't do it all on my own, Mel. You've got to give me a chance."

I stared at him. "How have I not given you a chance?"

"Yesterday, for example. When your house was broken into, I had to find out about it from Peg. Why didn't you call me yourself? Why didn't you let me be the one who was there for you?"

"I didn't think of it," I said honestly.

Sam winced as if the truth hurt. Any pity I might have felt was tempered by the fact that I was hurting, too. Once, Sam would have been the first call I'd made, and we both knew it.

"You didn't think of it?" His tone hardened. "*You didn't think of it?* If that's the best answer you can come up with, then something is seriously wrong —"

"Sam, be a dear and get the door for me, would you?" Aunt Rose sang out. Her voice

327

was filled with fake cheer. It was also unnaturally loud. She appeared on the other side of the screen door, both hands clasping a tray filled with cheese and crackers, wine and glasses.

Sam threw me a glance to let me know that our discussion wasn't finished. Not by a long shot, I thought in agreement as he crossed the porch and drew the door open.

Rose smiled at the two of us gaily. "Peter's just spooning some marinade over the steaks. He'll be out to join us in a minute. In the meantime, Melanie, why don't you pour?"

Aunt Rose, ever the organizer, was at her best when it came to whipping people into action. Having gone to school at Divine Mercy myself, I knew for a fact that the convent ran like clockwork. The sisters had little patience with slackers and Rose was no exception.

The wine bottle was already open. It was an easy task to half-fill the four goblets. While I was doing that, Aunt Rose placed slices of cheese on several crackers. When Sam looked as though he was about to speak, she hurriedly handed him one. In fact, she all but jammed it into his mouth.

"There now," she said, surveying us both with satisfaction. "That's much better, isn't it?"

Détente, Aunt Rose style. And pity the poor fool who didn't leap to follow her lead.

"Everything fine out here?" asked Peter, coming to join us.

"Just dandy," Sam agreed. Unless he wanted to be silenced with another wedge of cheddar, what choice did he have?

"That's what I thought." Peter poked at the coals with a long-handled fork. Gray on top, they glowed red underneath. "These look just about ready. Let's get this show on the road."

While the steaks cooked and were subsequently served, we discussed Dox's disappearance. Peter wanted to know whether I'd spoken to George Firth. Rose asked if I had any leads. Sam was concerned for the little Dachshund's welfare.

"Bottom line," I said, "I have to think that whoever has Dox is probably taking good care of him, because they certainly went to enough trouble to get him. Breaking into my house in broad daylight was a pretty bold move. It was just the thief's good luck that nobody saw anything, especially as Jill Prescott arrived on the scene only a short time later."

"That reporter from the dog show?" Sam looked up. "Don't tell me she's still hanging around."

I nodded unhappily. "I saw her earlier today."

Both Rose and Peter needed to be filled in. I helped myself to some more Caesar salad and obliged them. By the time I was finished, Peter was chuckling to himself.

"That woman must have a wonderful imagination," he said, patting his mouth with his napkin. "Imagine thinking you actually go around falling over dead bodies."

Rose, Sam, and I shared a look. Belatedly, Peter caught on that we weren't laughing with him.

"What?" he asked.

"It's just . . . I do seem to have become entangled in more than my share of mysteries."

"Oh, that." Peter dismissed the issue with a wave of his hand.

Oh, that? Like me, Rose and Sam seemed stunned into silence. After a long moment, during which none of us said a word, Peter felt compelled to explain.

"I've met Peg, haven't I? That woman's a force of nature all on her own. Let's just say that a taste for the unusual seems to run in your family. Not to mention a propensity for trouble."

Peter's brown eyes were twinkling. Sam was beginning to look amused as well. Suddenly I couldn't help but wonder whether he was thinking about our broken engagement and coming to the conclusion that he'd had a narrow escape.

"Even so," Peter continued, "I have to believe your reporter must be an optimist. Look at the law of averages. How often can things like that crop up?"

Considering how pleased Peter seemed with his conclusions, I decided not to mention my missing wallet, the hang-up phone calls, or the specter who'd been wandering through my house in the dead of night. Optimist indeed. The way my life was going, Jill's investigative instincts might turn out to be right on the money. And the next body someone tripped over could well be mine.

"Who wants dessert?" Aunt Rose asked. It seemed to be her evening for smoothing over awkward moments. "I've got cheesecake!"

Taking our cue, we all pitched in and helped to clear the table. Thankfully, when we were settled in our seats once more with coffee and dessert, the conversation turned to less personal topics.

An hour later, as I was preparing to leave, Peter pulled me aside. "We're putting together the program for the auction and I'll be sending it to the printer later in the week.

What should I do about the Dachshund puppy?" he asked. "Is he in or out?"

Good question. And tough to answer on a number of levels. Before I could decide what to say, Peter went on without me. It was clear he'd given the issue quite a bit of thought.

"Rose tells me you and Peg think it's a terrible idea to offer a live animal as one of the prizes. Until she brought it up, I probably hadn't given the issue enough thought. George Firth offered a donation and I was happy to accept it. To tell the truth, I was more concerned about caring for the puppy in the meantime than I was about what would happen to it afterward.

"Of course, I can see now that I was wrong not to have thought things through. And the fact that the puppy is missing simply complicates matters. If I withdraw him from the charity event, I should, by rights, return him to Mr. Firth. Of course, that's not possible at the moment, either. What are the chances you're going to be able to find him?"

Fair, I thought.

"Pretty good," I said aloud. It was what Peter wanted to hear.

His expression brightened at the news. "Do your best, will you, and I'll try to stall

George Firth in the meantime. I'd love to see this problem resolved. The last thing a charity event needs is bad publicity. And Mr. Firth struck me as the kind of man who could make a lot of noise if he was so inclined."

"Ready to go?" Sam joined us in the hallway. He was wearing his jacket and holding mine. "Why don't I walk you to your car?"

"Umm . . . sure."

As Sam knew perfectly well, the Volvo was no more than twenty feet away at the other end of a well-lit walkway. Chivalry was hardly called for. Which probably meant that he planned to continue our earlier discussion.

"Perfect." Aunt Rose was beaming, her pleasure in our couple-dom as transparent as a sheet of glass. "Thank you both so much for coming."

Fully conscious of the fact that Rose and Peter were watching us through their front window, I still found myself walking out to the curb in silence. I knew what they were hoping to see, but I had no intention of putting on a performance.

When we reached the Volvo, Sam took the key out of my hand and fitted it into the lock. "I don't want you to take this the wrong way," he said, "but I'd like to see you home."

For a surprised moment, I couldn't quite think how to respond. I glanced toward his BMW, parked up ahead.

"I'll follow you in my car. When we get to your house, I can go in first and make sure everything's all right."

"Faith and Eve —" I started to say, then stopped. Yes, the two big Poodles were standing guard. For all the good that had done me before.

"Will both be glad to see me," Sam finished. "In fact, they'll probably be delighted. I'd like to spend the night, Melanie."

"No —"

"In your bed, on the couch. Hell, on the floor, if that's where you want to put me. I just don't think you should be alone."

Where had this sudden protective streak come from? I wondered. How much had Aunt Peg told him? I gazed up at Sam. His face was half in shadow, half in light, illuminated by the amber street lamp above. "Why?"

"In all the time I've known you, you've never sent Davey away before. You can tell me he went to Bob's for spring break, but I don't have to believe it. Something's going on, and since I don't hear you denying it, I'm betting things are even worse than I've been told. Bad enough for you to think you need to put your son somewhere out of harm's way. Whatever's going on, Melanie, you don't have to face it alone. Let me help you."

Lord, but I was tempted. Sam had no idea how much I simply wanted to melt into the security of his arms. How nice it would be to pass along the burden of my fears and let someone else do the worrying for a change. Mostly I just wanted to stop being afraid of whatever it was that was out there stalking me, disrupting my life, and making me second-guess my every move.

But even so, I knew this was wrong.

If I let Sam come home with me, I could pretty much count on the fact that nobody would end up sleeping on the floor, unless perhaps one of the Poodles found the bed too crowded. Going for the quick fix might help my short-term problems, but it wouldn't give us anything to build on for the future. It also wouldn't quiet that little voice that wondered if I allowed myself to lean on Sam now, what would I do the next time he decided he was feeling confined and needed to get away?

"Thank you." I lifted a hand and cradled the side of his jaw. The skin was unexpectedly smooth. He must have shaved again that evening before coming to dinner.

His hand came up to cover mine. "For what?"

"For caring."

I felt Sam sigh, rather than heard it. His hand slipped away. "You know I care, Melanie. I love you."

"I love you, too," I said.

Once upon a time, I'd thought that was enough. I'd believed that love could overcome any obstacle. But unfortunately, experience had taught me differently. Now I knew that no matter how much you believed, love didn't automatically lead to happily ever after.

"I appreciate your offer, but I'm sure I'll be fine. My locks are good, my dogs are big." I tried out a small smile. "And apparently the only thing worth stealing in my house is already gone."

"It's your call." Sam stepped back. "We'll handle this any way you want. If you'd rather be alone, I guess I'll just have to understand."

"Thank you." My throat tightened. Some independent woman. If I didn't get out of there soon, I was going to turn into a mound of quivering Jell-O.

"If you change your mind, call my cell phone. I'll come right away."

"I will," I said. Even though I didn't plan on taking him up on it, the offer meant a lot.

Sam stood by the curb and watched me drive away. I couldn't see his expression in the half-light, but I didn't need to. I could tell by the set of his shoulders, by the way he'd jammed his hands into his pockets, that he wasn't happy.

Well, since you're wondering, neither was I. Though we'd only parted moments earlier, I already missed him. I missed the way our thoughts connected so quickly that we could finish each other's sentences. I missed the way my body drew warmth and strength from his. I missed the feeling of well-being that surrounded me whenever we were together. Worse still was the knowledge that Sam had offered me all of that; and this time I had been the one who'd walked away.

My house was waiting for me just as I'd left it. An assortment of lights was on to keep the shadows at bay. The two Standard Poodles met me at the front door. I let them out back and went to the pantry for biscuits, performing the simple tasks by rote, and berating myself for not allowing Sam to be there to share them with me.

His presence was so indelibly imprinted on my thoughts that later, after I'd checked the locks on all the doors and climbed into

337

bed, I still had trouble concentrating on anything else. The book I was reading couldn't hold my interest. Its prose was unable to nudge other, more stimulating images from my mind.

I was so caught up in the spell of the fantasies, so sure that Sam must have been thinking of me too, that when the phone beside the bed rang, I wasn't even surprised. The fact that he would call to check on me again seemed almost inevitable.

I reached for the receiver eagerly and held it to my ear. "Sam?"

For a moment, there wasn't any answer. And then I heard it, the murmur of an indrawn breath, the quiet rasp as the air was exhaled.

No, not Sam.

My midnight caller was back.

25

I slammed down the phone and felt the jolt all the way up to my elbow. My stomach clenched. Goose bumps rose on my arms. The unnaturally loud thump of my heart filled my ears.

Almost immediately, the phone began to ring again.

Wildly I looked around the room. At least I wasn't groggy, half-awake and sitting in the dark as I'd been the night before. At least I wasn't trying to make sense of what was happening.

I tried to find some comfort in that. It didn't help much.

The repetitious sound was making my nerves scream. My fingers twitched, wanting to pick up the receiver . . . And do what? I wondered.

Throw it across the room, probably.

After the fifth ring, the machine downstairs in the kitchen picked up. Faintly I heard a voice speaking, my own message being relayed to the caller.

You have reached the Travis residence, I thought angrily. *Melanie can't come to the phone right now. She's upstairs cowering in her bed.*

Unless he was whispering, no one responded after the beep. Coward, I thought bitterly. I hated the feeling of not being in control. Of not knowing what might happen next.

I threw back the covers and rolled out of bed. Eve was still stretched out on the duvet, snoring softly. It takes more than a late-night phone call to spoil her beauty sleep.

Faith, who'd always been more attuned to my moods, was already up. She knew something was wrong, she just didn't know what. I looked at her and crooned, "Good girl." She whined anxiously in reply.

As I debated what to do, the phone began to ring again. The sound was shrill and grating, a clarion call shattering the stillness. The night before I'd been concerned the noise might wake up Davey. Now I just let it ring.

Talk to the machine, or don't, I thought. Up to you.

I'd gone to bed wearing a tee shirt and flannel pajama bottoms. Suddenly that didn't feel like enough clothing, enough protective armor. I crossed the room to the closet, pulled out a robe, and wrapped it tightly around me.

Phone calls could come from anywhere. The fact that he was calling me didn't mean he was close by. Still, I felt myself drawn to the windows.

Lacy curtains shrouded the panes of glass. They obstructed the view of my bedroom from outside, but didn't block it entirely. I'd never worried about that before. Now it seemed of paramount importance. Back-lit, my movements were entirely visible.

If anyone was watching.

The ringing stopped. I heard the machine downstairs click on again. Again, there was no reply.

I thought of suggestions I'd heard on how to deal with harassing calls. Unlisting your phone number was always first. Not a late-night fix, certainly, and a huge inconvenience, too. Another idea: get a whistle and blow it into the phone.

Like that was going to happen. Someone was calling me, and he knew where I lived. Did I really want to make him mad?

He'd already visited my house once.

At least once, I amended.

Maybe I should have spent more time with the locksmith. Bars on the windows were sounding pretty good right about then.

So was a moat and a barricaded drawbridge.

The phone began to ring. Again.

I stalked across the room and snatched up the receiver. "Look, you pervert," I yelled. A gasp of indrawn breath greeted my words. I guessed he hadn't been expecting a response. "Whoever you are, cut it out!"

I jammed the phone down, then stared at it, simmering with annoyance. *Cut it out?* That was intimidating. I bet I had him on the run now. The guy was probably thinking about upping his insurance.

For a long, blessed minute there was only silence. Like maybe my angry words had worked.

Then again, maybe not. The phone began to ring again.

Turning deliberately away from it, I went back to the front window. Padding quietly, I skulked around the edges of the frame like an intruder in my own home. Two fingers lifted the edge of the curtain aside. Cautiously I peered out into the darkness.

A street lamp in front of the house cast a muted glow over the front yard. All was quiet and still. No cars drove down the road. Lights were off at most of the houses I could see. Everything looked just as I'd have expected.

The spot across the street where Jill

Prescott had parked repeatedly during the last week was empty. Where's a reporter when you need one? I wondered. Nerves were making me giddy.

The phone stopped ringing. The machine came on. The pattern was becoming annoyingly familiar. I wondered how long it would take him to tire of the game.

My gaze slid farther down the street. Two houses away, in the hollow of darkness between two street lamps, a car was parked along the curb. Several trees blocked my view. It looked like some kind of SUV, but I couldn't be sure.

And even if it was, I thought, so what? Every other soccer mom in Fairfield County drove an SUV. Nor was it unheard of for my neighbors to have overnight visitors. A car parked on the street was nothing remarkable.

Unless you happened to be wandering around your bedroom in bare feet and a bathrobe, peering out of the window, looking for suspects, and beginning to feel seriously deranged. I let the curtain fall.

And yet again, the phone began to ring.

I considered calling the police, but I doubted they'd send someone over. If my break-in hadn't impressed them much, this surely wouldn't, either. I also thought about calling Sam. Miles away, home in Redding by now, there was nothing he could do. Aunt Peg would probably tell me to go back to sleep. Bob might be alarmed and that would alarm Davey, something I wanted to avoid at all costs.

In the end, I did the same thing I'd done the night before and simply took my phone off the hook. Maybe not the best idea, but one that finally led to silence. Then I turned off my light and went to sleep.

Well, not really, but that was the plan.

Instead I stayed up most of the night, listening for unexpected noises. The crackle of branches, a creak from the house settling, the squeal of a neighbor's cat; it's amazing how much goes on in the middle of the night. And every innocuous sound shot me straight up in bed. Eyes wide, heart pounding, I clenched the covers between whitened fingers and waited, straining to hear evidence that I wasn't alone.

It never came.

Dawn eventually saved me. That and three cups of strong black coffee. By seven-thirty, I was on the phone. Davey's an early riser. I knew he wouldn't mind.

"Hey sport, how are things going?"

"Great. Last night we went to the movies

and I got to stay up extra late. Dad's going to make chocolate chip pancakes for breakfast. After that, we're going over to the farm to ride Willow. We might even spend the whole day there. Or maybe we'll go back to the Bean Counter. Dad hasn't decided."

I guessed that meant my son hadn't had time to miss me yet.

"It sounds like you're having fun." I tried not to sound wistful, but I was too tired to put much effort into it. Besides, Davey knows me pretty well.

"I am," he said gamely. "What about you?"

"I was thinking I might come over to the pony farm and watch you ride. Would you like that?"

"Sure," said Davey. "Pam says I'm going to work on my posting trot today. That's almost as fast as a gallop."

"I'll bring the camera," I promised, and we made plans to meet in late morning.

Since I was already feeling pretty low, I decided to totally demoralize myself and start the day at the Department of Motor Vehicles. It wasn't until I'd worked my way to the front of the two-hour line that it dawned on me that I'd be having my driver's license picture taken looking just like what I was: someone who'd been up most of the night.

I opened my purse, pulled out a mirror

and applied some concealer to the bags under my eyes. Now I had pouches with highlighter on them. The photographer caught me mid-grimace, which seemed altogether fitting. I took the offending card and tucked it into my new wallet. At least I was once again legal to drive.

As I approached the pony farm, my spirits began to rise. It was a gorgeous spring day. Tulips and wild daffodils lined the road, leaves on the trees were just beginning to bud, and the air smelled wonderful.

I'd stopped at home and picked up the Poodles. Both Faith and Eve were bouncing around on the back seat. They didn't care where we were going, just as long as they weren't going to be left behind.

As I had on my last visit, I pulled up next to the barn and parked beside Bob's Trans Am. Lowering the windows a bit for air, I left the Poodles where they were and went inside to see how Pam felt about strange dogs on her property.

Willow was standing cross-tied in the center aisle of the barn. Davey was beside her. He'd leaned over and picked up one of her front feet, which he was trying to clean. I heard Pam and Bob's voices coming from the direction of the tack room.

"That looks like hard work," I said when

Davey had finished his task and placed the hoof carefully back on the ground.

He spun around, grinning with pride in his accomplishment. "It is. Pam showed me how to do it. I make sure Willow doesn't have any rocks caught in her hooves so she won't get hurt when I ride."

"Good plan. Aren't those hooves heavy?"

"Not as heavy as you might think," Pam answered for him, coming out of the tack room. She had a small saddle draped over one arm and was holding a bridle in her other hand. "Actually, the pony bears most of the weight, and I don't let Davey do the back feet unless I'm out here with him. I'm glad you were able to make time in your busy schedule to come and watch him ride. Davey's really happy with the progress he's made."

Huh? I stared after her as Pam walked past me and went to help Davey tack up. What busy schedule was that? I always had time for Davey and he knew it. The fact that my son was currently staying with Bob had nothing to do with how busy I was.

"Don't mind Pam," Bob said under his breath. He'd followed her out of the tack room. Now he came my way. "I think she got out of the wrong side of bed this morning."

"No problem," I muttered. I still had to

ask about my dogs. It was too warm to leave them in the car indefinitely.

I walked over to where Davey was now encouraging the palomino pony to open her mouth and take the bit. Her teeth looked awfully large in relation to my son's small hands, but Willow didn't seem to notice. She dropped her head and opened her mouth without any fuss. As Davey was buckling up the straps, I asked permission to go get the Poodles.

Pam frowned fleetingly. For a moment, she looked unexpectedly perturbed. "They're not going to fight with my dogs, are they?"

"Of course not."

"They won't chase anything, or bark at the ponies?"

"They wouldn't dream of it."

"I guess it's all right then." She sent an assessing look in my direction. "Speaking of dogs, you must be really worried about that Dachshund puppy you lost."

How did Pam know about Dox? I wondered. I didn't recall mentioning him when we'd spoken the day before.

"I am. How did you find out about that?"

"Bob told me." Pam walked around Willow's side and lowered the saddle onto the mare's back. "He talks to me about everything."

If I were a Poodle, I'd have been growling. It didn't bother me that Bob had a new girl-friend. It did bother me that he told her so much stuff about my family and my life. Stuff that was nobody else's business.

Not only that, but I was willing to bet Bob didn't bother telling Pam about all the things that were going *right* in my life. Not when the problems made a much better story. Come to think of it, recently they'd been pretty much the only story. But that still didn't mean Pam needed to know about them.

"We're just about ready," she said. "Go on and get your dogs. You can meet us around back at the ring."

Faith and Eve bounded out of the car as soon as I opened the door. Immediately two Jack Russells showed up to check out the in-terlopers. I stood by while all four dogs touched noses cautiously.

Though the terriers greeted the new ar-rivals on stiffened legs, their tails never stopped wagging. After a moment's hesita-tion, the Poodles were accepted as friends. The four dogs dashed away, the much shorter legs on the JRTs pumping up and down like crazy as they raced to keep up.

Keeping an eye on the Poodles' progress, I strolled around the barn and joined Bob beside the ring. Davey and Willow were already circling the arena at a sedate walk. Pam was standing in the middle. Davey was sporting chaps, a safety helmet, and a big smile. I pulled out the camera I'd picked up from the car and snapped a picture.

"I hope you don't mind a little constructive criticism," Bob said.

"Go ahead."

"You look like hell, Mel."

And here I'd thought he was going to criticize my photographic technique. "I didn't get much sleep last night."

"How come?"

"Someone thought it would be funny to keep calling me in the middle of the night."

"That's all? Just phone calls?"

"That was enough." I drew my gaze away from Davey and turned to face him. "But since we're on the subject of things that are bugging me, what's going on with you and Pam?"

"What do you mean?"

"How come you keep telling her things about me? Don't you have enough stuff to talk about on your own?"

"Sure we do. We hardly talk about you at all."

I looked back into the ring, snapped another photo of Davey and Willow, and let him ponder the wisdom of that answer.

"All right, maybe you come up now and then," Bob tried again. "What's the big deal? It's not like I say anything bad about you. Is that what you're worried about?"

"No. I'm just surprised that you talk about me at all. Pam's your new girlfriend. I'd think the last thing she'd want to discuss is your ex-wife."

"You'd think so." Bob shook his head slightly. "But to tell the truth, I guess maybe she's a little . . . fixated. Like, since you're the woman I married, that makes you special. She's always trying to figure out what made our relationship work."

"It didn't work." I leaned over the rail to take another shot. "Isn't that the point? If our marriage had worked, you wouldn't be with Pam."

"Yeah, but for some reason, that's not how she looks at things. She's curious about you. That, and probably a little jealous."

"Really."

"I know, it's silly. I've told her that myself. But she says that since you're the mother of my son, you and I are always going to have some sort of karmic connection."

I thought about that for a minute. "What exactly is a karmic connection?"

"I have no idea. And I was kind of afraid

351

to ask. Sometimes Pam goes off on these tangents . . . Let's just say, I've been known to tune her out a time or two."

It didn't sound as though Pam's and Bob's relationship was heading in a karmic direction. Or maybe that was just me.

"Anyway," I said, "Stop telling her about my life, things like Dox being stolen. The whole world doesn't have to hear about this stuff."

"I don't even think we talked about that." Bob was beginning to sound irritated. "It's not like we spend all our time discussing you. Maybe Davey mentioned it to her."

"Davey? When would he have talked to her?"

Bob shifted his gaze back to the ring. Pam had brought Davey into the middle and was slipping a halter over Willow's bridle. She attached a lunge line to one inner ring, then sent the pony back out onto a circle.

"You know, last night," he said. "After we went to the movies."

"I thought that was just you and Davey."

Bob shrugged, but the gesture looked too elaborately casual. Like maybe we were heading toward something he didn't want to discuss. "We all went."

"And afterwards?"

"What are you asking, Mel?"

"Did you take Pam home after the movie?"

"Not exactly." Bob was squirming now. He knew I wasn't going to like what he had to say.

"When exactly did Pam go home?"

"Ummm . . . This morning. About half an hour ago."

That was what I'd been afraid of.

26

"Mom, look!" Davey cried from the center of the ring. "I'm trotting."

That announcement saved his father from the scathing outburst he deserved. At least for the moment.

Our son was indeed trotting in a small circle. He was working on posting, too, although what he seemed to have accomplished was mostly a rhythmic, leg-swinging, bounce. One small hand held the reins. The other clutched firmly at the front of the saddle.

"Good job," I called back, taking three pictures in quick succession.

Bob began to clap. Pam grinned in appreciation. Willow, with the patience of a saint, simply trotted on.

Over in the shade by the barn, Faith and Eve, accompanied by the Jack Russells, flopped down in the grass to watch the proceedings. Pink tongues lolled from all four mouths. Beside me, Bob was beginning to relax. Thanks to Davey's distraction, he thought he'd dodged the bullet. No such luck.

"What were you thinking?" I asked calmly.

His gaze flickered my way, then retreated. "When?"

As if he didn't know.

"I can't believe you would let a woman sleep over when Davey was staying with you. Has this ever happened before?"

"No, never. And you don't have to worry. Davey didn't mind."

I stared at him incredulously. "Of course Davey didn't mind. You're his father, you're a grown-up. He thinks you know what you're doing. He's not supposed to be watching out for you, Bob. You're supposed to be taking care of him."

"I know that." Guilt shaded his tone. "Look, maybe it wasn't the best idea. Hell, it wasn't even my idea."

"Don't try and tell me it was Davey's."

"Actually, it was Pam's. She was sure you'd think it was okay."

Based on what? I wondered. Pam didn't know me well enough to have any idea what I might or might not think was okay.

"Why did she think that?"

"Well, you know . . ."

"No, I don't." I looked into the ring. Pam had brought Davey in off the circle and was unhooking the lunge line. The lesson was ending. "What are you talking about?"

"Because of Sam and all."

Maybe I was just dense, but I had no idea where this was going. "What about Sam?"

"He's been known to spend the night at your house, hasn't he?"

There were so many things wrong with that question that for a single, startled moment I almost couldn't think how to respond.

"That's totally different," I sputtered. "In the first place, Davey and I have both known Sam for several years. Whereas you and Pam have been seeing each other for what, a couple of weeks?

"And in the second place . . ." I realized my voice was rising precipitously and paused to regain control. "How does Pam have any idea what Sam and I do when we're alone?"

"Two weeks can be a long time when you're with the right person," Bob said piously.

Did you notice how he hadn't answered my question? So did I.

Pam was walking to the gate with Davey and Willow. When they went through and headed toward the barn, she paused, no more than half a dozen feet from us, and fumbled with the latch.

As if the latch mattered when there was nobody in the ring. Not only that, but I'd never seen Pam fumble with anything before. I wondered how much she'd already overheard, but I didn't particularly care. The fact that she was listening was not going to shut me up.

"Think about what you're saying, Bob. It's ludicrous. Two weeks isn't even long enough to know whether you're with the right person or not. And when you find out that you aren't, what's Davey going to think? Are you going to let the next girlfriend stay over when he's there? What about the one after that?"

"Now you're the one who's being ridiculous." Bob scowled. "You're taking one little thing and blowing it all out of proportion."

Davey was waiting by the barn to dismount. Lips curved in a small smile, Pam slipped through the gate and moved on.

"It's not a little thing —"

"She told me you might do something like this."

"*What?*"

That semi-shriek drew me an over-the-shoulder glance, but Pam didn't stop walking.

"She thinks you're too attached."

Only a moron could have made a comment like that with a straight face. I gave him the glare he fully deserved.

"Of course I'm attached to Davey. He's my son."

"Not Davey," Bob corrected. "Like I said a minute ago, she thought you'd be all right with that."

"Then who are we talking about?" Slowly comprehension dawned. "You? She thinks I'm too attached to you?"

A faint blush began to crawl up Bob's cheeks. I took that as affirmation.

"And that's why I mind women sleeping over at your house?"

"Something like that."

"Let's get something straight." I reached out with one finger and poked him in the chest.

Bob looked surprised. Frankly, so was I. He took a step back which gave me a fleeting, and totally unexpected, sensation of power. Briefly I was tempted to poke him again and see what would happen but I resisted.

"What you do on your own time is up to you. You can have a girlfriend, a dozen girlfriends. You can sleep with every woman in Stamford for all I care. But when you're with Davey, I expect you to behave like the moral, upstanding citizen we're trying to raise our son to be. No shoplifting. No dancing naked in the streets. And no bringing a succession of women into and out of his life."

Bob looked wounded. "I would never shoplift."

I wondered if I should take that to mean that he would consider dancing naked in the streets.

"You know what I'm talking about."

"Yeah," he admitted. "I guess I do. And you're probably right." He pushed away from the rail and began to walk toward the barn. Faith and Eve, who'd been watching us, got up, shook out, and prepared to follow. "I'll tell Pam we have to cool things off for a while."

"Good." Then mollified by his concession, I tried to soften my stance. "It's only until I figure out what's going on and Davey comes back home. After that you can throw yourself an orgy if you like."

Bob waited for me to catch up. "If I do, will you come?"

"Fat chance. While you're enjoying yourself I'll be sitting at home, setting a good example for the next generation."

"Yeah." He sighed. "That's what I thought."

★ ★ ★

Inside, the barn was cool and shady. Davey, with Pam's help, had untacked the pony. Willow was standing in the aisle munching on a carrot that my son was feeding her from his flattened palm.

"Here, Mom." Davey handed me a piece. "You try."

I held my hand out flat, like Davey's. Deftly Willow whisked the carrot away with her lips. Her dark brown eyes, every bit as expressive as Faith's or Eve's, watched me as she chewed. I reached up a hand and stroked the side of her jaw. When my fingers climbed higher to just below her ears, she leaned into the scratch, just as the Poodles would have done.

"What comes next?" I asked.

"When it's hot out, Willow will get a bath after I ride. But now she just gets to go outside and eat some grass until she's ready to go back in her stall."

"Do you do that part?"

Davey nodded. "I'm supposed to have a grown-up with me, though."

I looked around. Both Pam and Bob seemed to have disappeared. I wondered if he was taking the opportunity to tell her that his ex-wife had just laid down the law.

Meanwhile, Davey was gazing up at me

expectantly. I didn't know much about ponies, but I couldn't see how hard it would be to make one eat grass. Wasn't that something they just did naturally?

"Let's go," I said.

Willow didn't need any prodding to follow us outside. Though Davey was supposed to be the one leading, the palomino pony marched smartly over to a shaded area between house and barn. Reaching a patch of lush spring grass, Willow dropped her head and began to graze. Even the fact that the Poodles had come with us and were sniffing around the area didn't seem to bother her.

"So how are things going?" I asked Davey. He was holding the end of Willow's cotton lead rope, but aside from making sure that it didn't get tangled in her legs, little seemed to be required of him.

"Fine."

"Are you enjoying being with your dad?"

"Sure. Dad's lots of fun. Only . . ."

I waited and let him figure out how he wanted to phrase his thoughts. After a minute, Davey's slender shoulders rose and fell with a sigh. "It'd be nice if sometimes we could do things with just the two of us."

"And not Pam, you mean?"

"She's kind of been hanging around a lot. I guess Dad really likes her."

"What about you? Do you like her?"

"She's okay." Davey snuck me a glance, and I realized he was concerned about hurting my feelings.

"It's all right for your dad to have other women friends," I said slowly. "Just like it's okay for you and me to see Sam. Bob and I are always going to be your parents, and we're always going to be friends with each other. Nothing's ever going to change that, right?"

"I know. You've told me that like a million times, okay?"

I'd tell him a million and one times if that's what it took to keep my son feeling secure in his parents' love.

"Anyway," he continued, "Pam's pretty nice. It's just that she acts like she wants to be my best friend. She asks all sorts of questions about my life and school, and I know she doesn't really care about that stuff. She's just trying to impress Dad."

"I don't think you're going to have to worry about Pam anymore," I said. "I had a talk with your dad. He's not going to be spending as much time with her while you're staying with him, okay?"

"Okay," Davey agreed.

I had no idea how to tell when a pony was ready to go back to its stall. Luckily, when

Davey and I started walking toward the barn, Willow picked up her head and came along. We'd almost reached the barn when Pam came striding out through the open doorway.

Her shoulders were stiff, her features angry. She reminded me of the way her Jack Russells had looked when Faith and Eve arrived, minus the wagging tail. I guessed that meant Bob had had a talk with her. My impression was confirmed when Pam tossed a scathing glance in my direction and kept walking.

"Thank you for the lesson," Davey said politely.

The trainer didn't even break stride. Nor did she acknowledge that he'd spoken.

My son stared after her. "I think she's mad," he whispered.

"Don't worry. She's not mad at you."

"Who's she mad at?"

Bob has impeccable timing. He appeared in the doorway.

"I see you talked to Pam." I tried to sound sympathetic, but, unlike Jill Prescott, I'm not good with fake emotion.

"She'll get over it."

"Get over what?" Davey asked.

"Thinking that the world revolves around what she wants."

The sound of a door slamming hard made us all turn and look at the house. Pam had gone inside. It looked like it was time for us to leave.

Bob didn't seem to mind. "Let's go get some lunch," he said.

As usual, food sounded good to me. "Am I invited?"

"Always. Don't you know that?"

Lunch it was.

27

Of course we ended up at the Bean Counter.
I only let Bob take me back there on one condition.

"I know," he guessed. "No Mongolian chicken, right?"

"That sandwich wasn't a big hit?"

"Not with the paying customers. Frank thought it was delicious."

My brother would.

"He and Bertie will be eating coconut and raisins for the next month," said Bob.

Outside the coffeehouse, I found a place to park in the shade and left the windows open. Davey ran into the Bean Counter and returned with a bowl of water for the Poodles. After all the exercise they'd gotten at the pony farm, both dogs were perfectly content to nap for a while. Bob leaned against the hood of the Volvo and waited for me to get things set to my satisfaction with unexpected patience. I'd turn him into a dog person yet.

As Davey went on ahead to get us a table,

a blue Mazda pulled into the parking lot. Bob stared hard for a moment. "Is it my imagination, or did that car follow us over here from Long Ridge?"

I gave the Poodles one last pat and headed for the coffeehouse. "You're not imagining things. That's my TV crew."

"Your *what?*" He turned and had another look.

"I'm being shadowed by a cable television reporter who's hoping that I'll lead her to the story that will make her famous."

"Good luck." Bob snorted.

"That's what I said." I sketched a wave to Jill and followed him inside.

One thing led to another, and Bob, Davey, and I ended up spending the rest of the afternoon together. The Poodles have visited Bob's house before. By the time we got back there in the early evening, the two dogs were happy to make themselves at home. The fact that Bob keeps a box of their favorite peanut butter biscuits in his pantry never hurts.

Bob's answering machine had recorded three messages in his absence. As Eve and Faith munched on their biscuits, he hit the button to play them back. All three sounded the same. Beep, click. Beep, click. Beep, click. Three hang-ups.

"That's odd." I stared thoughtfully at the

machine. Apparently I wasn't the only one who'd been getting silent messages.

Bob just shrugged. "Probably some telemarketer wanting me to look at a time-share or buy his stock tips. I'm probably better off having missed them. It saved me the trouble of saying no."

He walked over to the refrigerator and started poking around. "It looks like Davey and I are doing burgers for dinner. Want to stay?"

"Thanks, but no. I should be going."

That morning when I'd phoned Davey, I'd been looking for any excuse to get out of my house. I'd wanted to leave the demons from the night before far behind me. An easy, nondemanding day was just what I'd needed. And just what I'd been lucky enough to get.

But now it was time to start putting my life back in order. The first thing I needed to do was talk to Sam. Last night's mystery caller had contributed to my insomnia, but I had to admit he wasn't the only cause. Thoughts of Sam, and the way I'd left him standing on the sidewalk outside Peter and Rose's, had also haunted me through the sleepless hours.

He'd told me to call him anytime.

I was finally ready to make that move.

Davey was sorry to hear that I wouldn't be staying, but his disappointment quickly faded when Bob offered to teach him how to barbeque hamburgers on a gas grill. Eyes shining in anticipation, my son sneaked a look in my direction, waiting for my response.

Trust doesn't come easily to me, but I was working on it. "You will be careful," I said to Bob.

"Of course." His wide grin all but negated the vow. Then he added in a lower tone, "He's my son, too, you know. I won't let anything go wrong."

Feeling very virtuous about my non-interference, I hugged Davey good-bye and told him I'd call again in the morning.

"Don't worry," he whispered in my ear as I held him close. "I won't let Dad singe his eyebrows this time."

Good thought. I held on to it all the way home.

The house was dark when I arrived. Not surprising really. When I'd left that morning it was light out, and I hadn't expected to be gone all day. Still, I didn't rush to go inside. Instead, I sat in the driveway for a few minutes, waiting and watching.

I also kept an eye on the road behind me. Unfortunately, no light blue Mazda pulled up to the curb. Jill must have gone off duty.

After five minutes, the Poodles were looking impatient and I was beginning to feel pretty stupid just sitting in my own driveway. Any action had to be better than this. I got out of the car, let the dogs out, and slammed the door.

"Come on, guys," I said in a loud voice. "Let's go inside."

As if that was going to scare anybody off. It did make me feel better, though. I unlocked the front door, reached inside, and flipped on a bunch of switches. Let there be light.

If you believe that dogs have a sixth sense about impending disaster, Eve and Faith were both doing their best to let me know that everything was all right. They ran past me into the house, chasing together through the darkened rooms without the slightest hesitation. I brought up the rear, turning on lights as we went.

By the time we reached the kitchen, I'd stopped holding my breath. The tension in my shoulders began to seep away. I tossed my purse on the counter and went straight to the phone.

At seven-thirty on a weeknight, Sam would usually be home. I dialed his number and waited expectantly. Anticipation hummed through me; I was almost giddy with it. Smiling eagerly, I held the receiver to my ear and waited.

And kept right on waiting, as things turned out. Sam's answering machine picked up after half a dozen rings.

"Hi, it's Melanie," I said. Compared to the conversation I'd envisioned, talking to a tape recorder was a distinct letdown. "I was hoping maybe we could get together tonight. I'd be happy to come to Redding if you like . . . if you're home . . . I mean, when you get home. Which you're obviously not now. Or you could come here. . . . I just wanted to see you, and maybe talk . . . well, maybe not. . . . Anyway, give me a call when you get this message. Or when you want to. You know, depending on how you feel . . . I'm sure you have the number. . . ."

Idiot, I thought. Of course Sam had my phone number.

Grimacing, I hung up before I could babble myself all the way into oblivion. Talking to machines is not my strong suit. Hopefully, I'd see Sam before he got that message. If he was out, maybe I could catch him on his cell phone.

I dialed that number and waited again. Only twenty-four hours earlier, Sam had assured me that he'd be carrying his cell phone. That he wanted to hear from me. That I could call him at any time.

Any time but now, apparently.

When the phone went to voice mail after the fourth ring, I swore loudly and hung up. One stupid message was my quota for the evening. Wherever Sam was, he obviously didn't want to be disturbed. When he got home, he'd find out I was looking for him. For now, I would have to be content with that.

I fixed myself a sandwich for dinner and mixed the Poodles' food so we could eat at the same time. Just one big happy family. That took up half an hour or so. And still I hadn't heard back from Sam.

With more time to fill, I turned automatically to the activity that has become second nature over the last several years. Aunt Peg has trained me well. I began to groom a Poodle.

At eight months of age, Eve's coat is mostly soft puppy fluff. It doesn't require the sort of time-intensive care that will come later as she matures. Even so, the hair isn't above forming mats, especially in the areas that tend to get rubbed and jostled when she and Faith play.

Aunt Peg has a luxurious grooming room on the ground floor of her house; I have to settle for working in my basement. I've cleared a space where the lighting is good. I leave my portable table set up and my equipment out on a nearby shelf.

Eve knows the routine almost as well as her mother. When I led the big black puppy downstairs, she knew what was up. Faith, looking relieved but also jealous that she hadn't been the chosen one, followed along behind to supervise.

Once you know what you're doing, maintenance work on a Poodle requires a lot more patience than skill. Predictably, my thoughts drifted. And since I was determined not to think about Sam — who *still* hadn't had the decency to return my calls — I worried about Dox instead.

Unfortunately, my visit with Marian Firth the day before had raised as many questions as it had answered. If she did have the Dachshund puppy, that was probably the best-case scenario. Dox would be home with the woman who'd bred and cared about him. His status would still be in limbo, but at least he'd be well looked after.

A nice possibility, I decided, but most likely wishful thinking. Because if Marian was the one who'd broken into my house and taken Dox, how could I explain all the other things that had happened lately? She couldn't have been behind all of them; she wouldn't have had any reason to be.

Which meant that Dox was probably still in jeopardy. Just as I would continue to be in jeopardy until I could figure out what was going on.

Lying on a dog bed in the corner, Faith lifted her head and cocked an ear. She was listening intently to something I couldn't hear. Not an unusual occurrence. I gave Eve a reassuring scratch so she wouldn't lift her head too and cause me to lose my line, and continued brushing.

Faith barked once. The sound was loud in the small room. It reverberated off the concrete walls. The Poodle sprang to her feet and trotted to the base of the steps.

"What?" I placed a steadying hand on Eve's flank.

Faith wagged her tail and looked up toward the open kitchen door at the top of the stairs, making her request as clearly as she knew how to. She wanted to go out.

"Can't it wait? I'll be done in a few minutes."

Faith barked again. This bark was deep and low, its tone closer to a growl. I grabbed for Eve as the older Poodle cast one last glance at me, then bounded up the steps. The puppy was well trained, but she wasn't perfect. She wanted to see what her mother was up to.

Come to think of it, so did I.

I looped a couple quick rubber bands into Eve's topknot to keep the hair from falling in her eyes while we went up and had a look. Lowered to the floor, the puppy immediately scrambled up the stairs. I was only a step behind her.

When we reached the kitchen, Faith was scratching at the back door.

"What's out there?" I asked.

It wasn't as if I expected an answer. But the sound of my own voice made me feel better. Less nervous. More in control. So I kept talking.

"Do you hear something? What is it?"

Eve joined her dam by the door. Of course, I already had all the lights on, both inside and out. I looked through window into the shadowy backyard and didn't see a thing.

What good are watchdogs if you don't let them do their job? I flipped the dead bolt and opened the door. Immediately both Poodles slithered through the opening and raced outside.

There was a flashlight in the cabinet beneath the sink. It was big enough to illuminate the areas of the yard where the house lights didn't reach. And big enough to serve as a rudimentary weapon should the need arise. Thus armed, I slipped out after the dogs.

Standing atop the step, I shined the light in a wide arc. My backyard, fully enclosed by a tall cedar fence, isn't that large. Two things quickly became clear, one good, one not so good. First, the yard was empty; it didn't hold any intruders, real or imagined. Second, the yard was empty. Faith and Eve were gone as well.

I hopped down off the step and strode quickly around the corner of the house. Once again, the gate was standing open.

Fortunately, this wasn't the crisis it could have been when I was away on Sunday. Fence or no fence, Faith and Eve were Standard Poodles. Though they might race through an open gate to enjoy a few minutes of unexpected freedom, they would never willingly leave the area as long as I was there.

All I had to do was round them up, which, in this case, entailed walking around to the front of the house and calling their names. It sounds simple, and it was. But the ease with which the problem would be solved didn't make me feel any better.

Because I knew that gate hadn't been

open earlier. Just as I was sure I hadn't left all my lights on when I left for the dog show the week before. Just as I'd thought Dox was safe and secure when I'd left him locked in his crate in my bedroom.

I found Faith next door, sniffing Mrs. Silano's tulips with the rapt attention of a dominant bitch who smells another dog's scent in an area she considers her own. As Faith squatted to remedy the situation, I spotted Eve out by the sidewalk. I called her, and she came trotting back.

"Good girl!" I praised. I'm a firm believer in the benefits of positive reinforcement. The big puppy's tail came up. Her body wriggled with pleasure at having done something right. "Let's go back inside and get a biscuit."

Faith heard that and came bounding over to join us. Biscuits rank higher than tulips on her list any day. I ushered both dogs through the gate and pulled it shut behind us.

As the Poodles ran on ahead into the house, I stopped and considered. There was plenty of twine in the garage. It might not hurt to simply tie the damn gate shut. The last thing I needed was to be back outside at midnight, looking for the dogs again.

With the aid of the flashlight, the job took

only a minute or two. I half expected Faith and Eve to come back out and see what I was up to. But by the time I'd finished and went trudging around the house, up the steps and inside, no eager black Poodles had come to seek me out.

I probably should have thought harder about that.

Instead I carefully closed the door behind me and reset the lock. As it clicked into place, I turned and surveyed the kitchen. No Poodles in sight.

Images imprinted themselves on my brain in an instant. The pantry door was standing open. The basement door was shut. I heard the sound of a muffled whine come from behind it. Nails scratched against the wood, sending a shiver up my spine.

Then the lights went out.

28

The disorientation was immediate.

I blinked, adjusted. Not every light in the house was out, just those in the kitchen. As my eyes accustomed themselves to the gloom, I pressed my back against the closed door behind me, waiting and listening.

Wondering what would happen next. Wishing Faith would read my mind and stop making noise. I didn't need the distraction.

A minute passed. It felt like an eternity. For now, whoever was in the house with me was remaining as still as I was. I wondered what he had in mind.

I'd put the flashlight down on the counter. When I reached for it, a voice snarled, "Don't move."

Not a man's voice, I realized. Surprise made me drop my hand. A woman's voice. Marian's? Maybe Pam's?

I exhaled slowly. Flexed my fingers, moved my shoulders, braced my feet. A woman didn't seem as threatening, as frightening in the dark. Maybe I had a chance.

"I have a gun," she said, and I recognized Pam's voice. "You're going to do everything I say."

"Why?"

She stepped into the doorway between kitchen and hall. She was back-lit by the lamps in the front of the house; I saw her only in silhouette. But the weapon she held in her hand glinted even in the half-light.

"Because if you don't, I'll shoot you."

The pronouncement was meant to frighten me. But now that I'd finally put a name to the faceless intruder who'd haunted my nights, my fear was beginning to ebb. Even though the gun was pointing in my direction, I couldn't make my brain accept the idea that Pam might actually use it. What could she possibly hope to gain?

"Why?" I asked again.

"You're in my way. You're a problem. And you keep messing things up for me. After tonight, problem solved."

I shook my head slightly, baffled, disbelieving. Nobody could think things were that simple, not even a twenty-something pony trainer with a history of problem relationships and access to artillery. I'd thought Pam wasn't the best choice Bob might have made, but I'd never seen this coming. Not even close.

"This has *all* been about Bob?" I didn't even try to hide my incredulity.

"Your ex-husband," Pam said sharply. "Emphasis on ex."

Under other circumstances, I might have had Terry give Pam his "lots of fish in the sea" lecture. Not that Bob wasn't a catch of sorts, but nobody merited this kind of obsession. Threatening the perceived competition with a gun? That was way over the top.

"Take him," I said. "You've got my blessing. Bob's all yours."

"It isn't as easy as that," Pam snapped. "You always think everything's up to you. Well, it's not. This time I'm the one making the decisions. Bobby loves me. The only thing that's holding him back is you. Once you're out of the way —"

"I *am* out of the way!" It was like talking to a blank wall. Pam didn't seem to be registering anything I said. "Bob and I are divorced. He's free to do anything he wants."

"Legally, yes. But not emotionally. He thinks he's still tied to you. And to Davey."

A chill of dread wrapped itself around my heart. "Where is Davey?"

"How should I know?" Pam didn't look concerned. The icy bands that had constricted my breathing loosened just a little. "Bobby told me we couldn't get together anymore while the kid was there. That was your doing. You kept me away from Bobby, so I figured it was only right that I should come here instead.

"You made me come here tonight, get it? I know what happened. You saw how much Bobby was beginning to care for me, and you couldn't stand it. You had to try to drive a wedge between us."

"That's not true." My tone was vehement; my voice rising. Somehow I had to find a way to get through to her. "Bob makes his own decisions. And his own mistakes."

First rule of negotiation: never anger the person holding the weapon.

Pam's hand shook. Her finger twitched, bracing against the trigger. The room exploded in sound. A brief flash of light stunned my eyes. The cabinet beside me splintered.

Reflex made me jump sideways. I landed wrong, and my ankle twisted beneath me. I stumbled to the floor, my elbow and shoulder hitting hard.

It was shock, though, more than pain, that held me immobile. Terror nipped at the edges of my control. I'd seen the gun in Pam's hand; I'd assumed it was loaded. But even so I'd never imagined — I hadn't been able to imagine — that she might actually shoot at me.

Even after the fact, the thought was simply inconceivable.

"Don't be such a baby," said Pam. "If I'd intended to hit you, you'd be dead now. I just wanted you to know that I was serious. Now get up."

I did. Slowly and painfully, I hauled myself to my feet.

I wondered how loud that gunshot might have sounded outside the house. I hoped the noise had carried; I hoped my neighbors had been listening. Down in the basement, Faith and Eve were barking now, a ferocious racket that filled the kitchen but was probably undetectable from the sidewalk. It was too early in the year for people to have their windows open. Maybe no one had heard a thing.

"Now what?" I asked.

"Now we go upstairs." Pam beckoned in my direction with the barrel of the gun. "Come on."

"What's upstairs?"

"Has anyone ever told you you ask too damn many questions?"

Funny the things that will make you laugh in a semihysterical way when your life seems to hang in the balance. "Yes. Lots of people, unfortunately."

Pam stepped aside and I edged past her, through the doorway and into the hall. The Poodles began to howl. The gunshot had upset them; my leaving magnified their distress.

She cast a withering glance toward the cellar door. "I thought Poodles were supposed to be smart. If you're going to have a dog that barks all the time you might as well get a Jack Russell."

Slowly I started down the hallway. No point in hurrying. If Pam wanted me upstairs, I was pretty sure I wanted to be down.

Besides, the first floor had doors that could serve as an escape route if I got the chance. Not that I'd be making any hasty exits; every door and window in the house was locked up tight. I'd seen to that myself.

I'd hoped to keep the menace out; instead I'd barred it in with me.

Keep her talking, I thought. Stall for time. It was all I could think to do.

"Speaking of dogs," I said, "how's Dox doing?"

"Fine," Pam answered readily enough. Like we were two friends engaged in a casual conversation. Like maybe I'd comment on the weather next. "That puppy's pretty cute. It wasn't part of the plan, but I'm thinking maybe I'll keep him for myself."

I nodded as if that made sense. Why not? She was the one holding the gun. Reaching the foot of the stairs, I paused. "If you don't mind my asking, what *was* your plan?"

Pam kept right on talking. She wanted me to know what she'd done. "In the beginning, it was just a game. You were annoying me, it seemed like I ought to annoy you back."

"So you tried out a couple of things," I suggested. "Turning on my lights? Fiddling with my TV in the middle of the night?"

"Yeah, silly stuff like that. I figured maybe I'd throw a scare into you. Give you something besides Bobby to concentrate on. Security around here isn't too tight, you know? You ought to think about fixing that." Her lips curved upward in a creepy pantomime of a smile. "Not that you'll have to worry about it much in the future."

I ignored the implication and kept going. "When did you take my wallet?"

"That was so easy it was a joke. You left your purse sitting in the kitchen when you and Bobby went upstairs at his house. It wasn't something I'd thought about in advance, but let's just say I wasn't thrilled with the idea of you dragging my guy on a tour of the bedrooms."

I could have argued that I hadn't dragged Bob anywhere. Or that Davey had been with us. Or that our days of making use of bedrooms together were well behind us. But it didn't seem as though logic was going to make a big impression on Pam.

"I'll give you one thing," she said. "You're pretty damn resilient. I figured it would take you at least a couple of days to replace all the stuff you'd lost. I was congratulating myself on what a brilliant, spur-of-the-moment idea that was for getting you out of the way. Except that then you didn't friggin' *get out of the way,* did you?"

Charting Pam's mood swings would have made a veteran sailor seasick. Suddenly she was remembering why she was so angry again. The barrel of the gun motioned up the stairs.

"Enough talk," she said. "Get moving."

Not if I could help it.

"I have to turn off the outside lights," I said in a sudden flash of dubious, not to mention transparently desperate inspiration. "If I don't, my neighbor Mrs. Silano will come and check on me. With all that's been happening around here, I asked her to keep an eye on things. If the lights stay on too late, she'll know something's wrong."

"Where's the switch?"

Instead of answering, I started toward the door. Pam wasn't stupid. She moved quickly to angle her body and head me off. I turned and went to the light switch near the front window instead.

"It's right here," I said innocently.

Cupping my hand around the switch, I used my fingers to raise and lower it. Up and down quickly, then more slowly, then fast again. The universal signal for SOS. Dot, dot, dot. Dash, dash, dash. Dot, dot, dot.

Inside the well-lit hallway, the exterior lights weren't that obvious. I didn't think Pam could see what I was up to. Still, a distraction wouldn't hurt.

"Tell me about Dox," I said. "Why did you take him?"

"Because he was little and cute." Pam snorted. "Like I said, it's not as though a lot of planning went into this."

Just what I wanted to hear. The woman holding a gun on me was prone to impulsive behavior. Still, the fact that she wasn't big on making plans might be made to work in my favor.

"What were you after? Why did you break into my house in the first place?"

"I was just upping the ante, okay? Playing the game for higher stakes. When snitching your wallet didn't get your attention, I decided to go for something bigger. Bobby told me your dogs were really important to you, and I knew how upset I'd be if one of my animals went missing. I figured looking for Dox would take your mind off me and Bobby. Give you something else to do so you'd stop hounding us."

I'd asked Bob to stop broadcasting every detail about my life. Now maybe he'd listen to me. Now maybe he'd understand why. If I ever got the chance to tell him.

"I was going to take one of the Poodles," said Pam. "But it's not like they come when they're called." She gave me an accusing look. "Hasn't anyone ever told you that dogs ought to wear collars? Where are their tags? What if they got lost?"

I could have told her that Faith and Eve were microchipped, but what would be the point? I suspected the irony of this whole topic was going right over Pam's head.

"And then I saw the Dachshund, all crated up and ready to go. I've never liked big dogs much anyway. Little dogs are more my style. So I picked him up and off we went."

Just like that. As though breaking in and stealing something was the most natural thing in the world. The reasonable next step.

In Pam's mind, every time I hadn't responded the way she'd wanted me to, I'd goaded her into taking more drastic action. I supposed, in a demented way, that explained why we were now standing in my hallway with a gun pointed at my heart. Have you noticed how many times I've mentioned that a gun was pointing at me? Yeah, so have I.

"Lights out." Pam chuckled snidely. "You're done."

My hand slipped away from the switch, my last chance gone.

"Get it?" she asked, amusing herself.

I got it all right.

29

"Why are we going upstairs?" I asked.

"More questions." Pam heaved a dramatic sigh. "Don't you ever stop asking questions?"

"No." Right now, the questions were what was keeping me alive.

"First you're going to write a nice long letter," Pam said, "saying how depressed you are about the breakup of your marriage and the loss of your dog. Not to mention that other guy who dumped you last year. You've been having a real run of bad luck lately, haven't you?"

If and when I saw Bob again, I was going to strangle him. I couldn't believe he'd told Pam about my problems with Sam, too.

"Bob and I broke up years ago," I pointed out. "And the dog you took wasn't even mine."

Doubt flickered ever so briefly in Pam's eyes. I liked that. I kept talking.

"And that guy who dumped me? He's back. Or didn't Bob mention that? So if you think anyone's going to believe that I was unhappy enough to want to kill myself, you're nuts."

"It won't matter what they want to believe," Pam said determinedly. "Because you'll be dead and they won't have any choice."

You'll be dead. The words were all the more chilling for the matter-of-fact tone in which they'd been spoken.

I was not going to let that happen. I was *not* going to be defeated by Pam. I just had to figure out how to prevent it.

"Go on," she said. The muzzle of the gun nudged against my side. "Up the stairs."

The Poodles were still barking frantically. I've always known that Faith and I were attuned on a level that transcended mere physical communication. She knew something was wrong and she wanted to help. If only I could come up with a way to let her.

A loud thump came from the direction of the kitchen. Several moments later, the bruising sound was repeated. It sounded as though the big Poodle was throwing herself against the basement door. What a good girl. Faith wasn't going to give up and neither was I.

"No," I said.

"What you mean, no?"

Let her figure it out. The statement sounded self-explanatory to me. Not only that, but I was damn sick and tired of that gun poking me in the ribs. Without her stupid weapon, Pam was nothing. With it, she thought she owned the world. Well, not my world. Not that day. It was time to make a stand.

"What are you going to do?" I said, my voice as hard as I could make it. "Shoot me right here? That'll mess up your suicide scenario, won't it?"

Pam backed away a step, eyeing me warily. "It will still work. I'll just have to change things a bit, that's all."

"And I'm not writing any letter either."

Her lips pursed. Pam growled under her breath. "Then I'll just have to type one. There must be a computer around here somewhere."

There was, but I wasn't about to help her by pointing that out. Now that there was space between us, I was feeling better. At least I could take a deep breath. I forced myself to draw oxygen, lots of it, into my lungs.

"Let me think a minute," said Pam.

Another thump came from the back of the house. Her eyes shifted briefly in that direction. It wasn't much, but it might be the only chance I was going to get.

Back braced against the newel post, I kicked upward hard. Too late, Pam looked back. Her eyes widened as my foot connected with her outstretched wrist. As if in slow motion, I saw her fingers open, release. Her index finger was twined around the trigger, caught there even as the gun began to fall. The weapon wobbled briefly in midair, then fired.

For a moment, I couldn't do anything but stare. Sound was suspended, time as well. My shirt seemed to part magically as a streak of crimson appeared across my upper arm. The bullet punched me like a blow. I stumbled backward, but felt no pain.

Crumpled on the steps, I watched the gun skitter across the hardwood floor. Vaguely, I heard another crash. It sounded like breaking glass, but I couldn't be sure. Black spots were dancing in front of my eyes; maybe I was hearing things too.

Pam dropped to her knees, scrambling to get to the gun, determined to finish what she'd started. Some part of my brain was yelling at me to get up, to reach the weapon first, but I couldn't seem to make it happen.

A stream of dark red blood ran down my arm, soaking into my shirt, dripping over my fingertips. I stared at it in fascination. Every move I made seemed to take forever.

There was a rushing sound in my ears; it pulsed with the beating of my heart.

It occurred to me that this was an incredibly stupid way to die. I thought about Davey and I wanted to cry. But it was too late for that now . . . too late for anything. When Pam came up with the gun a second time, there was nothing I could do to stop her.

"Now look what you made me do," she snapped.

There was blood around me on the stairs, on the floor. Pam's fake suicide was turning out to be messier than she'd intended. I clutched my arm to my side. The wound was beginning to sting as if someone had applied a burning brand to my flesh.

"You're a real pain in the ass, you know that?" She didn't bother to train the gun on me now. Her hand hung down at her side; she was holding all the cards and we both knew it. "All you do is cause trouble. I can't imagine what Bobby ever saw in you."

"I can," said a quiet voice from the doorway.

Sam was holding a shovel he must have picked up outside. His shirt was torn; his jeans, streaked with mud. His eyes swept around the hallway, narrowing at the sight of blood. He swung the shovel with more anger than finesse, and when it connected with Pam's gun arm, we both heard the bone crack.

Under the circumstances, it was an enormously satisfying sound.

Pam shrieked and grasped her hurt wrist with her other hand, holding it to her chest. The weapon fell. Quickly Sam retrieved it. I heard the wail of sirens drawing near. The Poodles began to howl anew.

"Don't move," Sam said to Pam. He pointed the shovel for emphasis. "Just stay right there."

He crossed the room and sat, with infinite care, beside me on the steps. He looked like he wanted to put his arms around me, but didn't dare. "You're going to be all right. Help will be here in just a minute."

"I think it's just a flesh wound." In truth, I wasn't sure, but I was trying to sound brave. My voice quivered.

"Don't talk." Sam reached up and brushed the hair back off my brow. His fingers were cool and strong. "Don't worry about a thing. Everything's going to be fine."

A wave of dizziness washed over me. My head spun. My eyelids fluttered.

"I think I'm going to faint," I whispered.

Sam held out his arms and caught me.

30

Dox got his happy ending after all. Retrieved from Pam's house early the next morning, the little Dachshund was none the worse for the adventures he'd been through. Say what you would about Pam — and by the time the police were finished interviewing me, I'd said plenty — she did treat her animals right.

The first call she'd made after her arrest had been to make arrangements for the care of her ponies and dogs. The second had gone to a lawyer. The third call was to Bob. By that time, he'd talked to me, and he declined to speak with her.

I know he feels guilty. I know he thinks he should have seen some sort of sign. But Pam fooled all of us, not just my ex-husband.

Later, when I developed the roll of film that had pictures of Davey and Willow on it, I stopped and stared at the very first shot, taken the day the palomino pony had arrived in my front yard. Davey was sitting astride Willow. Pam and Bob were standing on either side, their arms intertwined behind him. If I didn't know better, I'd have thought they were a happy family group. So I guess some indications were there from the beginning, if only I'd known to look for them.

Peter called George Firth the next day and officially declined his donation, offering to return the puppy that afternoon. George, of course, was in his office, hard at work when Peter spoke with him. I'm sure my uncle planned it that way. George had a date that evening with Lynda French; the two of them were going to go boat shopping. On such short notice, it was tough to see how Dox could be made to fit into his busy schedule.

"Puppies are like babies," Peter pointed out. "They make their own schedules and you have to adjust to them." Into the silence that followed, he added, "If I might make a suggestion, I know of a home where this puppy would be much appreciated and very well cared for."

"Marian, right?" George had grumbled.

"Sometimes it isn't easy to do the right thing." Peter's years in the priesthood served him well at times like this. He always knew just what to say. It took him less than ten minutes to talk George into giving up the puppy, registration papers and all. Best of all, he left George feeling virtuous about the decision he'd made.

Marian received Dox back with open arms and tears in her eyes. She registered him with the AKC as Tulip Tree Pandemonium, a name that seemed to suit just fine. She calls him Panda for short and promised Aunt Peg we'd be seeing him in the show ring next year.

Peter's silent auction, held the next month, was a huge event, raising more money for his Outreach program than he and Rose had even dared dream. In part that success was due to the efforts of cable news reporter Jill Prescott. I finally gave her the interview she wanted, my capitulation based on the condition that the piece also highlight Peter's very worthwhile charity.

With no dead bodies to catapult the segment to the national news, it remained a local story. But while Jill didn't get the career bump she'd been hoping for, her follow-up piece on Peter's program and the inner-city kids it benefits was well received in humanitarian circles, bringing them both a great deal of exposure. There's been talk of an award and Jill's on-air time has increased dramatically.

As for me, luckily I did have just a flesh wound. The bullet creased my upper arm, leaving a track that stung like fire. As it healed, it turned into a scar that reminds me daily just how fragile life can be. Something like that tends to put everything into perspective.

When we got home from the hospital in the early hours of the morning, after Faith and Eve had been placated and walked, Sam and I finally got a chance to talk. We sat down on the couch in the living room. My head was fuzzy from the painkillers they'd given me in the emergency room, but my sense of resolve was very clear.

"How did you know that I was in trouble?" I asked. "I tried calling you at home. Did you get my message?"

Sam snuggled close. "I haven't been home. Not for more than a couple of hours in the last few days."

That surprised me. I lifted my head from the cushion. "Where have you been?"

"You may not like the answer to that question."

"Tell me anyway."

"I've been outside, sitting in my car, keeping an eye on things. I parked a couple houses down, hoping you wouldn't notice. You didn't want me to come in, but I couldn't just leave you alone here. I knew something was wrong, I had to try and help."

The SUV I'd seen parked in the shadows the night before had been Sam's, I realized suddenly. He'd been outside, sleeping in his car, while I'd been prowling around the house, thinking about him.

"Were you out there when Pam arrived tonight?"

"No," Sam said, frowning. "Jill had pulled up earlier, Rich was with her. I'd begun to wonder if the fact that the two of them were always hanging around at the wrong time was more than coincidence. But when I walked over to their car to confront them, they took off. That made them look even guiltier, so I ran back to my car and followed them. That's where I was when you got home. You tried to reach me on my cell phone, right?"

I nodded. Thanks to the painkillers, I felt as though I were floating along on a very pleasant cloud. I was more than happy to let Sam keep talking.

"I caught up with Jill and Rich at the cable station in Norwalk and we had it out," he said. "After that, I saw that I'd missed a call. I must have been driving through a dead zone when you tried. There wasn't any message, and I was heading back here anyway, so I didn't bother to call back.

"I was just pulling up when your lights

started to flash on and off. As I got out of the car, I could hear the Poodles howling. I dialed 911 and then damn near killed myself trying to get in here."

He'd used the shovel to break through the windows on the top of the kitchen door. I'd seen the evidence of that on my way to the hospital.

"I've never been so scared in my life as when I finally got inside and saw Pam holding a gun and you lying on the steps covered in blood." Sam wrapped an arm carefully around my shoulders and cradled me to him. "I couldn't stand the thought of losing you. I pushed you away once. It won't ever happen again."

I heard the words. I felt their import. I let the message sink in and couldn't seem to say a thing. Just as well, because Sam still wasn't finished.

His fingers threaded through my hair, stroking the silky strands and rubbing the back of my neck. He spoke slowly, choosing his words with care. "I've always known that you were one of the bravest, most resourceful women I'd ever met. I saw the way you'd picked yourself up after Bob left and made things work. You were good at your job, you were a terrific parent, raising a son that anyone would be proud of. You didn't need anyone to make your life complete."

I sat up suddenly. "That's not true."

"You loved me," Sam said gently. "I never doubted that. But you didn't need me. Not really. You were so strong, so capable, so damn competent . . . When I started having problems of my own, I couldn't deal with them here. I couldn't stand the thought that you might think less of me. After I left, you didn't call, you wouldn't answer my letters. . . . I stayed away so long because you had me half-convinced that you didn't want me back."

A lump was forming in my throat. I swallowed heavily. I'd never known how close I'd come to losing everything that mattered.

"I wanted you back," I said. "I *needed* you to come back."

"In the end, I never had a choice. No matter how far away I went, no matter how long I stayed away, my heart was always yours."

"You saved my life," I said.

"I saved my own," said Sam.

It turned out he'd held onto that diamond ring. Sam gave it back to me the next day, but I'm not wearing it yet. Sam says he doesn't mind.

For now, the ring is sitting in a box in my

dresser. Our relationship is a work in progress; I figure its status is the same. This time around Sam and I are talking more, working harder. This time, we're going to get everything right.

Sometimes I take the ring out just to look at it. The facets catch the light; the stone feels heavy in my hand. I find myself staring in wonder and thinking this must be what true happiness feels like.

We'll find out.

About the Author

Laurien Berenson is an Agatha and Macavity nominee, and a four-time winner of the Maxwell Award for Fiction, given by the Dog Writers Association of America. She lives in Georgia with her husband, her son, and six Poodles. Visit her Web site at http://members.aol.com/LTBerenson.